What's in the Rear View Mirror?

By

E.G. Lander

WCP

World Castle Publishing, LLC
Pensacola, Florida

Print ISBN: 9781629890920
eBook ISBN: 9781629890937
First Edition World Castle Publishing, LLC, May 15, 2014
http://www.worldcastlepublishing.com

Licensing Notes

Cover: Karen Fuller
Editor: Maxine Bringenberg

Dedication

Everything I do, everything I feel, everything I have,
Everything is because of my princess wife Nancy.
I miss her so. Every second.
I miss her smile, her eyes, her heart.
Her love.
God is so lucky
To have her with Him.
She must light up His heaven
Like few have ever done.

Chapter 1
The Funeral

Steve Summers slid his dented toolbox into the back of his truck, closing his tailgate so hard it sent two sawhorses halfway up to the cab. He turned around, spotting Willie Bob Reynolds walking towards him with his usual sliding gait. Willy was cradling a white creamy pie in his hands, proudly smiling at his friend.

"Steve, the little woman made you a pie. You always say you won't take money for helping me, so at least you can take this home with you." Willie handed him his fluffy dessert.

Steve looked down at his gift. "That is really something; what kind is it?"

"Mabel said your wife's favorite is lemon meringue, so that's what she made. I guess she thinks you'll need a peacemaker after you get home. My God, you've been working on that dock of mine for what, over six hours? And just last week you spent two full days helping me repaint my truck. I can still see the green paint on your boots. I owe you big time, Steve."

"You don't owe me a thing. I'm just being a good neighbor, that's all. Who knows? Maybe someday I'll need something and I can count on you being there." Steve put his fancy present on the passenger seat of his red Ford pickup, then walked around and got in on the driver's side.

Willie pushed Steve's door closed and leaned on the side of the truck. "Hey, Steve, that was some football game last night. That grandson of yours made some catch there at the end. I didn't think he had a prayer to snag that throw—it looked like it was about eight feet over his head. You've got to be proud as hell of him, I bet."

"Yeah, Billy is something else. Well, I gotta go." Steve looked at his watch. "It's pushing nine. Mary always fixes me something special on Saturday nights, and I'm starving." He started his truck. "I might even sneak a handful of that fancy pie on the way home."

"You take care Steve, and thanks again for the help with the dock. Remember now, if there's anything I can do for you, just give me a holler."

Steve laughed. "You already did something for me. Thanks for the pie, Willie."

Willie snickered as he watched his friend back out of his driveway. Steve had that fifties music blaring again, and the whole neighborhood could hear Pat Boone sing about some love letters in the sand.

"What a guy," Willie said, loud enough to cover up the fading music as Steve drove away.

***

It was unusually dark as Steve pulled out onto Highway 21, one of those cloudy South Carolina September nights that didn't allow a single star to brighten the skies, let alone save any space for the moon. He was glad to see farmhouses in the distance with their yard lights glowing, just to give him something to look at.

About four miles from Willie's place, Steve felt a bump. Maybe he'd run over something? He looked in the rearview mirror, hoping to see a pothole or a branch in the road instead of some animal fighting for its life, but he saw nothing.

Then he felt another thump. This time he could barely make out the silhouette of a vehicle of some kind in his mirror. The car, or truck, or whatever it was, didn't have any headlights on. Steve reached over and pulled his headlight lever in and out, trying to signal the driver behind him that he had forgotten to turn his lights on.

Steve's head jerked back after the third bump as his truck was propelled over the embankment guarding the big curve two miles from home. He instinctively reached over to keep Mary's pie from sliding off the seat, not knowing where it would land. There was a giant oak coming at him fast. Within seconds, it was over, and Steve Summers was gone.

***

Billy Summers couldn't believe how hot it was. He expected it be hot, but not this bad. Little balls of sweat sprinted down his back, not even trying to stick to his shirt. Grandma was right…he should have worn the tan suit, it would have been cooler. But today was a day he wanted to look his best, and his tan coat had some threads coming out of one of the sleeves. So he had to wear the black suit, no matter how hot it was.

He looked around at the crowd at the cemetery. It looked like all of Rymont had come to say goodbye to Grandpa. The entire football team, as well as most of his teachers, were standing in a semi-circle to the left of the red Davis Brothers funeral tent. A lot of them didn't know Steve Summers very well, but they had come for Billy, knowing he had just lost his best friend. Almost all of them tried not to make eye contact with the family; just like the night before, when they had paraded past Grandma and the boys at the visitation, not knowing what to say.

Billy noticed some of the older people standing next to the tent, leaning on their canes and walkers. He could name a lot of them, as they used to come to Grandpa's porch on Sunday nights, talking about old times. The wondrous stories they would tell made Billy laugh as he laid behind Grandpa's recliner, eavesdropping through the half-open window. Billy felt like a special unknown guest, listening to their sometimes R-rated tales. But that all ended when Grandma had caught him snickering at a dirty joke, and pulled him away from his listening post.

But one Sunday a few months ago, Steve had invited Billy to sit with him and his porch buddies. Grandpa had said that Billy became a man that night. It was a small thing to the rest of the world, but Billy thought it was an incredible achievement, a special gift from Grandpa. Now he looked around, noticing tears tracking down the cheeks of those old-timers, the same friends that had rolled with laughter on those special Sunday nights.

The family sat in the front row under the funeral tent next to Grandma, with Billy wrapping an arm around her shoulders. Almost everyone in Rymont called her "Granny" because she was so frail but feisty, like the character in *The Beverly Hillbillies*. She even looked the part, with her grey hair pulled back into a little bun and her glasses on the tip of her nose. But she wasn't feisty now, she was just frail. She had been through so much the last four days. Her whole world had been ripped apart. She stared at Grandpa's coffin, never wavering, watching it glisten in the blazing South Carolina sun. Every few minutes she would squeeze Billy's sweaty hand, as if to confirm that Grandpa was really gone, really lying in that casket.

Billy thought back to Saturday night when that state trooper had sheepishly come to their house, half-heartedly knocking on their front door. He could still hear his grandmother's screams in his head. Somehow, he knew at once what it meant. It was the day of the big nightmare, a day that shattered the Summers's worlds forever.

He thought his grandfather would always be there for him. He'd never imagined a life without either of his grandparents. They were the center of his world since his parents had died when he was four. Since then, Grandpa and

Grandma were his parents, and probably better parents than any kid had in Rymont. "This has to be just a bad dream, it can't be real," he whispered as he stared at the green outdoor carpet covering the dirt pile next to Grandpa's coffin. He realized it wasn't a dream when he looked up at Preacher Jack, noticing him move his lips, then someone always nodded back at the bearded minister. Billy closed his eyes hard, hoping to open them and find things changed. But they didn't change. Grandpa was dead.

Billy's little brother Gary was sitting on the other side of Grandma. The kids in school called him "Opie." He was almost a foot shorter than Billy, with a head full of red, stringy hair. The blistering sun made his hair look even redder, while brightening most of his freckles. Gary kept looking around like he was on display. Every few minutes, he'd reach up to loosen the collar on his new white shirt.

Gary wasn't very comforting to his grandmother. Billy thought he could at least hug her a little bit, as she was having trouble trying not to sob. Tears were cascading down her cheeks, landing on her breast, and Gary wouldn't even look at her. It made Billy mad.

Sitting next to Gary was Grandpa's twin brother Ray. He looked a lot younger than his sixty-eight years. What did look old was his blue pin-striped suit. It must have been his only suit; it was all he ever wore for anything important. It had wide, old-fashioned lapels, as well as a small tear under the right sleeve just below the armpit, and it was missing two buttons. Billy looked over at Ray, noticing his zipper was down. He tried to make eye contact with his uncle, but Ray kept looking down at his tattered brown work shoes, slowly twisting them back and forth.

Billy had dozens of thoughts crisscrossing through his mind as he stared at the shiny coffin that held such an important part of his world. Why did this happen, and how? He thought about what Grandpa had told him after the game

Friday night. "Billy, you're the man. See, I told you practice pays off, and guess what, son? You are one great football player."

Now the football game was the last thing on Billy's mind. One thought kept popping up over and over in his brain. He wanted five more minutes with Grandpa, just five more minutes, to tell him how much he loved him, and that he was the best dad ever. But he realized he would never get that chance. All because of what?

There were crazy rumors flying around Rymont. People said that after Grandpa found out he had colon cancer, he had rammed his truck into that tree to save everyone from watching him die. Billy knew that couldn't be true. Grandpa told everyone he was going to "whip that goddamn cancer," and he meant it. He even heard Grandpa might have been drunk, but that didn't make sense either. Grandpa used to spin tales on Sunday nights about how much drinking he did when he was in high school, but Billy never saw even a single can of beer touch his grandfather's lips.

He gazed at the special box holding Grandpa, wondering how there could really be a God. How could a loving God do this...first take his parents, and now his grandfather? What kind of a God could do that? It didn't make sense. Grandpa was the greatest man Billy had ever known, and was always there to help anyone. Since he'd retired from the insulation plant eight years ago, he'd spent hours helping neighbors with anything, without even asking for a "thank you" in return. How could anyone that good be taken away?

Billy found a small smile as he thought about all the times they'd played together; how Grandpa could take a piece of paper, or a cardboard box, and make games out of them. Or, when they went fishing, how they'd talked about so many private things. Grandpa would tell him some of the crazy stuff he'd done in high school as they laid back, watching their fishing bobbers bounce up and down on the waves at the lake. Grandpa wasn't proud of everything he'd done, but he wanted to be sure the boys learned from his mistakes, so he wasn't bashful talking about those mistakes.

Billy was a senior at Rymont High, and its most decorated football player…the first Rymont player ever to be named All-State. He took sports seriously, learning that from his grandfather. Steve had made sure that the boys did their homework right after school, so he could practice with them, spending hours and hours showing the boys how to throw a baseball, shoot a jump shot, or catch a football. Grandpa had told them almost every day that "practice is all it takes for anyone to be a superstar, to be great." Billy had taken that to heart, but Gary didn't.

Grandpa had worked hard with Gary, trying to build up his confidence. After the game Friday night, he had made as big a deal about Gary's three tackles as he did Billy's incredible winning touchdown catch, but that catch meant nothing to Billy now as they left the cemetery.

Grandma and the two boys drove home without talking, like they were in a fog. Billy couldn't focus on anything until they turned onto their street. When they got to their driveway, everything they could see brought back memories of Grandpa.

He had built the entire house from the ground up. Grandma said he even did the electrical and plumbing all by himself. While his friends were off to college, he was working on her "dream home." It took him over three years to finish their castle. He had laid every red and brown brick, shingled the roof, and poured all the sidewalks. It was his masterpiece, and it became a Rymont landmark.

The newspaper had done a story about how Grandpa built the first "Charleston-looking" house in the county. Billy heard stories about cars that had slowed down to gaze at the unique structure, even taking pictures, sometimes asking Grandpa to pose for them in front of his homemade palace.

After Grandma stopped the car, Billy noticed the rusty old porch swing. He thought back to all the times he had sat there with Grandpa, sharing so many secrets, like a father and son would do. It was their special place to be friends (and to play with Grandpa's shiny watch).

Looking up at the basketball hoop, Billy remembered all the nights Grandpa had worked with the boys on their shooting and rebounding. They would practice so late they could barely see the basket. Grandpa wouldn't let up, wanting one more pass or one more free throw, then Grandma would get mad because dinner got cold. The boys thought it was cool when they walked in, expecting her to yell at them, but Grandpa always beat her to the punch by squeezing her and laying a big kiss on her cheek, followed with, "Oh, hush up, old woman, you know you still love me." He must have said that fifty times. She blushed and melted all fifty times.

Chapter 2
A Fifty Year Old Secret

After Grandma and the boys walked quietly into the house, she said she had to talk to both of them in private, starting with Gary. She made her way up to her bedroom, with Gary a few steps behind.

"Gary, honey, have a seat, I've got something to tell you." She halfway closed the door as he sat on the edge of her bed. She sat down next to him, putting her hand on one of his knees. "Gary, you know how much your grandfather loved you. To him, you and Billy were his sons, not his grandsons. But he always worried about one thing with you, Gary; seeing that you got to go to college."

She turned, looking into his eyes. "Billy's got that scholarship to Georgia Tech, and your grandfather wanted you to get the same chance. But you know we don't have the money for that, so he took out a fifty thousand dollar life insurance policy so that when he died, you would get all of it for school." By now, tears were racing down her cheeks. She nodded, giving him the best smile she could find. "So Gary, after you graduate, you make your grandfather proud and go to a good college somewhere."

Gary opened his mouth, then lowered his shoulders. He turned his head, looking out the open window. "I don't know what to say. I've been thinking all day about all the times I was mean to him. I feel awful, Grandma; I feel real awful." He shook his head. "I just don't know what to say."

Grandma looked into his green eyes, expecting to see some tears, but there were none. She knew he was hurting. "It's okay, Gary; now, you just go ahead and let it out. Go ahead and cry. You'll feel better if you do."

Gary looked down at his feet, wiggling them nervously as he bit his upper lip. Tears began to swell up in his eyes, but he wasn't going to break loose. No one was going to see him cry. It was a battle he was determined to win.

She put an arm around him, squeezing as hard as she could. He didn't react at all. A few seconds later, she stood up, wiping her eyes with the sleeve of her special black dress. "Now Gary, do me a favor and go downstairs and bring in the rest of the flowers. Just put them on the back porch so they can get some sun. Oh, and get your brother up here. I need to talk to him."

Gary shrugged his shoulders, putting his hands on his knees. After taking an elongated deep breath, he got up and left, leaving his grandmother staring at her husband's picture on the top of the dresser. While she was waiting for Billy, she walked over to the little wooden desk in the corner, opened a small drawer, and pulled out one of Grandpa's treasures. She looked at the sparkling keepsake, shaking her head. "Why God, why? Why did You take him from me? Why?"

"I've been asking that question every damn minute for the last three days, Grandma," Billy said, walking up behind her, putting his arms around her waist. "It doesn't make sense, does it? I mean, with all the scumbags in the world, why did he have to die? He never hurt anyone."

She turned around and they hugged for over a minute. After she patted him on his back twice, she looked directly into his eyes, grabbing both of his arms. "Billy, I've got something to give you and I've got something to tell you. So, let's start with your present from Steve." She wrapped her hands around his, placing Grandpa's dented gold watch and chain into his palms. "He didn't have anything else to give you but his father's old watch. He told me to be sure you got it if something happened to him. He said you'd know why and you'd take care of it."

Billy stared at the old timepiece. "You know something, Grandma? He knew this was important to me. He always let me play with it when we were on the front porch, when I was little. I thought he was joking when he said he'd give it to me one day. I'm going to put it in a very special place. God, I miss him so much." Tears started pouring out of his eyes. They hugged again.

Grandma reached over, pushing her bedroom door closed. Turning back to Billy, she grabbed his arm as they both sat down on her bed. "Billy, I told you I had something to tell you." She lowered her voice to almost a whisper. "I want this to stay between us. I don't want you talking to anyone about what I'm going to tell you…not your brother, Uncle Ray, or even Nancy. Do you hear? You've got to tell me you won't tell a single soul."

Billy lowered his eyebrows, giving her a puzzled look. "Sure, Grandma, I promise. What is it?"

She took a deep breath, then turned her head towards her husband's picture. "Billy, I don't think your grandfather died by accident, I think someone killed him. I don't know who or how, but I don't think he ran into that tree on his own, I think he was pushed off the side of the road. He didn't kill himself like some folks are saying, and you know how good of a driver he was. He wouldn't have driven off road by accident, I know it."

"But Grandma, what are you…?"

She interrupted him. "Now you just hear me out, then I think you'll understand." She looked down at her feet, then back towards Billy. "Billy, now listen to me. I knew Steve better than anyone. He didn't want to die. He kept talking about the things he was going to do after he got his cancer fixed. He told me a hundred times how much he was looking forward to seeing both you boys go to college and walking the campuses with you, and he even said that after he found out about his cancer two weeks ago."

"But Grandma, why do you think someone would kill him?" Billy was anxious to hear what she was about to tell him.

She reached over, grabbing Billy's hand. "Steve told me last week that he had to clear up something he did when he was a senior in high school. He said he had to fix it his way, and that he couldn't tell me about it. I was really puzzled. I mean, why would he tell me about doing something really bad, but not tell me what it was? I nagged and nagged at him to tell me what he was talking about."

"So, what'd he say?"

"He said he wanted to prepare me; that someone may want to hurt him, or us, once he straightened out whatever it was he did, but he was going to fix it, and soon."

"But Grandma, I don't understand. If he thought he would get hurt, why didn't he just tell you the whole story, or why didn't he go to the police?"

"That's exactly what I asked him. He said he didn't want me or you boys harmed in any way, and the more people who knew what happened, the more people would get hurt. That's when he told me to forget about anything he'd said, and to just trust him. That was probably the strangest conversation we ever had, Billy. But he sure convinced me he was going to do something that might put him or us in danger."

He looked into her wrinkled, tired face. "Did you ever ask him about it again?"

She lowered her head, exhaling slowly. "Oh yeah, I asked him about it the next day and he wouldn't tell me anything, so I dropped it." She stood up, then turned back to her grandson. "I should have tried harder to get the truth out of him. He might still be alive today if I would have bugged him about it."

"Grandma, you don't know if he would ever tell you what was bothering him. The cops said it was an accident. How can you be so sure they were wrong?"

"I'm not sure of anything." She spread her arms apart. "But it's got to make you think. I mean, he tells me about someone hurting him, or us, once he fixed a problem, and a week later he dies running off the highway. A man who never even got a speeding ticket, and never had an accident, runs into a tree and dies instantly? It's too much of a coincidence for me, Billy. I think he may have been trying to take care of what he was hiding and the wrong person found out."

"So, Grandma, what can we do about it anyway? The cops are sure no one else was involved and it was an accident. Maybe he just took his eyes off the road and hit a tree. Even if someone pushed him off the road, what can we do about it?"

She was silent for a few moments, collecting her thoughts. "I thought about not telling anyone about all this, but I've got to find out what really happened to Steve. Don't you see? That's why I told you about it. I trust you more than anyone else in the world, and I need your help sorting all this out."

Grandma walked over to the window, opening the yellow and white curtains, looking down at the back yard. "Maybe we don't want to find out what he did in high school, I don't know. But Billy, what keeps bothering me is that it's a hell of a coincidence…I mean, all within one week. What if he was right, and whoever hurt him thinks we know something and comes after us? I think we've got to find out what we can about what he was hiding, don't you?"

Billy rubbed his forehead back and forth, trying to think of the right words to tell her. "I understand why all that bothers you, Grandma, I really do. I'll tell you what I'll do…I'll try to find out what Grandpa might have done back when he was in high school and see if that leads to anything. I really don't think I'll find anything, but I'll try."

He walked over next to her, twisting his head to look out the window over her shoulder. "I think I'll just tell people I'm doing a report for school about his life. That way no one can think we know anything. But we don't need to worry about anyone coming after us. We'll be okay."

***

Billy tossed and turned all night after his conversation with his grandmother. His body needed sleep, but his mind kept him awake. Where was he going to begin looking for answers about what Grandpa may have done in high school, or how that could have tied into his accident? Who would be able to help uncover Grandpa's secret? Uncle Ray; sure, Uncle Ray…after all, they were twins. They must have known everything about each other back then. This might be easier than Grandma thought. All he had to do was talk to his uncle, without coming out and telling him the whole story. Maybe that would give him a clue to what Grandpa was hiding and wanted cleared up.

The next day in school Billy kept thinking about what he was going to ask Ray. After he finished his last class, he started pulling out of the school's parking lot when he saw Nancy. She was the most popular girl in school, and had been his girlfriend for over two years. She was on her way to cheerleader practice when she spotted Billy and started running towards his "hot" burgundy Mustang. Man, she looked good. He watched her little black skirt dance from side to side and her long blonde hair jump up and down on her shoulders with every stride she made towards him.

"Hey, Billy, hold on," she hollered. She got to his car, putting both hands on his open window edge, catching her breath. "Where are you going? I thought you had practice tonight."

Billy reached over and turned his radio off. "Hey, baby. I've got some stuff to do for the family. You know, with everything going on about Grandpa. I'm going to miss some practices, but Coach Fatha is fine with it. He told me I could skip out today right after school."

"Oh, okay. Well, how about calling me when you get done? I haven't seen you much since Friday, and I miss you." She leaned into his car and gave him one of her soft, warm kisses.

"Maybe we can get together tonight, Nancy. I'm sorry everything is messed up right now, but I'll make it up to you." Billy reached out, pulling her back into his Mustang, kissing her again.

"I'll remember you said that, Billy. Listen, I've got to go, I'm running late for practice. Love you." She smiled, then turned and ran back to the other cheerleaders.

***

His uncle's farm was ten miles out of town, giving Billy more time to think about how he was going to ask his questions. So many thoughts were going through his head as he turned into Ray's place off Old Smithfield Road. He hadn't been out there in weeks, ignoring his tomato patch on the acre Uncle Ray had given him.

He could feel the bumps of the little cattle bridge bounce his tires up and down as he spotted Uncle Ray's green truck parked under the big tree with the tire swing. That swing was one of the biggest reasons he'd loved going to the farm when he was little. Now, it was nothing more than a place to park Ray's truck.

Billy pulled up in front of the tattered farmhouse, walking through the porch into the living room. He could hear his uncle doing something in the back. He picked up an old People magazine laying on the tan recliner, then threw it on the coffee table that was already loaded with stacks of newspapers and books. "Hey, Uncle Ray, where are you?"

"Is that you, Billy? Come on in, I'll be right out, Bud. I'm just finishing up a little project."

A couple of minutes later, Ray appeared, drying his hands on an old greasy towel. He looked up, throwing the towel on a rocking chair next to the white stone fireplace. "So, what's up, Billy? Are you going to work on your tomatoes out back?"

"No, not today. I just wanted to come out here to talk, that's all."

"Sure, sit down. What's on your mind, son?" Ray threw three purple pillows on the floor as they both sat on the brown velvet couch.

Billy took a deep breath, looking down. "Uncle Ray, I was thinking about Grandpa, and how neat a guy he was, so I decided to write a story about his life for my advanced writing class. I think it would be cool to find out more about him, like when he was in high school, and what you kids did back then."

"So, what do you want to know, Billy? I guess I would know as much about him as anyone, except of course for your grandmother."

"Well, can I start by asking you about his friends in high school, especially his senior year? Oh, and what kind of stuff he liked to do back then."

Ray leaned back on the sofa. "Steve was very popular in school, probably the most popular kid in our class. But all of us were a little crazy back then. He wasn't the wildest of the bunch, that's for sure, but he had his moments. I guess he had to be a little careful because he was so big into sports he didn't want to get into trouble and not be able to play. All he talked about was sports...sports this, sports that, everything was about sports."

Billy's uncle raised his eyebrows, shaking his head. "I'll tell you one thing…for being twins, we weren't much alike. He never studied, but still got all A's. Me, I had to work my ass off just to get C's. But he wasn't perfect; he was a partier. He sure liked the drinking parties."

"Uncle Ray, I heard him talking about drinking when he was in school, but you know something? I've never seen him drink anything, not even beer or a glass of wine. Do you think he had a drinking problem back then? And if he did, what made him quit?"

Ray leaned up, putting his elbows on his knees. "I don't know if you would call it a drinking problem, but he sure liked his beer…that is, until he got hooked on vodka. You know, Billy, it's kind of strange how he ended up not touching the stuff after he graduated. You're right, it's been a long time since he drank anything."

Billy crossed his arms. "So, tell me, who'd he hang out with in high school?"

"Steve had his own clique, and I wasn't part of it. We had our own circles of friends. I'd say his best friend was Brad Tillin. They were always together, the best I can remember. I thought they'd be friends forever, but Brad left Rymont right after graduation." Ray tilted his head up. "I think he went into the Army or Navy, I don't remember."

"Do you know if Grandpa ever got in trouble in high school?"

"Trouble?" Ray paused, cocking his chin up. "Why would you think he would get into trouble? He was wild, but he wasn't a troublemaker. We all did things that weren't exactly kosher, so I guess he probably did some dumb stuff, but I don't remember what. Why would you ask that?"

"I just wanted to find out what Grandpa's senior year was like compared to mine, that's all."

Ray gave his nephew a quizzical look. "Why, did you do something wrong, boy?"

"No, no, Uncle Ray. I just thought it would juice up my story if he did something crazy."

Ray held both hands out up to his shoulders and shrugged. "Billy, I can't remember anything crazy he did back then, I really can't. And no offense, Billy, you are kind of talking in circles. Steve was a good guy, when he was little, when he was in high school, and every day since."

"I know he was a good guy, Uncle Ray, but that's not stuff kids want to read about in my writing class. I'm looking for wild stuff to write about to make my paper more interesting. So, if you can think of anything crazy he did, or if he got into trouble in high school, let me know."

Ray seemed agitated. "I don't follow you, Billy. Why would you want to know all the dumb stuff he did, and not be interested in all the good things he might have done? That seems kind of one-sided to me."

"Oh, I don't know. I uh…I just figured the weird stuff might uh…make my paper better. Well, anyway, thanks for your help." Billy got up, heading for the front door, knowing the conversation was not going in the direction he wanted.

"I'll try to remember more stuff for you, Billy. You just kind of caught me off guard. Oh, how about showing me that paper when you get it done?"

Billy turned back to Ray. "Will do; see you later. Take care, Uncle Ray." He got in his Mustang, found a yellow napkin between the seats, and wrote "Brad Tillin" on it.

Chapter 3
The Yearbook

Billy drove home, spotting Grandma sitting on the back porch, taking a break from her gardening. She was wearing the same old orange gloves she always wore when she worked on her roses. When she saw Billy, she started to get up, but had to sit back down. Since she'd broken her hip two years ago, she struggled getting up and down. Billy helped her get back to her feet.

"Thanks, Billy. How about giving me a hand so I can get back to my roses?"

"You bet, Grandma," he answered as they started walking. "Say, I was wondering, did you ever hear of a Brad Tillin? I heard he was Grandpa's best friend in high school."

"I didn't go to the same high school as Steve." They both sat down on the wooden bench in front of her roses. "We met after high school, remember? I told you about all that. I did hear Steve talk about some kids from high school, but I don't remember anyone named Brad...what did you say his last name was?"

"Tillin, Grandma, Brad Tillin."

"No, that doesn't ring a bell at all."

"Grandma, I was wondering; do you think we've got any of Grandpa's stuff from when he was in high school?"

She turned towards him, taking a tired breath. "I think there are some old boxes in the attic from his high school days. Come to think of it, I think there's even a box marked 'Rymont High' up there somewhere." She shook her head. "I never opened it, but I'm sure it's your grandfather's stuff. It's been up there too long to belong to either one of you boys. You'll probably find it if you look long enough. But the attic's a big mess. I've been meaning to ask one of you boys to help me fix it up, but it keeps slipping my mind." She looked into her grandson's eyes. "Do you think there's anything up there about what we talked about after the funeral?"

Billy stood up, looking at her roses. "Who knows? It won't hurt to look, I guess. I think I'll just go up there and see if I can find anything neat about Grandpa."

He patted her on her shoulder and went into the house, pulling the rope down to the attic stairs. Making his way to the top step, he looked around. Grandma was right, the attic was so full of junk it was going to be hard for him to even walk up there. There were stacks of magazines and newspapers everywhere, and he could see big tan crates, old Christmas trees, piles of clothes, and a ton of cardboard boxes of all sizes.

Billy shuffled around for twenty minutes, finally finding the box marked "Rymont High." He took it near the attic window and sat down on an old folding chair. After tearing the box open, he knew it was Grandpa's stuff. There was a Rymont Ravens 1951 team football picture on the top.

His eyes moved across the photo. Grandpa was easy to find. He was in the second row, wearing jersey number twenty. Under the photo were some old school papers—each one with a big red "A" on it—a black leather Rymont jacket, and a red and black felt book. He turned it over, recognizing it at once. It was Grandpa's 1951 yearbook. Opening it carefully, he started looking for anything about his grandfather.

The senior class pictures were on the second page. There were only seventeen seniors that year. Billy looked at all the kid's photos, spotting Grandpa at once. He had that sparkle in his eyes like he was planning something, as Grandma used to say. His hair was loaded with grease, parted on the right side of his head, just above his temple, and he was wearing the ugliest checkered shirt Billy had ever seen.

Brad Tillin's picture was next to Grandpa's. He looked like a bookworm. He had on a pair of Buddy Holly-looking black glasses, a pocket protector with three pens in it tucked into his right shirt pocket, and he was looking up for his picture. "Now, there's a real nerd," Billy mumbled, as he started reading what was written over the photo. "Don't ever forget all the fun we had, and don't forget the Four Raven Promise. Your friend, Brad."

What could that mean? He studied the rest of the pictures. Most of the other photos had a short "good luck" or "I'll miss you" message written over them, except for what was written on the picture of a Tim Sanders. It read, "Don't ever forget, Steve, I mean Ditto to B.T."

Billy thought about it for a few seconds, then realized that meant "Ditto to Brad Tillin."

Sanders must have been part of the Four Ravens Promise, too. But what was the Four Raven's Promise? Could that have anything to do with what Grandpa may have done in high school, or maybe his accident?

He took the yearbook down to his room, looking for more clues. That Promise kept bouncing around in his brain. Someone had to know about it, but who? He had to find Tillin or Sanders. He picked up his cell phone, punching in Uncle Ray's number.

"Hey, Uncle Ray."

"What's up, Billy?" Ray asked, catching his breath.

"Uncle Ray, I have a couple more questions for you about Grandpa."

"Fire away, Billy."

"Have you ever heard of the Four Raven Promise?"

Uncle Ray took a second, then replied, "Four Raven Promise? No, uh...that doesn't ring a bell. Where'd you hear about that?"

"Oh, I was just looking at Grandpa's yearbook. It was up in the attic. It's kind of neat looking at all the notes and stuff in it. That's just something that was written on Brad Tillin's picture."

"I wish I could help you, but I have no idea."

"Okay. Do you remember Tim Sanders? It looks like he made that Promise, too."

"Hell yes, I remember Tim. He was a wild man. I always thought he'd get your grandpa into big trouble one day. I never could figure out why Steve ran with Tim. There weren't many kids who liked Sanders, except for Steve and Tillin. Sanders was nuts. If there was any kind of trouble at school, you could bet Tim was involved. He was drunk half the time, and the rest of the time he was just plain mean. Problems seemed to follow him everywhere.

"And Sanders wasn't all that smart. One day he spray-painted graffiti on a cement wall at the back of the school, and put the spray can in Steve's locker. Of course, your grandfather didn't have anything to do with it. The principal was fixing to call our folks when a teacher came by and told him that Sanders had the same color spray paint all over his hands. Now, you'd think anyone with any brains would be sure he cleaned off the paint from his hands after he got done. No, not Tim Sanders. He was not only a jerk, but he was dumb jerk."

"So, what happened to him...I mean, after school? Do you think he still lives here in Rymont, or is there a way I can find him to talk to?"

"Tim just kind of vanished after graduation. I never heard where he went. In fact, over the last forty years, I don't think

I've heard his name mentioned by anyone until now. No, he ain't in Rymont, that's for sure. I'll bet you even Steve never heard from him after we graduated. Oh, Billy, can I call you back? I've got something in the oven and the timer's going off."

"Sure, don't worry about it. That's all I needed to ask you, anyway. Thanks, I'll talk to you later."

Billy hung up, wondering who else might know about Tillin or Sanders. Coach Fatha; sure, Coach Fatha. He was a whiz on the computer. If anyone could find out about anyone in Rymont, he could, and Fatha would do anything for Billy. Everyone said Billy got special treatment because he was the team's star player, and they were right.

He got into his car, heading over to the high school. He parked next to Fatha's brown Murano, then made his way into the gym, peeking into the coach's office. Fatha was looking over some football plays on his laptop.

"Hey Coach, you got a minute?" Billy asked, knocking lightly on the half-open office door.

Fatha leaned back in his chair, turning towards Billy. "Sure, I always got a minute for you."

Billy took a deep breath. "I need a favor, Coach. I'm doing a paper for school about my grandfather. It's going to be about what he did in high school in the fifties and how that compares to what us kids do now. I guess it's kind of my testimonial to him. I figure it will be fun figuring out what kids were like back then."

Fatha sat back up in his chair, closing his laptop. "Well, it sounds like you picked the right guy to write about. I've sure heard a lot of nice things about him since he died."

"Yeah, he was a special guy, and even a more special dad. That's why I'm doing a paper about him. But I'm having a hard time finding out about his buddies back then, especially what happened to two of his best friends. I was hoping you could do some magic on your computer and find out how I can get in touch with them. That would really help me."

"You got it, Billy, just give me their names." Fatha leaned up, picking up a pen. "I'll check it out. If I can't find anything on my computer, I'll try the admin office or even the police station. Those guys owe me a favor or two. It's worth a try. So, what's their names?"

Billy pulled the napkin from his back pocket. "The first one is…here, let me see…oh yeah, Brad Tillin. That's T-i-l-l-i-n. The other guy was Tim Sanders, that's S-a-n-d-e-r-s. They were both in the Rymont High Class of 1951, but no one seems to know where they are now."

The coach wrote down their names on a piece of graph paper loaded with x's and o's. "Maybe they're dead, Billy. I mean, they have to be what—seventy now if they are alive? Maybe that's why you can't find them."

"I never thought of that. Can you find out about that, too?"

"Sure, no problem, I should be able to get you some info pretty quick. How does tomorrow morning sound? Why don't you drop by and see me say, right before first period?"

"How about if I call you then? I'm not going to school tomorrow."

"What do you mean? You said you'd miss a few practices, but now you won't be in school at all?"

"I can't. I've got a lot to do…you know, family stuff. I'll give you a ring about nine or so in the morning, okay?"

Fatha reopened his laptop, nodding at Billy, who turned towards the door.

"Thanks, Coach, you're the best. I'll talk to you tomorrow."

When Billy called him the next morning, Fatha told him he had found out a little. Tillin joined the Marine Corps right after high school. He was a war hero, getting four medals before he was killed in a helicopter wreck in 1963.

Billy shook his head. "The Marines, huh? Wow, he came a long way from that nerdy picture in the yearbook."

"What does that mean?" Fatha asked.

"Oh, nothing. So, what did you find out about Sanders?"

Fatha told Billy he couldn't find out anything about Sanders after he graduated. He even called a buddy of his in the Social Security Office in Columbia, who told him there were no records on Tim Sanders since 1951. His friend assured Fatha that it was almost impossible to vanish from their files, but Sanders had done just that.

Billy now knew that Tillin was dead, but there was no place to begin looking for Sanders. Where was he going to find a man that disappeared fifty years ago?

He drove by the Rymont Cemetery, glancing at the taller family markers near the road, like he'd done hundreds of times. Then he pulled back on the Mustang's reins, slamming on the brakes, remembering what Fatha told him. Maybe if Sanders was dead, he was right there in the cemetery? It couldn't hurt to look.

He stopped his car in front of the cemetery building, then walked up to the office door. There was a handwritten sign taped to the door telling the world that, "I'll be back in two hours." Billy chuckled, wondering if the sign had been up there all day. He turned, starting to walk down the rows between the graves, looking for any Sanders. Thirty minutes later, he finished walking the last row. There were no Sanders buried in that cemetery, that was for sure. But how could that be? If Sanders was in high school in 1951, his parents or grandparents must be buried somewhere.

Then he remembered the graves behind the Baptist church, on the other side of town. He drove over to the church, parked, and started walking down the paths between the graves. In the middle of the third row, he saw a large gray marker with "Sanders" engraved on it. There were two small headstones on each side of the marker. On the right side, there was one that read "Thomas James Sanders, Father, Born 6/19/1909, Died 7/14/1965." Next to it was one that was engraved, "Cindy Ann Sanders, Daughter, Born 2/22/1935," but it didn't have a death date. On the left side, there was a grave with a headstone for "Teresa Sue Sanders, Mother, Born 10/02/1916, Died 4/28/ 1976." Beside Teresa's grave was a gravestone for "Timothy John Sanders, Son, Born 4/26/1933," but no death date.

Grandpa was born in 1933, too. This had to be the guy, and it looked like he could be alive. But where was he, and how was Billy going to find him? His sister Cindy must be alive, too. Maybe that was where to start. The answer was finding her. She would know about her brother.

He left the cemetery, wondering if he should bother Uncle Ray about Cindy Sanders. Maybe he would remember her, but Coach Fatha knew how to find people on the computer, and he always did that fast.

Chapter 4
A Young Detective

Billy drove back to the coach's office. Fatha wasn't there, so he walked into the locker room, noticing Connor Jerric, the best linebacker on the team, stretching his arm. Billy took a drink out of the water fountain by the lockers, then turned towards Connor. "Hey, big guy, what's happening? Are you here by yourself?"

"Yep, just me. I'm working some crazy kinks out of my shoulder," Connor said, without looking up. "I woke up this morning with some real stinging. I hope it's not the same nerve thing that kept bugging me last month."

"God, I hope not, Connor; we've got some big games coming up, and we're going to need you."

"Hey, don't worry about me. There ain't nothing that will keep me from playing Friday, you'll see."

Billy leaned down, patting Connor on the back. "Have you seen Coach Fatha?"

"Sure, I saw him heading towards the gym a few minutes ago," Connor answered, wrapping his left shoulder with a long, tan elastic bandage. "He's probably still there, Billy. I haven't seen him come back this way."

"Thanks, Connor. Take care and get that shoulder right. We've got to kick ass Friday."

Billy walked into the gym, spotting Coach Fatha talking to a policeman in the corner. "Hey Coach, can I see you for a minute?"

Fatha walked away from the cop, heading towards his star player. "What's up, Billy?"

"I didn't catch you at a bad time, did I?"

"Uh, no, I'm fine. I just, uh, had some personal business to take care of, that's all. So, what's on your mind, Billy?" he asked, putting his arms behind his back.

"There's one more student I need to check on. Her name was Cindy Sanders. I think she graduated around 1954. I promise this is the last name I need help with. Is there any way you can find out about her?" Billy gave Fatha a pleading look.

The coach took a deep breath, nodding his head. "I'll give it a shot." He pulled a pen from his shirt collar, writing Cindy's name on his hand, then looked at his watch. "How about giving me a call, say, in an hour?"

"Thanks, Coach; and by the way, I think I'll be making practice pretty soon. It looks like I'll finish all the family business in a day or two. Then everything should be back to normal."

Fatha shook his head. "No problem. You go ahead and take as much time as you need this week…you need to take care of your grandmother. Don't worry about it." He put his hand on Billy's shoulder. "When you get back, you get back. Just be ready by Friday. We're going to need you against Washington. They're good this year."

"I'll be there, you can count on it."

The coach shook Billy's hand. "I hope you're right, Billy, I really do." He turned, heading back to where the cop was still waiting for him.

Billy was thinking about his grandfather all the way home. He parked the Mustang in front of the house instead of on the driveway. He walked into the garage, finding both of his basketballs, the new orange one and the scratched-up brown bouncer. He picked up the brown one and looked at it, thinking about all the times Grandpa had thrown chest passes at him with that ball. He could feel his grandfather watching him as he started shooting. After making a long shot, he hollered out, "How about that one, Grandpa?" Tears were welling up in his eyes, but he kept shooting. "Watch this, Grandpa."

He ran as fast as he could down the driveway, stopped, and jumped up, sinking a twenty-foot shot. "That's for you, Grandpa; that's for you," he shouted through gritted teeth.

Billy rolled the ball back into the garage, then sat on the porch swing. He pulled out the old gold watch from his pocket, wrapping the chain around his wrist, and cried for a few minutes, constantly wondering when this bad dream would end. He laid his head back on the swing, looking at the blue sky that spread across the heavens. There was not a single cloud to interfere with the blueness.

He opened up his grandfather's watch, noticing it was still running, and it had been over an hour since he talked to Fatha. Pulling out his cell phone, he dialed the coach's number, asking him what he'd found out about Cindy Sanders. Fatha told him that she was now a widow by the name of Cindy Archdale, living at 113 Blueberry Avenue over in Fort Ridge.

Finally, he had a starting point; someone connected to Tim Sanders was still around. He was sure she would lead him to her brother.

Fort Ridge was only ten miles away. Driving as fast as he dared, he found Blueberry Avenue, pulling up in front of a house with 113 on the mailbox. Jumping out of the Mustang, he made his way up the sidewalk to the front door, ringing the doorbell that was dangling loosely from the cracked door frame. No one answered. He rang it again, still no answer. He pounded his fist on the door. Finally, his efforts paid off and the door opened just a crack.

"What you want?" a voice asked from behind the door. A few seconds later, a dark-skinned Hispanic woman with long black, braided hair peeked around the door. "I ain't buying nothing from you, so goed away."

"I'm looking for Cindy Archdale; is she here?"

"She used to be, but not no more. Now, leaved me alone. I gotted work to do," she snapped, trying to close the door.

Billy slid his foot inside the door, not allowing her to close it. "I'm sorry, lady, but I didn't catch your name."

"That's because it's none of your beesiness; now git your foot away or I'll breaked it with this door."

"Please, all I'm asking is your name, and I only have two or three questions, that's all."

"Well, okay, if that's how I can git rid of you. My name is Niveat."

"Niveat, can you tell me if Mrs. Archdale is here?"

"If you want to see her, you got to go to da morgue. She was keeled about a week ago. The cops say she just died, but I think she was keeled. I know she didn't stop breathing on her own. You go to da morgue. Go see her over there. Just leaved me alone."

Billy leaned in closer to her. "Do you think I can come in for a minute or two?"

"No way. You gotted a hearing problem? I said she died, and I don't want no trouble. If you want to talk to me, do it right here." She paused, peeking her head around Billy, making sure he was alone. "But only for a meenut."

"How can you be so sure Mrs. Archdale was killed?"

"Because I ain't stupid. She thought I was stupid, but I ain't. I was her maid for over twenty years and I've been seen some strange stuff going on around here. But I don't care no more. I'm glad she died, I hated her. Whoever keeled her did the world a big favor. Now, go away."

"I just have one more question. Do you know if she had a brother, or where he lives?"

Niveat looked up and down the street. "Yeah, I knowed about her brother. She tolded me about him, and tolded me not to tell anyone. But who cares? She eees gone now. I can't get in no trouble now."

"I'm talking about Tim Sanders. Wasn't he her brother?"

She shook her head. "He ain't Sanders no more, he eees Casey, Robert Casey, and he eees in a nursing home up in Charloote. Won't do no good to see him. He hadded a stroke, a bad one. Sometimes hees awake, sometimes he ain't. I really don't care about him. He eees a beeg loser."

Billy pulled his head back, squinting his eyes. "Niveat, do you have any idea why he changed his name?"

"He gotted into some trouble with some other boys in school and got drunked. They drowned a retarded kid the night they gradudated. That's why he went to being called Casey now and moved up to Charloote. Now he eees dying up there. Okay, your minute eees up, goodbye," she said, again trying to close the door.

Billy pulled his foot out, but held his hand on the door edge. "Which nursing home in Charlotte?"

"Go away. Leaved me alone." She closed the door, scraping his hand, then turned the deadbolt.

At least now Billy had a lead. He just had to find the right nursing home in Charlotte. Sanders, or Casey, or whatever his name was, must know about the Promise. It was starting to look like maybe the Promise was about four kids killing a classmate on graduation night. Maybe that was Grandpa's long dark secret. If only he could talk to Sanders, maybe he could find out everything that happened that night back in 1951.

He drove up to Charlotte, pulling into the first gas station he saw with a payphone. He began flipping the yellow pages until he found "Nursing Homes." There were hundreds of them.

"I might as well get started," Billy whispered, taking a deep breath. He dialed the first one listed (AAA Rehabilitation), asking if Robert Casey was there.

"I'm not allowed to give out the names of our patients," a grumpy old voice said. "You can come by and talk to our administrator if you want, but I can't give you any of that information over the phone."

"But I need to find him; he's a friend of the family, and there's about a hundred nursing homes in Charlotte. I can't go to all hundred of them." He pounded his fist on the side of the phone booth. "Don't you people have some kind of data base on all the patients up there?"

She giggled. "You got to be kidding me. I'm sorry, sir. I already told you more than I am supposed to say over the phone. I got to go," the voice said, hanging up.

He knew he couldn't drive all over Charlotte checking out nursing homes. That would take days and days. But he had to find out about the drowning…if it was a murder, and whether Grandpa was involved. That just couldn't be. Billy knew his grandfather couldn't hurt anyone, even if he was drinking. There must be another answer. Who else would have any information about a drowning that happened fifty years ago?

Then it came to him. Maybe the newspaper would have a record of that night? But where could he find newspapers that old? "I know…at the library," he muttered.

He drove to the main Charlotte library and walked in the front door, seeing a well-dressed older lady behind the counter. She looked like she was about sixty with her gray and white hair brushed down over her ears. Her left wrist was loaded with colorful rubber bands. As he got closer to her, he became amazed by how she kept her crooked wire reading glasses on the very tip of her nose. It looked like they would fall off with her next breath.

Billy lightly tapped his knuckles on the counter, trying to get her attention.

"I see you, young man. What can I do for you?" She continued stacking index cards without looking up.

"I was wondering if I could look at some old newspapers."

"Sure you can," she answered, finally raising her head, giving him an obviously fake smile. "So tell me, what newspaper did you want to see, and what was the date?"

"I was wondering if I could check out the first few pages of the Charlotte paper…I think it was called the Charlotte Daily Sun back then. I need to look at the May and June papers from 1951."

She stopped playing with the index cards, looked up at Billy, and laughed. "1951? You've got to be kidding me. We don't have papers that old here. I think the oldest paper we have on file is around 1980. Everything since then is on computerized storage. Anything before 1980 was stored on what was called microfiches. You see those old green machines in the back?" She pointed to the back right corner of the library. "I suppose you might get lucky and find what you're looking for on one of them."

"Thank you," Billy responded, then turned back to her. "By the way, how do I know which one of those machines has copies of the Charlotte Daily Sun?"

She shook her head, taking a deep breath. "None of them have any papers in them. They're all empty. You have to find the right microfiche from the file cabinets next to them."

"Okay, what are microfiches?"

She looked down at her index cards. "They look like a negative. You know, like a negative of a picture, except they're full of information. Just put one of them into a green machines, and scroll down until you find what you are looking for. If you have any problem or need some copy paper, let me know."

"Will do, thanks." Billy made his way to the back, finding a five-drawer file cabinet next to the first microfiche machine. There was nothing about the newspapers in any drawer. He tried the next cabinet, spotting a drawer labeled, "Charlotte Daily Sun." Pulling the drawer open, he found hundreds of fiches, not in any order.

It took him over an hour to find the May 1951 fiche. After figuring out how to put the fiche in the machine, he started spinning the dial to look as fast as he could at all the front pages. Finally, he found what he was looking for; a front page story about the Rymont drowning. A small headline near the bottom of the page, dated 5/27/1951, read: "Rymont Youth Drowns at Graduation Party."

There was a black and white photo of the drowned kid next to the article.

Billy swallowed hard, starting to read the short story. "An eighteen-year old Rymont senior drowned during a graduation party at approximately 10:00 PM last night at Buckley Lake, near Rymont. The dead teen was identified as Brian Kelly. The police are investigating whether or not it was an accident or a homicide. Sheriff John 'Buzz' Harris indicated there were some suspicious facts surrounding the drowning, saying, 'The investigation will continue, as we are not certain at this point if there might have been some foul play here.'"

He made a copy of the news story and the photo of Brian Kelly, folded them up, put them in his back pocket, and started back to Rymont.

Chapter 5
The Break-In

Billy's mind was swirling all the way home. Was Grandpa really involved in a suspicious drowning? How could Grandpa do anything like that? But what about the Promise? Was it a pact to keep it quiet? And who were all the Ravens? Grandpa, Tillin, and Sanders looked like three of them, so who was the fourth? Maybe what he'd learned so far would trigger some answers from Grandma or Uncle Ray.

When he turned onto his street, his heart stopped when he saw flashing lights coming from three police cars parked in front of their house.

"Oh my God, oh my God, Grandma," Billy screamed, slamming on the brakes, his tires smoking when he slid onto the driveway. He jumped from his Mustang, running towards the front door.

"Hold on there, young man." Billy heard a deep voice shouting into his ear as he felt a vice-like grip around his arm. He turned to the side, shielding his eyes from the sunlight creeping over the garage. All he could see was a dark blue uniform and the sparkle of a silver badge.

"It's okay, he's my brother," Gary hollered from inside the house.

Billy jerked his arm free from the cop and entered their house. "What's going on, Gary? What happened?"

"It's fine now, Billy. Don't have a cardiac on me. Someone broke in while Grandma and I were at the store. The cops are trying to get fingerprints and figure out what happened. They say they're about done."

Billy looked at his brother, trying to clear the cobwebs. "Is Grandma all right?"

"Yeah, she's fine, she's just scared, that's all. I made her go outside after we got home so I could go through the house. I checked everything out, making sure no one was here, then I called 911. The best we can tell, nothing's missing. But man, whoever did this sure was looking for something. They tore up every room in the house…and you should see your room, it's destroyed."

"Where's Grandma?" Billy asked, looking around.

"She's in the kitchen," Gary answered as he went back to cleaning up the broken picture frames that were scattered all over the floor, throwing them into the brown garbage can that was normally in the garage.

Billy found Grandma sitting next to the small dinner table in the kitchen, bending over, picking up silverware and putting it on a pile on the table. Newspapers and plastic bags were mixed with broken dishes and her old recipe books behind her in the corner. She was crying.

He put an arm around his grandmother. "How you doing? Are you okay?"

"I guess I'm all right, Billy, but why would anyone do this? They tore the whole house up, and for what? They didn't take any of my best stuff. What were they looking for?" She looked around the kitchen, taking in a deep breath. "Billy, this doesn't have anything to do with what we talked about, does it?"

"No, Grandma, it can't. Nobody knows what you told me, I promise. Besides, what would anyone think they could find here about that? We don't know anything about Grandpa's secret to begin with." He was silent for a few moments, trying to find the right thing to say to her. "Maybe it was just our turn to get broken into." He patted her on the back. "It's going to be fine, you'll see. You just leave the cleaning to Gary and me. Why don't you go relax on the porch?"

"Billy, maybe you ought to just leave everything alone. Besides, it's your senior year. You need to get back to schoolwork and football. You don't want to lose focus on that with that scholarship and all." She stood up, bracing herself on the table. "And don't forget Nancy. She is hurting now, too. She loved Steve more than you think. Just let it go, Billy." She wiped the tears off her cheeks with a lace handkerchief. "I'm sorry I even told you about everything. Besides, whatever you find out won't bring your grandfather back. Maybe it's meant to be that we won't ever find out what happened to him. I don't know."

Billy grabbed her arm, helping her walk out of the kitchen. "Grandma, no one knows what I'm doing. I've only told a couple of people that I'm working on a school paper about Grandpa. There's only a few more things to follow up on, that's all. If they turn out to be dead ends, I promise I'll just drop the whole thing. Now, please, just go outside and rest."

He let loose of Grandma after seeing her regain some strength, and he felt a tap on his shoulder. He turned, seeing the same policeman that had stopped him at the front door.

"I need to ask you some questions," the cop said as he scratched his chin. "Is there a place we can have a private talk?"

"Sure, let's go out back," Billy answered, turning towards the back door.

The officer nodded his head, motioning for Billy to lead the way.

Billy finally got a good look at the cop. He thought he looked a lot like the one that was talking to Coach Fatha in the gym. He wondered if there was any connection.

"Let's sit over there," the policeman said, pointing to an old wooden picnic table about twenty feet from the back door. They sat across from each other. The cop pulled a pad and pen out of his right shirt pocket, looking into Billy's eyes. "Okay, what's your full name?"

"William Eric Summers."

"All right, William Eric Summers, tell me where you've been the last three hours?"

"I was up in Charlotte doing some research for a school paper," Billy answered as he looked at the name badge on the cop's uniform, seeing the name "Gunders." He had heard that name before, but couldn't remember where.

"Is there anyone that can verify that? Before you answer, let me give you a warning…I'm going to check out everything you say."

"There sure is. There's a lady at the library who'd remember me. She helped me find some old newspaper articles. I also talked to a maid over in Fort Ridge."

"Oh, you did? Well, tell me her name and where she lived in Fort Ridge."

Billy pulled a paper out of his pocket, sighed, then unfolded it. "She worked for a woman named Cindy Archdale, who lives, or used to live, at 113 Blueberry Avenue. The maid's name is Niveat. I didn't get her last name."

Gunders was silent for a few seconds, jotting the names and addresses down. "Do you know why anyone would break into your home, or what they might be looking for?"

"No and no."

"Don't get an attitude with me," Gunders responded, tapping his pen on his pad. "Okay, smart guy, I've been hearing that you're playing teenybopper cop, trying to dig up info on some old dead cases. I even heard you're looking into police business from over fifty years ago. Is that true?"

Billy thought for a minute before answering. "I'm not trying to be any teeny bopper cop, or dig up anything. I'm just trying to put together a paper about my grandfather. He just died, so I decided to do a little story about him and what kids did back then, that's all. I wasn't hurting anyone."

"Let me tell you something, buster. If you're trying to play high school detective and start stirring folks up, I'm not going to appreciate it one bit; got it?" Gunders pointed his finger in Billy's face.

"Yeah, yeah, I got it. Can I go now?" Billy leaned away from Gunders's finger.

Gunders got to his feet and pulled his shoulders back. "Just remember what I said. Let the police do the investigating. You're just a kid. You don't know what you're doing anyway. Quit wasting your time and my time on all this old bullshit that doesn't mean anything." He turned, heading back to the house, then spun around, facing Billy again. "Everything I said to you was meant to help you; got it, son?"

Billy grimaced, then nodded. He watched the cop re-enter the house, then leaned forward, holding his chin in his hands, with his elbows on the table. What was all that about? Why was he being grilled anyway? The whole mess was starting to get to him. He hadn't figured out anything, but it seemed like his world was coming apart. Maybe Grandma was right; maybe he should just forget everything and just get back to being a kid.

Billy finally got up, walking through the back porch, past the kitchen into the dining room. It looked just as bad as the kitchen. Shaking his head, he continued his tour upstairs, peeking into Grandma's room, where it looked like a herd of pigs had gotten loose, bent on destruction. As he turned the corner, he could tell his bedroom was destroyed even before he looked in, with remnants of his closet spilled out into the hallway. Grabbing the door frame, he leaned in, seeing no resemblance to the room he had slept in for over ten years. It was like some powerful being had picked up his whole room and tossed it in the air, laughing as he watched it splatter all over the entire upstairs.

"I told you your room was destroyed," Gary said, standing in the doorway. "You win the blue ribbon, Billy; you got the biggest mess to clean up. So, where do you think we should start? We've got a lot of work to do getting this house back to normal."

Billy picked a dresser drawer from the floor, shaking his head. "We might as well start right here."

"What do you think they wanted?" Gary started grabbing Billy's clothes off the floor.

Billy wanted to tell him what he thought, but he couldn't. He knew there wasn't much to tell him anyway. "Gosh, Gary, maybe they wanted my baseball card collection. That's the only thing of value I can think of, but it's up in the attic."

Gary picked up a shoe, throwing it into Billy's closet. "Hey, we better check out the attic. Maybe whoever broke in went up there too. I'll tell you one thing, it would be hard for anyone to find anything up there. That's a real shit house."

Billy didn't want to tell his brother he was just up in the attic. "Well, I doubt—"

"Billy, Nancy's here," Grandma screamed from downstairs.

"Go ahead and send her up, Grandma," Billy hollered back as he picked up his desk lamp that was broken in half.

Billy could hear Nancy coming up the stairs. He was anxious to see her. As soon as she turned the corner, he watched her in his desk mirror. She was still wearing her red and black cheerleader outfit. Her eyes had a special sparkle. Her blonde hair was perfect, flowing down, resting on her shoulders. She looked like she belonged on the cover of a modeling magazine, and she was exactly what he needed.

When she got to Billy's door, she almost ran into Gary, who was leaving. She stepped back, surveying Billy's room. "Wow, your house sure is trashed. What happened?" She plopped down on his bed, looking around like her head was on a swivel, trying to take in the entire disaster.

Billy sat next to her, nodding. "Someone broke in, and we have no idea what they wanted." He looked around the room again. "We don't have much of anything to steal; it doesn't look like they took anything, but they sure looked hard."

Nancy shook her head. "We need to talk. What's this all about? First, you basically ignore me for three days, then your house gets tore up. I've tried and tried to talk to you since your grandfather died, and I keep getting shut out. Don't you want me in your life anymore?" She picked up his hand and held it on her lap.

He turned and looked at her, raising his eyebrows. "Of course I want you in my life, baby. You're just as important to me as ever. I've just got some personal family issues going on that don't involve you. I was hoping you'd understand and trust me."

She leaned on his shoulder, looking up into his eyes. "Are you sure you don't want to talk to me about what's going on? I bet I can help; I'd love to help."

He didn't answer. He just raised his shoulders, chewing on his lower lip.

"I'll tell you what, Billy…when you feel like sharing your life with me, I'll share mine with you." She pushed his arm aside, stood up, and walked out the door, stomping loudly down the stairs.

Billy lowered and shook his head, hearing someone pull into his driveway. He got up and looked out the window, seeing Uncle Ray getting out of his truck. Ray stood there, scratching his head, watching the police cruisers leave.

A couple of seconds later, Ray came in the front door. "Anybody home? Hello?"

"We're up here, Uncle Ray," Billy answered, trying to collect himself from what Nancy had just said.

Ray walked up the stairs, heading directly to Billy's room. "My God, Billy, what in the world happened?"

Billy raised his shoulders, spreading his arms out.

Ray kept shaking his head. "I mean, all this happening in the middle of the day. I can't remember anyone ever getting broke into before here in Rymont. And look at this mess...I don't think anyone could make a bigger mess, even if there were twenty of them. Deputy Williams told me you had a break in, but I never figured it to be like this." He picked up Billy's desk chair, turned it right-side-up, then sat in it, drooping his shoulders. "Say, where's Gary, and how's Granny doing?"

"Gary's in his bedroom. He's a got a big mess in there, too. Grandma's fine, she's just a little shook up. I think she's resting out on the back porch."

"So, what do you think this is all about, Billy?"

Billy closed his bedroom door, leaning towards his uncle. "I think someone was after Grandpa's yearbook. Why else would my bedroom be the most tore up?"

"I have no idea what you're saying son; slow down."

"Uncle Ray, I need an honest answer. Did you tell anyone about the yearbook, or that I was looking into what Grandpa did in high school?"

Ray leaned back, crossing his arms. "I didn't know it was supposed to be a secret. You told me you were writing a paper about Steve, using stuff from his high school days, and you found his yearbook. I thought that was great. Sure, I told some guys about what you were doing. I guess I was a little proud." He rubbed the bottom of his chin. "Maybe I had a few too many beers and I was bragging some, that's all."

Billy raised his eyebrows, shaking his head. "So, who did you brag to?"

After taking a deep breath, Ray nodded. "Well, I mentioned it to Jim Ford. He dropped by last night and we talked a while on the front porch. I had no idea you didn't want me to tell anyone about what you we doing. You should have told me not to talk about it if that's what you wanted."

Billy moved closer to his uncle, lowering his voice. "You mean you told the chief of police I was looking into what Grandpa did in 1951? I can't believe that. Who else did you talk to about it?"

"I ran into a couple of old buddies at the liquor store, and I guess I might have mentioned what you were doing. I didn't know that wasn't the right thing to do. I can't undo it, so it's your fault if I did something wrong. You didn't warn me not to talk to anyone about anything."

"You're right, Uncle Ray. I'm sorry I blamed you. It's really nothing. I'm just guessing that someone is looking for the yearbook, anyway. I guess I was just reaching for answers, that's all."

Ray twisted a finger in his ear, looking puzzled. "Answers for what, and why would anyone want Steve's yearbook?"

"I'm not sure. Like I said, I was just guessing." He stood up, patting Ray on the shoulder. "Well, I better get back to cleaning this mess up. Do me a favor, Uncle Ray, just keep my project quiet, will you? I want it to be a surprise when I finish writing it."

"You got it. Oh, Billy, I just saw Nancy leave. She didn't look happy. Is everything okay on the love front?"

"I don't know…it's just been a terrible week all the way around. I think things will get better for everyone in a day or two; at least I hope so."

Ray patted Billy on his shoulder as he got up. "Now I need to find Granny and make sure she's all right."

The boys finished cleaning up the house, taking three hours to get it to look somewhat close to its normal condition.

Grandma walked back into the living room just as they were finishing. She was cried out. She laid down on the couch and Gary covered her with the special brown and white quilt she made when she was in the hospital. It had become part of the couch…no one used it but her. That was Grandpa's rule.

Billy put a damp washcloth on her forehead and she went right to sleep. He went out to his car, pulling up the carpet from the trunk. The yearbook was still there. He was determined to find a private place to study it. There must be something in that book that someone was looking for. He had to find the clue.

Chapter 6
Kaylee Jones

Billy drove to Oak Ridge Park, next to Buckley Lake, looking for a picnic table away from everyone. He spotted a table hidden in the corner under a massive pine tree. From there, he could see the Rymont City Pier. There were pieces missing from the hand rail on the steps going up to the pier, with a Closed/Unsafe hand-painted sign stretching across the entrance. He wondered if he was close to where that Kelly kid had drowned in 1951.

He held the yearbook flat on his lap, determined to look at every square inch. Studying the pictures of the girls in Grandpa's class, he started comparing them to Nancy, as she kept creeping back into his head. A girlfriend that caring shouldn't be shut out. Maybe he should fill her in on everything he was doing…it couldn't hurt. But he remembered the promise he'd made to his grandmother. "Nah, it can wait," he mumbled.

Looking at all the girls' pictures, he wondered which one may have been Grandpa's girlfriend. Maybe his girlfriend was with him on graduation night. If there was anyone who would know about any girlfriend, it would be Uncle Ray. He pulled his cell phone out of his back pocket.

"Hello," Ray answered after the second ring.

"Uncle Ray, I know I've been a pain, but you got to answer one more question about Grandpa. Do you remember who his girlfriend was when he was a senior?"

"That's an easy one, Billy. Your grandfather dated a lot of girls that year, but I'd only call one of them his girlfriend. That was Kaylee Jones. I remember her so well because Kaylee and I were going together until Steve stole her away."

Billy was silent for a few moments. "Uncle Ray, if you don't mind, can I ask what…uh, I mean, what was the deal with him stealing your girlfriend?"

"Well, I was head over heels in love with Kaylee. I thought she loved me, too. She sure told me enough that she wanted to marry me. She even had a closet full of things like dishes and towels…you know, girly stuff for our first house. Anyway, it looked like we'd end up getting married."

"So how did Grandpa steal her away?"

"We double-dated a lot. Steve played the field…he had a different girl every time we went out. He kept saying he needed to find a girl like Kaylee, but I didn't pay much attention to any of that. Looking back, I guess I should have. Anyway, one night Kaylee and I were going out, but Steve didn't have a date. She told us that was okay, just the three of us would have fun." Ray took a deep breath. "Oh, yeah, that was the night we got into that big fight."

Billy's eyes got bigger. "What fight?"

"Let me back up for a minute. We stopped at a 7-11 to get some beer. I had the fake ID, so I went in to get a twelve pack. When I came out, I thought I saw them kissing. They acted real nervous, so I asked them if they were kissing. They both said 'no,' but I could tell they were lying."

"Then you got into a fight with Grandpa?"

"Not right away. Things were kind of quiet until I took Steve home, then I drove Kaylee back to her house. I asked her that night to marry me. I thought she would automatically just say yes, but she said she had to think about it. That really set me back, after all that talk about getting married and buying all that stuff. I left pissed, and when I got home I confronted your grandfather. I asked him if he was trying to steal my girl. He said he liked her a lot but he wasn't going to do anything because she was my girlfriend. I asked him again if he'd kissed her and he said she'd started it, but they did kiss."

Billy sat down on the picnic table bench. "So, what happened next?"

"Well, what do you think happened? I went crazy. I hit Steve square on the nose and broke it. Dad came into the room, got between us, and started to scream at me. There was blood all over. Billy, that's the maddest I ever got in my life. I went to hit Dad, and he…." Ray rolled out one of his famous belly laughs. "Dad ducked, so instead of hitting him, I hit Steve, right on his nose again. I broke it for the second time. Mom and Dad took him to the hospital, and I stayed home. I called Kaylee and she got upset, telling me she wanted Steve and not me."

"What did you tell her?"

"I told her to put it where the sun don't shine. It took me months to get over losing her, but I never let her know that. I learned my lesson. Now, I don't let any woman mess with me. When they start talking marriage, it's bye-bye time."

"Uncle Ray, did all that happen right around graduation?"

"Let me think…no, it was right before Christmas. I remember because when we talked on her porch, I could see their Christmas tree through their front window. No, it had to be in December sometime."

"So, Grandpa and Kaylee went together your whole senior year?"

"Oh no, they had a big fallout a few months after all that happened. She kind of dumped him. I think it was over his drinking. He was devastated. In fact, he didn't even go to our senior prom because he was so broken up over her."

"So, he wasn't going with anyone around the time you all graduated?"

"Not really, Billy. He felt shafted by Kaylee and nobody else could measure up to her. I could tell he wanted her back. He tried to ignore her in school, but he lit up every time he saw her. It took a big toll on Steve, especially after she went to that girl's college in Atlanta right after graduation. I think he thought they'd get back together one day, but he gave up after she left. But he never stopped loving her. Now, don't you go and tell your grandmother that."

"I won't, Uncle Ray. Thanks for the info. Take care."

Billy hung up, glancing back at the yearbook. Thinking that was a wasted call, he went back to looking at the seventeen seniors in that class. All he had to do was find one of them still living in Rymont who could solve the riddles about the Promise.

He studied the photos. Uncle Ray's picture was next to Grandpa's. There was no writing on it. Next to Uncle Ray was Betty Thomas. She must have never married…her name didn't change. Betty was still in town, just retired from the post office. She'd be a good one to talk to. He noticed Bob Atlas, from over at the bank, was also in that class. Bob was a good friend and a regular on their front porch on Sundays. "Best of luck, Steve, Your Friend Bob," was written over Atlas's photo.

Kaylee Jones's photo was directly above Uncle Ray's on the second page, but there was nothing written over her picture. It was easy to see why Uncle Ray and Grandpa had fought over her. She was gorgeous. She had long brown hair, big dimples, and an incredible smile. Her eyes were a little crossed, but she was something.

Billy didn't recognize anyone else in the yearbook, but the fourth Promiser's picture must be there. It had to be one of the other eight or nine he didn't know. Not bad odds. Billy had to find out more about that class. He made a list of all seventeen names, crossed through the ones he knew, and put the list back into his pocket.

He looked over the rest of the book, noticing Brian Kelly was in the football team photo. Kelly wasn't wearing a uniform, just a sweatshirt with a big RHS on it. He looked like he was a midget standing next to the other players. Maybe he was a team equipment guy or a ball guy. Grandpa was towering over Brian, standing behind him.

Billy found his grandfather in the glee club, the basketball team, and the Spanish club photos. Brad Tillin was in all three photos, and so was Brian Kelly. Why was he in every picture with Grandpa and Tillin? The three of them must have been close, or at least good friends. So, why would Grandpa, Tillin, Sanders, and a fourth person be involved in Kelly's drowning? Could there have been something else, besides the Kelly thing? But that maid, Niveat, said Sanders changed his name because of the drowning.

All those thoughts were going through Billy's head. He felt like his brain was going to explode. Then something caught his eye. "IRWY-JS" was written in small letters under the Spanish Club photo. What did that mean? Did "IRWY" stand for something, and was "JS" someone's initials? Flipping back to the senior class photos, he found only one person with those initials…a Jessica Stanger. Billy went back to the Spanish Club picture. She was there. She had to have written that.

Billy's heart jumped, knowing he had found another clue to add to the drowning and the Four Raven Promise. But how could he find out about "IRWY" and Jessica Stanger? "I guess it's time to find Coach Fatha again," he muttered, shutting the yearbook and making his way back to the Mustang.

Driving back to the high school, Billy found Fatha in his office, shaking his head as he glared at his laptop.

He knocked on the window next to the door, leaning in. "Coach, can you help me find one more person from the '51 class?"

"Sorry." Fatha looked up from his computer. "I really can't get involved with any more of that fifty-year-old stuff. I'm just too busy with the big game coming up Friday. Besides, I shouldn't be using school computers for personal stuff. You understand, don't you, Billy?"

"Sure, Coach, I understand. I won't bother you about anything else again. I guess I should be talking to Uncle Ray, anyway. After all, he would know what happened back then; he was Grandpa's twin."

"I knew you'd understand. You got a good head on your shoulders, Billy. And you know I'd help you with anything, but right now I just can't."

Chapter 7
How Many Are Still Alive?

Billy left Fatha's office with more questions bouncing around in his mind than he'd brought. Why was Fatha shutting him out? After all, he was the best football player ever at Rymont High. Did it have anything to do with him talking to that cop? What was his hang up?

"I don't need him anyway," Billy mumbled, determined to find people in town from his grandfather's class himself. There was always Bob Atlas at the bank. Bob wouldn't push Billy aside like Coach Fatha did. He looked at his watch, hoping Bob would still be at the bank.

Billy pulled up to Rymont Farmer's Regional Bank, parking close to the ATM machine. He walked through the lobby, finding the office with Robert Atlas, Vice-President painted on a frosted glass door. Billy had known Atlas for years. He not only was a Sunday night regular, but he would stop by and see Grandpa any day of the week, just to talk about their high school days together.

He knocked on Bob's door, hearing the familiar deep voice telling him to come in.

"How you doing, Mr. Atlas?" Billy asked as he walked in.

"Well, if it isn't my favorite football player of all time. How am I doing? The important question is how are you doing, and Granny, and Gary?" He motioned to Billy to sit in the chair in front of his desk.

"Oh, we're doing all right, I guess. It's been a tough week, Mr. Atlas."

"I know, son, I know. We lost a wonderful man. What a shame. But it's great seeing you. I sure wish I was sitting on your front porch with you and Steve, though."

Young Mr. Summers looked around the big office, noticing a picture on the wall of Grandpa, Atlas, and two other men kneeling next to a dead deer. They were all wearing camouflage outfits. "I know, I miss him, too. He was one of a kind. Say, Mr. Atlas, is that a picture of you and Grandpa hunting?" He pointed to the photo on the wall.

Atlas swirled his chair around, looking at the four hunters. "Yeah, that's me and Steve. Hell, that was over twenty years ago. It was the only time I went hunting with your grandpa. He shot that big old buck right at daybreak." He turned back around to his young visitor. "Billy, I never hunted after that. I just didn't have the stomach for killing something. It made Steve mad that I didn't like to hunt, but it just wasn't my thing. Some guys like that stuff; I'm just not one of them."

Billy stood up to get a closer look at the photo. "I'm with you. I never really liked shooting things either. By the way, who are the other two guys? I'll bet you they're some of your old high school buddies, huh?"

"No…uh, that's just two guys…uh, that worked with Steve at the plant." He turned back to look at the hunters. "The guy to your grandpa's right is Forrest Stephenson. He was probably Steve's best friend in the world back then."

Billy took another step closer to the photo. "I never heard of him. If he was Grandpa's best friend, how come I never heard of him?"

"Forrest left town before you were born, but that whole deal was a big mystery. You have no idea how tight Forrest and Steve were. Forrest was even the emcee at Steve's twenty year party at the plant, but something happened that your grandfather could never figure out."

"What was that?" Billy asked, sitting back down on his chair.

"Forrest just went into a shell. He wouldn't talk to Steve or anyone else. He must have had something happen in his life that changed him. I know he went through a bloody divorce, but it had to be something bigger than that to turn his back on Steve. It really bothered a lot of folks. Finally, Forrest just picked up and moved away, and no one's heard from him since. It broke your grandfather's heart."

"Was Forrest in high school with you and Grandpa?"

"Oh no, they got to know each other at work."

"So, who's the other guy in the picture, Mr. Atlas?"

"Uh, let me look." Bob got up and lifted his glasses, looking at the picture. "I'm not sure who that was…uh, that must have been another worker at the plant." He sat down in his chair, turning towards Billy. "Billy, I'm so glad you came to see me. I've been thinking a lot about your family lately. I've been kind of leaving you all alone so you'd have some time to heal. Are things getting any better?"

Billy felt uneasy about the quick change of subjects. He could feel that Atlas really did know the fourth guy in the picture. "Well, we're doing about the best anyone could expect. Every day is hard, but we got each other, and we got a lot of good friends. That helps a lot."

"So, what can I do for you? I figure you came to see me about something. Heaven knows, I've got the time." Atlas snickered, leaning back in his chair. "They think I'm too old to do anything around here, so I spend a lot of time talking to friends like you, Billy. So, tell me, what's up?"

Billy rolled his tongue over his upper lip, then sat up in his chair. "Well, Mr. Atlas, I need a favor. I'm putting some stuff together about Grandpa for my creative writing class. I don't know much about his high school days, or what kids did back then. I remember you talking to Grandpa on our porch about stuff you all did at Rymont High, but I can't remember the details."

"What kind of details are you looking for?"

What an opening. Billy took a few seconds, biting the side of his lower lip, searching for the first question. "Okay, Mr. Atlas, have you ever heard of a Four Raven Promise?"

"A Four Raven what?"

"A Four Raven Promise? It was kind of a clique I think Grandpa was in."

Atlas was quiet for a few seconds, raising his eyebrows up and down. "I think I heard about something like that, but I'm not sure about that. What else do you want to know?"

"I was wondering, do you know what IRWY means?"

"I sure do, I remember IRWY. We did some weird things in those days. Kids wrote IRWY on their books, then flashed it to someone they liked. It stands for 'I really want you.'" He slapped the palm of his hands onto his big oak desk, laughing. "See, we were just as forward as you kids are today, we just had different ways to show it, I guess. Anyway, when we liked someone, we showed them an IRWY."

Atlas looked out the window, rubbing his hands together. "Why, that's how I got my wife, Beverly, God rest her soul. She wrote that on a piece of paper and handed it to me when we were juniors in chemistry class. It sure worked for me. But, Billy, I'm kind of interested, where did you learn about IRWY?"

"I don't know. I heard it somewhere and it kind of stuck with me, that's all. Uh, okay, here's one for you. Do you remember a girl named Jessica in your senior class?"

"Jessica?" Atlas turned his head to the side, squinting his brown eyes. "I remember a Jessica, I sure do. I just can't get all my memory cells to work." He paused, leaning closer to

Billy with a confused look. "Now, what was her last name? Let me think, it's on the tip of my tongue."

"Could it have been Stanger?"

Bob snapped his fingers, leaned back, smiling. "Yeah, that's her, Jessica Stanger. She sure had a big crush on Steve. And she was a very big drinker. She'd do anything for a drink. Oh, uh, she was kind of easy, if you know what I mean. Jessica hung out with Tim Sanders, but she wanted your grandfather. But I don't think Steve really liked her all that much."

"Does she still live here?"

"Oh, no, she got married right after graduation and moved up north somewhere."

"By the way, you mentioned Tim Sanders. Did you know him very well?"

"Sure, I knew him. Your grandfather knew him better, though. You'd always see Tim hanging out with Steve, and Brad Tillin, usually with some girls. No offense, Billy, but that was a pretty wild bunch, with all that drinking and stuff. It wasn't my kind of crowd, that's for sure. I'd rather hang out with Beverly. Besides, Tim was always in the middle of some kind of trouble. He wasn't a very nice person."

"Mr. Atlas, do you remember the kid who drowned at your graduation party out at Buckley Lake?"

"You mean Brian Kelly? Sure I remember him, poor kid." Atlas paused, looking down. "He was retarded, you know? I felt so sorry for him. He wanted to be part of the group, but he never fit in. They made him the ball boy for the football team. He just wanted to be involved in anything Steve's group did." Bob slowly shook his head. "Kelly used to worship all the players, tried to be like them, act like them, stuff like that. I think they kind of felt sorry for him so they let him be part of the gang."

"So, how did he drown?"

"You know, to this day, I still wonder about that night." Atlas interlocked his fingers, laying them on the desk in front of him. "They said it was an accident, but I'm still not sure. He was hanging around with Sanders and Brad Tillin that night. Say, didn't your grandfather ever talk to you about Brian, or what happened that night?"

"No, he never did. Were you very close to Kelly when he drowned?"

Atlas laughed, shaking his head. "No, I'm not much of a swimmer. I didn't go into the water that night or any night. You probably didn't know it, but I wasn't much of a partier. I hardly ever drank in high school. I guess you could say I was a nerd. I was more interested in getting into college than I was about any party. No, I wasn't in your grandfather's clique, that's for sure. That was way too much drinking and troublemaking for me."

"So, do you keep up with the kids from your senior class?"

"Oh, I see the ones still living in Rymont every so often. A few of them have died, and some of them have moved away. I guess I should have kept up with them more." He sighed, smiling at Billy. "Gosh, that was such a small class, you'd think I'd know everything about all of them, but I don't."

Billy pulled out the list he'd made at the park, sliding it across the desk. "Mr. Atlas, can you do me a favor?"

Atlas held the list up in front of his face, pushing his glasses up from the tip of his nose. "What's this, Billy?"

"That is a list of all seventeen seniors in your graduating class. I've crossed out the ones I know something about. I was wondering if you know anything about the ones I didn't cross out. That would help me a lot with my paper."

"Well, let's see. Wow, does this ever bring back memories. Some of these folks are dead." He scanned down the list. "He's gone," he said, drawing a line through the name. "And she's gone," again crossing out the name.

He picked up his phone, hitting a button. "Marty, whatever happened to Beth Winston?"

Atlas nodded. "You're right, I remember now. Yeah, that was awful. Thanks." He hung up the phone, drawing a line through her name. "She's gone; she died a cruel death, Billy. Beth got bit by a slew of water moccasins when she was water skiing about twenty years ago. She tried to jump over a floating branch, not knowing it had all those snakes around it. It was terrible."

He stopped his eyes on another name and squinted, clearing his throat. "She's gone, too." His eyes began to water, showing signs of a tear forming. "That was my wife Beverly." He didn't draw a line through her name.

It was silent for a few moments as Atlas composed himself. "What's that, five people for sure that are dead? That leaves four. I really don't know what happened to them, Billy. I guess they must have moved away, I don't know…oh, but wait, Gloria Wilson. I know her, she married Todd Stillers." He nodded. "Sure, she did. She's Gloria Stillers now. Come to think of it, she hung out with Steve and his crowd. I'd talk to her about your grandfather's group."

"Do you know where Gloria is now? And what was her last name again?"

"Stillers…she's Gloria Stillers. Here, I'll write her married name over her maiden name on your list. She works over at the city office. She's who you see when you want your electric turned on." He looked at his watch. "She's probably there right now." He handed Billy the list.

Billy stood up, shaking his old friend's hand. "Thanks, Mr. Atlas, you were a lot of help."

"I'll always be here if you need me," Atlas said, watching Billy leave.

After a short drive across town, Billy walked into the city building, asking the guard where he needed to go to get his electric turned on. The guard told him to go up to the third floor and look for a door marked City Utilities. He found the office and walked in, asking the girl at the counter if Gloria Stillers worked there.

She pointed to a desk about halfway across the room. "Gloria is over there; see her? She's working in her file cabinet. I'll hit the buzzer and the door next to you will unlock. Just go ahead and walk in, Billy."

Billy walked through the door after he heard it unlock, looking back at the girl who'd let him in. "How did you know my name?"

"I go to the football games on Fridays. I'd bet most people in Rymont have watched you play one time or another over the last two or three years."

He didn't know what to say. He just smiled and nodded, turning back to walk over to Stillers's desk, seeing a silver-haired lady standing with her back to him going through some papers in a file cabinet. She was wearing the same kind of long, flowery dress that Grandma always wore. "Excuse me, are you Gloria Stillers?" he asked, with both hands leaning on her desk.

"That's me." She turned around to Billy. "What can I do for you?"

"I was wondering if I could talk to you a minute? My name is Billy Summers. My grandpa was Steve Summers."

"Oh, I'm sorry I didn't recognize you, Billy. I should have remembered you from Steve's funeral. Wow, I sure can see the resemblance up close. Have a seat, Billy." She closed the file drawer, sitting in her rolling black chair behind her desk, while he pulled over a brown folding chair from the desk one cubicle over.

Billy cleared his throat. "Mrs. Stillers, I heard you were a good friend of Grandpa's in high school. I'm doing a paper about him, and I was wondering if you could help me with it."

"You bet we were friends. He was a super guy and a lot of fun. I was shocked to hear about his accident last week." She looked over Billy's head, staring out the back window. "I hung out a lot with Steve back in the fifties, but I haven't seen him much since then. I guess we all got caught up in our own little worlds, and just sat back and watched time go by. So, tell me, young man, how can I help you?"

Billy wiggled his chair closer to the desk. "I've got a few questions about your senior year. Since I'm a senior, I figured I'd write about his life as a senior, too, for my school writing class. But it's been hard to find out much, seeing as how just a couple of people from your class are still in town."

"Did you know Bob Atlas over at the bank graduated with us?"

He nodded. "I already talked to him. He helped me quite a bit, but I want to talk to as many people as I can from the class of 1951."

"Fire away," she said, making a stack of white folders and putting them aside.

"Mrs. Stillers, what kind of a classmate was Grandpa?"

She chuckled, leaning back, shaking her head. "Wow, what a question. Your grandpa was always the center of attention. He had such a great personality, and what a kidder. Everyone really liked being around him, with that sense of humor of his. Why am I telling you that? I'm sure you knew him a lot better than I did."

"Yeah, he made me laugh a lot. But what I'm looking for is what he liked to do back then."

"Well, let's see; he loved sports, but I think he liked to party as much as anything. We had some great times, him and me." She smiled, showing a bright twinkle in her eyes. "Someone would pull a case of beer out of a trunk, and the party would start. You'd never know what might happen next with our group. I loved Steve. He was one of the good guys." Her eyes got watery as she wiped them with a tissue. "It just tore me up when I heard he died."

Billy leaned closer to Gloria. "Do you remember anything wild he did in school? You know, like anything he'd want to keep secret? I need something to juice up my paper."

"Not that I can think of. He was unpredictable, but he wouldn't do anything that he'd have to keep quiet about." She smiled again, running her tongue over her bottom lip. "The only thing crazy I remember Steve doing was bringing a bum into our house."

"When was that?"

"Oh, I guess it must have been in December of our senior year. I remember because it was a real cold night, and he was taking me home from a big Christmas party at school. I mean, we weren't dating or anything, he was just giving me a ride. What we did that night was dumb, but I'll never forget it. I still crack up thinking about it." She started laughing.

Billy's eyes got bigger as he scooted his chair closer again. "So, what happened?"

"Well, before he took me home, we had to stop at the laundromat to get some clothes for my folks. We pulled all the clothes out of a washer, and went to put them in a big dryer...you know, the super-sized ones. When we opened the door on this one dryer, a bum was sleeping inside of it." She laughed again. "Yep, a bum. It was a guy named L.D., the town drunk. He must have got cold, climbed in the dryer, and went to sleep. Steve pulled him out, then L.D. collapsed on the floor. We laughed and laughed. Then I got an idea." She stared into Billy's face. "I don't know if I should tell you about all this."

Billy smiled, giving her an anxious look. "You got me interested now, Mrs. Stillers; you've got to tell me the rest. It sounds like this is something to add some spice to my paper. So, what did you do?"

"Oh, okay. Well, I've got this little sister. Her name is Beckie, and she was almost seventeen back then. We didn't get along too good. Anyway, her bedroom had a light over the bed with a string on it. We lived in an old house that didn't have light switches, so we turned the lights on and off with a string. Most of the time when Beckie went to bed, she didn't even turn the light on. She'd come home, start taking her clothes off going up the stairs, then jump into her bed. Do you see where I'm going with this?" she asked Billy, leaning in, almost whispering.

"I think so. I like where it's heading. So, what happened next?"

"Steve and I snuck L.D. upstairs. He didn't care, he was passed out. My parents' room was on the other side of the house, so they didn't hear a thing." Her chest was bouncing with laughter. "We put him in Beckie's bed and went out on the front porch, watching for her to come home. Well, she came in the back door like always and headed up the stairs, taking her clothes off. By the time she got to the top, she was almost naked.

"The next thing you know, she's screaming, I mean a blood-curdling scream that had to wake up the whole town. Then my dad ran up the stairs, in his underwear no less." Gloria was laughing so hard tears were running down her face. "Beckie flew down the stairs, buck-ass naked, still screaming. It was incredible."

"So, what did your dad say?"

"He didn't know who put him up there. He just threw L.D. out the back door. I still get tickled when I think about it. But really, that was the craziest thing I remember Steve doing. Just do me a favor; go ahead and put that in your paper, but don't mention my name. Beckie, to this day, doesn't know who did that."

Billy caught a breath between laughs. "You've got my word, I won't tell anyone who told me that story."

Gloria took a deep breath. "Yeah, that's the only silly thing I remember Steve doing. So, do you have any more questions, Billy?"

"Sure. Have you ever heard of the Four Raven Promise?"

Stillers thought for a moment, pulling on her right ear. "Those boys always were doing things like that, making promises, having clubs, stuff like that. I don't remember a Raven Promise…not to say there wasn't one, I just don't remember it."

"Okay, do you remember anyone in your group that got into trouble?"

She nodded. "If there was ever anyone who would get into trouble, it would have been Tim Sanders. But to tell you the truth, I can't recall anyone doing anything real bad, at least not bad enough to call it trouble."

"Do you remember the drowning on your graduation night?"

Her friendly smile turned into an instant frown. "I don't know anything about any drowning. You have to talk to Tim Sanders about that." She looked down at some papers on her desk, starting to stack them.

"What do you mean, talk to Sanders?"

She started writing on a paper. "That's all I know. I'm kind of busy today, and I already said too much. Maybe you can come back and we can talk again, okay? I don't want to get too far behind on all these new accounts."

"I just wanted to know—"

She cut him off. "That's all I can tell you."

Billy waited for a second, then tried to make eye contact. She would not look up. "I just need to ask you one more question."

"Sorry, but I've got to get back to work. I've got a lot to do today."

"I understand, Mrs. Stillers, but do you know anything else about the drowning?"

"No, I told you I don't know about that. Just find Tim, he'll tell you."

"But I already tried that. He's up in Charlotte in a nursing home in a coma. I found that out from someone, but she won't tell me which nursing home."

It was silent. It was obvious that news bothered her. She sighed hard, staring at a yellow and black clock sitting on her desk. "What do you mean, he's in a coma? Was he in an accident?"

Billy shook his head. "What I heard is that he had a stroke. That's why I came to see you about what happened on your graduation night. Everybody keeps saying to talk to Sanders, but I can't even find him; and if I could, it sounds like I won't find out anything anyway. If I only knew what nursing home he was in up in Charlotte, maybe I could try to get some answers from him while he still can give them to me."

Stillers took in a deep breath, leaning back in her chair with her hands behind her head. "You seem like a very persistent young man. Why don't you go find your source and ask again?"

"I'll do that," Billy answered, extending his hand to her. She shook it, got up, and went back to looking through the top door of her filing cabinet. She watched him leave out the corner of her eyes, then plopped down in her chair, putting her hands over her face.

Billy got to his car, wondering why she had gotten so uptight about the drowning. What was that all about? Why would someone who thought so much about Grandpa get so defensive about what he may have done? Something was fishy, and she seemed to know a lot more than she let on.

But she did give Billy an idea. He should never have left Niveat without getting the name of that nursing home. It was time to go and find his favorite maid. There would be no stopping him now. Look out Tim Sanders, Billy Summers was on his way.

Chapter 8
Talking to a Dead Man

The next morning Billy got up with only one thing on his mind. He wasn't going to school, he wasn't going to football practice, he was going to find Tim Sanders. It was going to happen.

He drove back to Fort Ridge, pulling up in front of the familiar mailbox at 113 Blueberry, anxious to find Niveat again. When he pushed the doorbell, no one answered. He waited, ringing it again, and again, but there was still no response. He pounded on the wooden door with the bottom of his fist.

"You can beat on that door all day, but no one's gonna answer," a voice shouted from next door.

Billy turned, seeing a woman bending over, pulling weeds out of a flower bed loaded with yellow and white daises.. He walked halfway to her. "Excuse me?"

She stood up, putting a handful of weeds into a black plastic bag. "I said, you can beat and beat on that door and no one will answer."

"I'm looking for the maid that works here. Her name is Niveat."

The neighbor shielded her eyes with a dirty gray glove. "Young man, why would anyone want to see that woman? Now, there's a real loser. I never could understand how

Cindy put up with her. That is the meanest and most selfish woman I have ever seen in my life, and that covers over seventy years. She thinks she knows everything and doesn't know anything. She bossed Cindy around all day long. She was something. Well, anyway, I'm just glad she's gone."

Billy walked a couple of steps closer. "What do you mean she's gone?"

"She's working for the Morrisons now. Once Cindy died, Niveat started cleaning the place out, so I told the cops about her and they took her key away."

"You said she's working for the Morrisons. Where do they live?"

"They live three blocks over on Baymont…289 Baymont, I think." She pointed up the street. "Just go to that stop sign, turn right, and the third street is Baymont. Make a left and she should be there…that is unless Vera Morrison listened to me and sent her packing."

"289 Baymont, got it. Thanks, take care," Billy ran back to his car, and after making a quick, squealing U-turn, he found Baymont Street, following the house numbers on the mailboxes until he spotted 289. He jumped out of the Mustang, taking giant steps until he reached the front door. He pounded on the door just below the brass knocker. No one answered. He grabbed the knocker, striking its plate on the door hard three times, and the door opened slightly. He stepped back as he noticed a finger holding the door edge.

"What you wanted now? I tolded you before I ain't got nothing to talk to you about. Now goed away before I call the cops."

Billy knew instantly who was talking to him. He put his foot between the door and the frame, keeping her from shutting the door. "I've just got one question, Niveat."

"I don't know nothing, and I'm tired of people asking me about Mrs. Archdale and her brother. What eees everybody looking for? Like I tolded that asshole in the big truck yesterday, I just wanted to be left alone. Now, go away or I'll get my gun and shoot you."

"Come on, I just got one question. What's the name of the nursing home Casey is at? I'm not going anywhere until you tell me."

"Bradley. Bradley. It's the Bradley Hospice. There, I tolded you, now goed away."

Billy pulled his foot back, hearing her slam the door closed as he ran to his car. All he had to do was find the Bradley Hospice up in Charlotte and see if Casey would talk. He eased out of the driveway, then hit the gas. The Mustang went into a fishtail, leaving black marks in front of the mailbox, followed by a trail of black smoke for Niveat.

He stopped at a pay phone in Charlotte, finding the yellow pages and the number to the Bradley Hospice. He called and got directions, and ten minutes later, he walked into the lobby, seeing Visitors Sign In Here over a closed frosted window. He tapped on the window frame, peeking between the panes of glass. He could see someone sitting down with his back to him. He rapped the window again, this time with a car key.

A very large, round man dressed in white turned around without getting out of his chair, sliding the window open. "What do you want?"

"I was wondering if there is any way I can see an old friend of the family. His name is Robert Casey. He's supposed to be here."

The attendant sighed, leaning his head back, showing his half grown beard under his chin. "Who?"

Billy repeated the name.

"Why would anyone want to see him? He's out of it. He can't even talk. Even if I let you go back and see him, he won't know you're there."

"Sir, I'm doing a paper in school about his high school, so I just wanted to ask him a couple of questions."

The guy in white laughed. "High school? Are you crazy? Casey must be seventy years old. Even if he could understand anything, he won't remember anything about his high school."

"Not about when he was in high school, just if he knows where some of his friends are that went to high school with him."

The attendant unrolled a piece of peppermint candy and threw the wrapper on the floor, popping the treat into his mouth. "Go ahead, sign in here. I don't give a shit. He's in room 155, just down the hall, next to the water fountain."

Billy walked as fast as he could without running, finally finding room 155. Casey's name was written on a small white chalkboard next to the door. He tried to open the door, but someone was pushing it from the inside. He stood back as a nurse came out of the room.

"Can I help you, young man?"

"I want to see Mr. Casey. They told me up front I could talk to him."

The nurse raised her eyebrows. "Be my guest, but let me tell you something. Casey will try to fool you. He's a sly old fox. I think he's awake more than he shows, playing games with all the nurses. Go ahead, go on in." She smiled and turned away, heading down the hall. "Oh, and good luck," she muttered, turning her head back towards Billy.

Billy entered the room, seeing Casey laying in a bed next to the window, surrounded by silver bed rails. The room was dark, and smelled like musty old clothes. He walked over to Casey, looking down at the small old man. Tubes were coming out of him everywhere. There was nothing in the room showing any kind of life—no flowers, no chairs, no TV—just a bed holding a pitiful-looking old person.

"This guy looks a hell of a lot older than seventy," Billy mumbled, as he tapped on the headboard, hoping to wake Casey up. There was no response. He leaned down and patted the old man on the shoulder. "Hello, Mr. Casey, my name is Billy Summers. My grandpa was Steve Summers. He died last week."

Casey moved his lips slightly, giving Billy hope that maybe he could understand him.

"I found out you were a good friend of Grandpa's in high school and you hung out together. Is that true?"

Billy got no reaction. "I'm doing a school paper about his life. Do you think you can answer some questions about him?"

Casey gave Billy a small nod.

"Can you talk?"

Casey struggled to barely shake his head, but now Billy had a way to communicate with him, getting yes or no answers from a nod or a head shake.

"You and Grandpa were best friends in high school, right?"

Casey nodded again, this time with a small smile.

"And your name was Tim Sanders back then?"

The old man's little smile left his face as he forced out an almost undetectable nod.

"Do you remember something called a Four Raven Promise?"

He got a nod.

"I figured out that promise was made with Grandpa, you, Brad Tillin, and someone else. Is that someone else still alive?"

Casey gave him another nod.

"Does that person still live in Rymont?"

There was no reaction.

"Maybe you didn't hear me, Mr. Casey. I asked you if that person still lives in Rymont?" Billy waited for a minute, then realized he wasn't going to get an answer.

"Okay, Mr. Casey, if I give you some names, will you tell me who it is?"

Casey shook his head.

Billy raised his shoulders, realizing he had to go in a different direction. "All right, do you remember your graduation night?"

Casey quickly nodded.

"How about Brian Kelly, do you remember him?"

Casey didn't nod or shake his head, but a couple of facial muscles twitched, and a small tear formed in his right eye.

"Mr. Casey, I'm not here to cause you any trouble. I know Kelly drowned that night, and I'm not saying it was or wasn't an accident. I just need to know if Grandpa had anything to do with it, that's all."

The old man worked hard to slowly shake his head.

Billy took a deep breath. "Did you have anything to do with it?" There was no response. "Can you hear me?"

Casey nodded.

"Okay, how about Gloria Wilson, who is Gloria Stillers now…do you remember her?"

Billy got a small smile and a nod.

"Was she the Fourth Promiser?"

Casey didn't do anything.

"You're not going to tell me who that person is, are you?"

Casey shook his head.

Billy turned after hearing a light knock on the door, and watched a very young nurse walk in.

"I've got to give him a bath." She shook her head. It was obvious she didn't want to give him that bath. "I don't think you want to be here for that, so just wait outside and I'll tell you when I'm done."

"Sure," Billy replied. "I'll go out and get a burger and come back." He paused, looking at his watch. "How about twenty minutes, does that sound okay?"

"That should be fine," she answered, starting to work on Casey.

Now Billy had more time to think about other questions he would ask the old man. He walked across the street to McDonalds, ordering a cheeseburger combo. After getting his food, he sat on an outside bench, trying to collect his thoughts. It didn't look like he was going to get the name of the other Promiser, or anything about the drowning, but maybe Casey would give him the name of someone else to talk to. Why didn't he pull out the list of names from his pocket?

He glanced at the traffic going by, going over possible questions for the old man in his head, when he looked at his watch. He'd been gone for almost thirty minutes. After throwing his half-eaten lunch into a trash can, he walked back to the hospice.

This time Billy headed right to Casey, without stopping at the front counter. When he entered the room, it was empty. He stuck his head out the door, looking both ways. There was no sign of anyone.

He went back to the big guy up front, finding him reading a magazine behind the glass, with his feet propped up on the desk. "Excuse me, sir, I was talking to Mr. Casey and I had to leave so he could get a bath. But he's not there now. Is there any way I can see him again?"

The attendant turned a page of the magazine without looking up. "You can come back tomorrow. Casey is down at therapy, getting some of his dead muscles worked on. I don't know why they waste time doing that, but they do." He sighed, turning another page. "He'll be there, I'd say, about two or three hours, and after that, visiting hours will be over. Just come back tomorrow."

"Why didn't the nurse tell me that? She said I could go get a bite to eat and talk to him after his bath."

"She doesn't control schedules here. All she does is give baths, clean bed pans, and change sheets on their beds. Anyway, who cares what she said to you? We make all the decisions around here, not some stupid nurse. So, forget about it, unless you want to talk to my boss, sonny."

Billy shook his head, deciding not to push his luck. After he went to the Mustang and started it, he headed for the interstate as soon as he entered traffic. After merging onto the highway, he glanced at his rearview mirror, which was cockeyed, so he straightened it up, and immediately noticed a big black car behind him. He remembered seeing a car like that following him after he'd left Rymont, almost all the way up to Charlotte. He tried to make out who was driving, but he couldn't tell, as the driver's face was hidden by a hat and sunglasses.

He decided to get off at the next exit just to see if the black car followed him, and sure enough it did. Billy pulled into the first gas station, watching the other car go by. He leaned back in his seat, taking a deep breath, and wiped his sweaty forehead with the back of a hand. A few minutes later, he pulled back onto the freeway, glancing in his rearview mirror again. Three cars back was the same black Cadillac. Billy hit the gas, freeing all the horsepower in his Mustang, gripping the steering wheel as tight as he could, cutting in and out of traffic.

By now, it was obvious he was being followed, so he backed off, moving to the right lane, waiting for the mystery car to pass him. The Cadillac stayed in the outside lane, going by Billy so fast there was no way to see his tag number. All Billy could tell was that it had a South Carolina license plate.

Billy was getting scared. Why would anyone follow him to Charlotte, then tail him back to Rymont? Maybe what happened in 1951 really was something no one needed to know about. He decided to give the whole mess a breather and get his life back to normal. He had to get ready for the big game, and he sure had to make up with Nancy. She was on his mind all the way back to Rymont, and his damn cell phone was out of juice.

When he got home, he ran up the stairs and called her, tapping his foot on the floor waiting for an answer. Finally, she picked up.

"Hey, Billy, how you doing, honey? It's for me, Mom, it's Billy." She sighed. "I get so sick of her wanting to know who I'm talking to all the time."

"That's okay. Grandma does that to me sometimes, too. Nancy, I've been meaning to call you."

"I've been thinking about you, too. I'm sorry for what I said yesterday, Billy. I didn't mean any of it. I guess I was just worrying about you after the break in. I wanted to know what was going on, and I kind of lost it. Do you think you can ever forgive me?"

"There's nothing to forgive. All you were trying to do was help, and I should have been more patient. Let's just forget about yesterday. I was wondering, how about you and me going over to the 'hill' tonight after the game? What do you think?"

"I'd like that. We need to spend more time together, Billy. I want everything back like it was. I know you've had a tough week, but it's been a long week for me too, not being able to see you very much. Plus, I kind of feel I was left out of a lot of stuff this week."

"I'll tell you what, Nancy…meet me after the game outside the locker room. Then we'll get some time together alone. Oh, I'm going to score a touchdown for you tonight, you'll see."

"That sounds awesome. Maybe we can celebrate that tonight, and maybe you'll score again later…who knows? Listen, I got to go, Billy. I'll see you tonight. Love you."

Billy hung up, thinking about what she'd just said. Every time he touched her, she would say "no." Now, she was talking about him scoring at the "hill." It looked like some good things were finally about to happen in his life.

Chapter 9
The Big Game

An hour later, Billy drove to Rymont Raven Stadium and walked into the locker room. His teammates were shocked, but excited, to see him, as all his private eye stuff had kept him from practice all week. Just seeing Billy instantly raised the spirits of the whole team.

"Welcome back, Billy," Coach Fatha said, rounding the corner. "We're really going to need you tonight, son."

"It's good to be back, Coach. I'm really looking forward to the game. I promised Nancy I'd score a touchdown for her."

Fatha smiled and patted Billy on the back. "I hope you get her two or three, and maybe one for me, too. Listen, I need to talk to you in my office for a minute."

Billy put his cleats on the bench and followed his coach to his office.

Fatha closed the door, picking up a paper off his desk. "Billy, you know I can't start you tonight. You missed practice all week and you know the rules…no practice, no starting. I can't make any exceptions for you. You'll watch the first fifteen minutes, then you can play the last three quarters."

Billy nodded. "I understand. I expected that. No big deal, Coach."

"Good. And listen, I wanted to talk to you about our conversation the other day. I didn't mean to cut you off. Of course, I want to help you any way I can. That was just a bad day. Besides, I think all that stuff from fifty years ago is not doing anyone any good." He paused, turning his back to Billy. "I understand the story you're working on is important to you, but sometimes when we look into the past, we find more than we need to know. Do you get what I'm saying?"

Billy didn't have a clue what the coach was talking about. All he could think to do was to agree. "I know what you mean, Coach. Anyway, my school paper's almost done."

"Great. I knew you'd understand. Now, go get ready for the game."

As Billy was putting on his uniform, he was still wondering what the hell Fatha had meant. He shook his head, grabbed his helmet, and went out and found a place on the bench, wanting to get his mind right doing what he loved...playing ball.

Washington High was a tough opponent. Every year, the game with them was close. Billy knew he had to play a great game, or they might lose. He had the first quarter to concentrate on football, clearing his head of everything that had happened during the week. He was antsy to get on the field, but he had to wait, watching his teammates play without him.

Gary was playing the best game of his life. He made three tackles and even sacked the quarterback, all in the first quarter. *At least one Summers is making a difference,* Billy thought as he watched the scoreboard tick down to the time he could get into the game. Finally, the second quarter was ready to start. He strapped his helmet on tight, sprinting to the huddle. He was nervous, looking around at the other players, who all were smiling. Their superstar was back. After his first play, Billy felt normal, with all of his thoughts finally being only on football.

Washington obviously had a game plan to stop Billy. They double-teamed him on every play. He was still able to help Rymont score, catching two balls on the first drive of the second half, but he didn't get Nancy's touchdown.

The game was tight. Washington led by five points with two minutes to play. Rymont was moving the ball, heading towards a winning score, probably to be made by Billy. They had the ball on Washington's thirty-yard line. It was fourth down and six yards to go. The next play would determine who would win.

Joe Howard, the Rymont quarterback, squatted in the huddle, looking at every player. "This is it, guys. We have got to score on this play. Make it happen—BSG 15 Right." It was the one play that never failed. It meant, "Billy, stop and go, 15 yards out." It was a play designed only for their hero.

The quarterback took the snap, rolling to the right. His eyes were locked on Billy, who was streaking down the sideline. Howard reared back, throwing a perfect spiral, leaving a victory celebration to Billy and his hands. Billy sidestepped the defender, who fell down, leaving him wide open. The ball spun into his hands just how Coach Fatha had designed the play. The Rymont crowd was standing, ready to cheer for the upcoming touchdown.

Billy dropped the ball. It was deadly silent. He fell to the ground, out of breath, not believing what had just happened. His nostrils started to burn, filling his eyes with tears. He picked up his helmet and threw it towards the goal line, knowing he'd blown the game.

Washington took possession of the ball, and their quarterback dropped to his knee four times to end the game. The excited screaming gave way to shock for the Raven faithful that night.

The Rymont team walked off the field, their heads hanging like a parade of penguins, all afraid to look up at the sun. When they walked into the locker room, the only thing anyone heard was cleats hitting concrete. The players looked around, wondering what had just happened. Before long, their tearful eyes were focusing on Billy. They weren't used to seeing their superstar mess up a play late in a game…not Billy Summers.

"Gather round," Coach Fatha barked out. "Listen up guys, we gave it our all. A few plays here or there, and we'd be celebrating now. I don't want anyone thinking they lost the game by themselves. We win as a team, and we lose as a team." He paused, looking at his team without focusing on any player. "Just learn from tonight. Plan on giving your school some extra effort next week during practices, and we'll get back to winning next Friday. Now, go on and get your showers."

Billy sat on the bench in front of his locker, looking down. He knew the coach's speech was about him. He lost the game, no one else did. Now everyone on the team, especially Gary, was probably mad. If they only knew what he'd been through all week, maybe they would understand and forgive him. Billy hoped Nancy, at least, would be there for him, even if no one else was.

He took his shower, got dressed, and walked out the back door of the locker room. Nancy was waiting for him.

"It's okay, baby, I still love you." She smiled as Billy walked up to her. "I've got a surprise for you."

"What is it? I need something special tonight." He hugged her hard as she put her head on his shoulder.

Nancy pulled back, looking up into his eyes. "It's in your car. It's something you really need, especially tonight."

They walked to his car, arm in arm. "Now, you just look in the back seat," she said, giving him a big beautiful smile.

Billy turned, seeing his surprise. It was exactly what the doctor ordered. Her red and white cooler was on the back seat. He reached back, lifting the lid, and saw that it was full of iced-down beer. "Baby, you're something. How did you do that, and how'd you know I needed a surprise like that after letting the whole town down tonight?"

"First off, Billy, you didn't let the whole town down. Think of all the times you made everyone proud right out there on that same football field." Her eyes got wider as she shook her head, smiling at Billy. "And I'm not going to tell you how I got the beer. I put it there before the game started...you can tell by the melted ice. I did it because you had a tough week; who cares about the game? Besides, you promised me a score tonight. Maybe you still will. Let's go over to the 'hill.'"

By now, Billy had almost forgotten about the game, or how it ended. Nancy was still talking about scoring. He was anxious to get to their favorite spot at the "hill."

The "hill" was an undeveloped subdivision eight miles out of Rymont. It was called the "hill" because a guy named Walter Hill bought six hundred acres and planned on building nearly a thousand homes out there, so he cleared the land, put in streets, and even put up street signs. When he found out the soil was contaminated and he couldn't get the okay to start construction, he just left. Now, the whole area was loaded with weeds over six feet tall. There were no lights anywhere. It was the perfect place for kids to go for a party, especially after football games.

Billy and Nancy both had two beers by the time they got to the "hill." Billy could feel his problems floating away each time he took a swig of his frosted brew. Now, about all he could think about was Nancy. As they turned onto Bobolink Lane, their usual corner, he turned off his headlights.

"Come here, baby," Billy said, as he moved his seat back, reaching out to grab her.

She moved up against him, kissing his ear, whispering, "It's gonna be okay, sweetheart. One thing's for sure, you can always count on me being here for you, to love you forever."

He turned and kissed her like never before, the mother of all kisses. He felt like a wild man as the scent of her perfume filled the car. She was breathing harder and faster as he reached under her left arm, starting to rub a breast. She kissed him even harder, giving him the sign to keep going. Billy slid a hand down her stomach, working his way to the top of her blue jeans, finding them unsnapped.

Nancy grabbed his arm. "This isn't very comfortable…it's so cramped in here. Do you still got that blanket in the trunk?"

"I sure do, baby. Do you want to go outside?"

"Let's do it," she answered, pulling her blouse down.

Billy wondered if she'd meant what she said. Did she really want "to do it"? He got out of the car, almost running to the trunk, watching her get out on her side. He grabbed the blanket and closed the trunk, spreading the soft cover on the pavement.

She reached into the back seat, pulling out the cooler, and dropped it on the blanket, then started to unbutton her blouse.

An intense light suddenly blinded both of them. Billy held his hand up, shielding his face, seeing the silhouette of a police car. The powerful light was coming from a spotlight on the side of the cruiser, and someone was standing behind that light.

"What the hell is going on?" Billy shouted, closing the cooler lid.

A husky voice boomed from behind the light. "Okay, I'm going to give you two lovebirds exactly thirty seconds to get your young asses out of here, or you're going to jail for underage drinking and trespassing; you got that? And don't leave any of your trash anywhere, either."

Billy and Nancy jumped up, loading everything back into the Mustang. They were both shaking as Billy turned on the headlights. He pulled out of their spot, turning left, constantly watching the police car in his mirror. They didn't say anything until the cop turned to the right. It was as if they weren't free until he was out of sight.

"Holy shit, Nancy, do you believe what happened? What was that all about?"

Nancy stared out the window. "Do you realize how much trouble we could have gotten to? I mean, we're eighteen and we were drinking. And if that cop would have waited five more minutes before he turned on that light, we would have had some bigger problems. Wow, we were lucky."

"You bet your ass; but where'd he come from? I didn't see him drive up. I sure didn't see any car there when we got there. How come we didn't hear him before he hit us with that light?"

"I don't know, Billy. Maybe he was there the whole time. Maybe we just missed seeing him." She shook her head. "Or maybe he just gets his kicks out of catching kids out there."

"Nancy baby, do you want me to take you home?"

"I guess so. I don't feel like doing anything now. That son of a bitch ruined our night. Maybe we can find a safer place tomorrow night."

"How about me picking you up tomorrow, say around noon? I'm going out to Uncle Ray's place to check on my tomatoes."

"Sure, I'd like that," she answered as they pulled onto her driveway.

Chapter 10
Tell Me About My Parents

As Billy drove home, all he could think about was what might have happened at the "hill." For the first time, it had looked like Nancy wanted to go all the way. "Damn that cop," he shouted, as he parked behind Grandma's beat-up yellow Chevy.

He peeked through the front window, seeing the television still on in the living room, thinking Grandma must be sleeping, so he quietly pushed the front door open.

Grandma was sleeping on the end of the couch, covered with her quilt. Her reading glasses were dangling from the top of her nose, so crooked it made him laugh. She was slumped over with a magazine on her lap.

The HGTV channel was on the TV. She loved that channel. Billy couldn't ever figure out why she liked it so much. It was boring, and she never did anything she saw there. Grandpa would tease her about not letting anyone watch sports in the living room, because she had to learn how to put up walls, or fix the plumbing, or insulate an attic.

Billy tiptoed over to her, gently pulling at her reading glasses.

She opened her eyes, smiling. "Oh, Billy, it's you. For a minute there, I thought it was Steve."

"No, it's just me, Grandma, and it's after midnight. Do you want me to help you get upstairs?"

"Nah, that's all right. Maybe you can get me a glass of water? My throat's so dry. I think I'm coming down with something. I felt a little dizzy tonight."

"How about if I get you some Advil, too?"

"I guess that wouldn't hurt, but just get me one. I took two of them a couple of hours ago."

A minute later Billy leaned over her, handing her a glass of water and an Advil.

"Billy, do I smell alcohol? Have you been drinking?" She asked, swallowing her pill.

"I just had a couple of beers. Me and Nancy went out after the game and had a little pity party. We lost the game because I dropped a ball at the end, so I screwed up and drank a little."

Granny took a deep breath, slowly shaking her head. "I just don't want you to turn out like your Uncle Ray. Your grandpa was so proud of you, but he always worried you'd drink. He always said alcohol did nothing but cause problems, and he was right."

"Grandma, you know I almost never drink. I had a tough night. It seemed like everyone was mad at me except Nancy. Gary even acted pissed off after the game. By the way, is he home?"

"He's upstairs. He got home hours ago, and he sure was upset. I asked why he was so mad, and he wouldn't answer. He just whizzed by me, heading to his room. He must be asleep by now."

"I know why he's mad. He had one of his best games ever, then his brother lost the game in the final seconds. I don't blame him for being pissed. I was hoping he'd still be up so I could tell him how sorry I am about the game."

"Billy, it's just one football game. It's not the end of the world. Besides, you've got a ton of stuff on your mind. Most of that is my fault, talking to you about Steve's death. I've thought about it a lot since we talked." She sighed, looking at the TV. "I shouldn't have put so much on your shoulders. You should be having fun your senior year, not worrying about crap that happened fifty years ago."

He sat down next to her. "Grandma, it wasn't too much on my shoulders. Besides, it's kind of been fun…I mean, trying to put the pieces together. But I'll tell you one thing, I think Grandpa was right saying it could be dangerous. Some weird stuff's been happening since he died."

She lifted her head up, staring at him. "What do you mean, 'weird stuff'?"

He leaned back on the couch. "I learned a lot in a week, starting with finding Grandpa's yearbook up in the attic. He was in a clique called the Four Ravens. They had a kind of oath they called the Four Raven Promise. I know who three of the four are. There was Grandpa and a Brad Tillin, who died a couple of years after graduation. The third one was a Tim Sanders. He's in a coma up in a hospice in Charlotte. He changed his name to Casey, because he drowned a retarded guy in high school."

He took a breath. "Grandma, I've been thinking, maybe the Promise is all about the drowning, and maybe all four of them were in on it, and they swore never to tell."

She shoved her magazine off her lap, tossing her beloved quilt onto the floor. "That's a bunch of bullshit. Steve wouldn't have been involved in any drowning of anyone on purpose." She shook her head, biting down hard on her lower lip.

"I don't think he was either, Grandma. I'm just telling you what I found out. What if he just knew about it and promised not to tell anyone? I found where this Tim Sanders, or now Robert Casey, was at and went to see him. He couldn't talk, but he could nod and shake his head." Billy paused for a few moments. "I came out and asked him if

Grandpa had any part in the drowning, and he shook his head 'no.' I had more questions for him, but I ran out of time. I'm going back to see him tomorrow or Sunday."

"But Billy, why did you say all this could be dangerous?" She bent over to pick up the fanned-out magazine and her quilt that probably had never seen the floor before.

"The break-in was the first thing. Someone sure wanted something bad, and I think it was the yearbook. And I don't mean to scare you, but someone's been following me all week."

She sat straight up. "Following you? What are you talking about?"

"There's a big, black Caddy that's been tailing me. I have no idea who it is, but it's definitely been behind me no matter where I went, even up to Charlotte. Oh, one other thing…some people have been acting real funny when I asked them about Grandpa."

"What are you talking about?"

"First off, Coach Fatha's been very strange about the whole thing, and there's a woman at the city office who was in Grandpa's senior class who was really nice until I asked her about graduation night and that drowning. Then she clammed up and couldn't wait to get rid of me."

"What's her name?" Grandma asked, putting her water glass on the coffee table.

"Gloria Stillers. Does that name ring a bell?"

"No, I don't think so," she said, shaking her head. "What does she do at the office?"

"She works in the utility department, handling electric bills, stuff like that."

"Nope, I don't know her. Was there anyone else you talked to?"

Billy nodded as he twisted his neck. "Well, when I was looking for Sanders, I found out his sister lived in Fort Ridge. I talked to her maid, who said his sister had just died. She passed away a week or so before Grandpa died. I'm sure there is no connection, but it's awfully strange."

Grandma scooted up on the couch. "Billy, did you learn anything from Uncle Ray?"

Billy laughed. "They didn't hang out together back then. When they were seniors, they had some problems over a girl they both liked, so Uncle Ray couldn't tell me much about Grandpa. The main thing he said was that Grandpa did a lot of drinking and got good grades."

She looked directly into her grandson's eyes. "You said you were being followed, and now you tell me some people have been acting strange when you talk to them. I'm starting to get a little frightened. Maybe you ought to go to the police."

Billy's eyes got big as he waved his hand. "No, I shouldn't. What can I tell them anyway? All I know is what a crazy maid and a man in a coma told me." He took a breath, exhaling slowly. "I've got to have more than that to go to the police. But I'm not going to stop now, I'm getting too close. Maybe going to see Sanders again will help."

She leaned back, giving his leg a light slap. "Billy, why don't you just drop the whole thing?

Why don't we just go about our lives and not worry about it anymore? If we do, maybe it will go away."

"But, Grandma, if we drop it, we'll have the rest of our lives to worry about who wants to do what to us. We can't live that way. Besides, Grandpa wanted to clear the air and get something fixed. I think we need to finish this for him, if for nothing else."

"Maybe you're right, but please be careful, Billy. Why don't you try to get some help?" She leaned up, putting her hands on her knees. "Have you thought about talking to Chief Ford in private? He seems honest."

"I don't know, Grandma; I don't know who I can trust. I think I'll give it a rest, then maybe I'll go see Sanders again up in Charlotte. After that, I'll put it all together and sit down with Uncle Ray and hope he keeps his mouth closed."

Granny shook her head. "I just hope he doesn't tie one on and it gets worse." She stood up, reaching for her cane. "Let's go to bed, Billy, I'm pooped."

"Grandma, before we go to bed, there's one other thing I wish we could talk about."

"What is it?"

"I've been wondering if Mom and Dad's accident had anything to do with what happened to Grandpa."

"Why would you think that?" She asked, sitting back down on the sofa.

"Oh, I don't know." He rubbed his chin, looking for the right words. "I don't know anything about their accident. No one's ever told Gary or me about it, and since Grandpa died, it's been on my mind a lot. Would you please tell me about them and how they died?"

She looked at the TV, then turned it off. "Your grandfather and I decided not to tell you about their accident until you were older. Besides, it was horrible, just horrible. Just thinking about it brings back so many bad memories." She let out a heavy sigh. "I'll tell you about that night under one condition...I don't want you talking to Gary about it. I want to do that myself when he is ready. Do you promise?"

Billy nodded. "I promise."

"All right. First of all, there wasn't any connection between the two accidents. Their deaths had nothing to do with anyone else." She leaned back, cupping her hands behind her head. "Your father and mother had a love-hate relationship. Oh, they were in love big-time when they got married. Then they got into some money problems that split them up. The big thing is that Andy was on the lazy side. Steve and I could see that when he was growing up. Don't get me wrong, we loved him—he was our only son—but just because we loved him didn't necessarily make him a good husband or father. He was not a go-getter. He wouldn't take responsibility for anything, like finding a good job, or starting a career somewhere."

"But I thought he went to college."

"Yeah, right," she snickered, looking down at her feet. "He went to college for one semester. I think he quit school because his teachers told him what to do. Andy never liked anyone telling him what to do, not even Steve or me. He always said he was going to be filthy rich one day, but he wanted it handed to him. He kept talking about 'get rich' schemes. It's a good thing there wasn't a lottery back then, or they never would have had any money. Did you know he even tried inventing things, looking for his big pot of gold?"

"No...you've got to be kidding me. So, what did he invent?"

Granny chuckled. "Oh, some crazy stuff. One time he got a patent on a machine to burp babies." She started giggling louder. "Yes sir, a baby burping machine. It was some deal. He built it in the garage. You should have seen it. It even had wheels and pieces of carpet on the inside."

"So, did he sell any?"

"Hell no. One night he wanted to show us how it worked. He even bought a doll to put in the thing. He cranked it up and it looked like it really would burp a baby. Then it kind of went haywire, knocking the doll's head off." She laughed so hard tears were rolling down her wrinkled cheeks. "So, that was the end of that invention."

"Did he ever invent anything else?"

"Let me think. Oh, did you ever hear about the eclipse box?"

"No, I haven't. How did that one go?"

She put her hand over her heart, taking a big breath. "Listen to this one. One year we were going to have a solar eclipse...you know, when the sun gets blocked out. Your dad heard it was coming and figured he would make a fortune on an eclipse box. He got some empty boxes from the liquor store. You should see what he did with those boxes."

"Did he ever finish it, Grandma? Did it work?"

"I'm not sure if it would have worked. You had to stand with your back to the sun and put this box over your head. There was a small hole in the back of the thing, so the sun could shine in a little dot to look at. He figured if you could see the dot inside, you could watch it eventually go away when the sun was covered. He thought it was the cat's meow."

"So, did he sell any of those?"

Grandma leaned forward, twisting her neck. "Yeah, he sold four. Me and Steve each bought one, and Bobbie and Jake Wright next door bought two. Your dad charged us twenty dollars for each one. He worked on his boxes for over four weeks solid, and all he got was eighty dollars for his trouble."

"Did it work?"

"No one ever saw the eclipse that day. It was too cloudy for any eclipse, box or no box." She tried to talk between laughs. "That was the end of his inventions. He was oh for two, Billy. He wasn't no Thomas Edison, that's for sure."

Billy caught his breath as the laughs subsided. "So, what did he do after that?"

"Oh, he went back to being lazy. Steve used to tell him if he would just get as excited about a career as he did with his inventions, he would have ended up a millionaire. But your father didn't care. He went back to mooching off us, watching his wife work. He was just flat out lazy."

"So, what did Mom see in him?" Billy asked, scratching his head.

Grandma leaned back on the couch, sighing. "Andy was a handsome man, and they had a lot of fun before they got married. But it didn't take long for Betsy to see how useless he was. Your mother was special...yeah, Betsy was like a daughter to me. I tried to warn her before they got married that he wouldn't hold down a job."

"Do you mean he never got a job after they got married?"

She laid back. "Hell yes, he got a job. About every six months he got a new one. Steve kept telling him to stick with one company and build a good reputation. But your dad always had an excuse to quit. Like I said before, he didn't like to take orders, and he thought he was smarter than any boss. By the time you came along, he'd had four or five jobs. It was a joke." She paused to cough into her hands.

"Do you want me to get you some cough syrup?" Billy asked, starting to get up.

"No, no." Grandma gave a quick wave with her hand as Billy sat down. "It'll go away, just give me a minute." She took another drink of water. "Now, where was I? Oh yeah, your dad. Well, he couldn't hold a job, while your mom, God bless her, kept plugging away down at the diner. Andy became kind of a mom for you boys while she worked, but he wasn't a good one. There were a lot of times we had to help them get by, and we gave them as much money as we could, but a lot of that went towards his booze. It made Steve so mad…he hated alcohol. He used to call it the 'devil's blood.'"

"Do you mean he would stay home all day while Mom worked?"

Grandma nodded. "But he got tired of that life real quick, and started feeling sorry for himself. That's when all the trouble started that led up to their accident."

"What do you mean?" Billy asked, moving closer to her.

"Well, your mom would get home from the diner and find the house all tore up and Andy asleep on the couch, with you and Gary watching TV. He didn't even have any kind of dinner made for Betsy after she worked all day. Then they'd get into big fights, especially after he took all her tip money to buy more beer."

"That must have been awful, Grandma."

"The word awful doesn't come close to describing everything. Do you know Steve and I would go over there just to give you kids breaks from all the screaming? You used to sit with your faces tight against the TV with the volume up as high as it would go when we got there, just so you could tune out the fights. Yeah, it was more than awful."

Billy could see tears building up in the corner of her eyes. "Are you all right, Grandma?"

"Sorry, I just have a hard time thinking about all that. Anyway, while all that was going on, your dad decided to get a girlfriend."

"No…really?"

"Yeah, really. One night your dad came by and asked us to watch you boys. He didn't know your mother got off early that night, and she spotted his truck at the Holiday Inn on her way home. She waited there until Andy came out of a room after kissing his girlfriend. That was the night they both got arrested."

"Wow, this story gets crazier and crazier, Grandma."

"When she got home, they got into a monster fight. They beat each other up terribly. We kept you two boys until they got out of jail. When your mother got released, she called us, wanting us to keep you boys overnight again. Steve and I had a feeling something was terribly wrong. I can still remember that night like it was yesterday." Tears were streaming down her face again, as Billy got her another tissue.

She caught her breath. "We got you and Gary ready for bed, then Steve put you both on his lap and read you a story. See that picture over there?" she asked, pointing to the fireplace mantel. "That's a picture from that night. Then a cop came to the door, asking us if we could put you kids to bed so he could talk to us."

"What'd the cop say?"

"It seems your parents went for a ride after they got out of jail. The cop said they were going very fast out on

Highway 33, and somehow swerved, hitting a car head-on. They were killed instantly…." Grandma began to sob.

Billy grabbed her hand as he put an arm around her shoulder.

She finally collected herself. "They also killed the Randall family, all five of them. I knew Betty Randall since she was a little girl; and my God, Billy, they had three kids, all under ten years old. It was terrible…that was a week from hell." She sobbed again.

"I'm sorry. If I'd have known all that, I wouldn't even have brought it up." He pulled her head onto his shoulder.

She nodded. "Steve and I had to carry that for so many years, seeing our son destroy his family and kill another family. What I regret the most is that you boys never had a chance to know your mother. She was a wonderful person. All she ever cared about was you boys. It was so sad."

Billy bent down and kissed her, noticing the big octagon-shaped wooden clock over the fireplace. "Wow, it's two o'clock. We better get to bed."

"Oh, my gosh, where did the night go? How about helping this old woman get up the stairs? They're getting harder and harder for me to climb. Oh, and fold up my quilt, will you?"

He helped her into bed, kissing her on the forehead. "Thanks for telling me about Mom and Dad. Now I understand why you never told us about that before. You are something, Grandma…I will always love you."

"I love you, too," she said, already half asleep.

He remembered her quilt, going downstairs to fold it and put it in its usual spot on the back of the couch. He thought for a moment, then pulled the quilt back, putting it over his face, and cried for over ten minutes.

He'd had a terrible and wild day, from the embarrassing football game, to being with Nancy, to the cop on the "hill," to hearing the story about how his parents died. The highlight of his day was talking to Grandma…she always made everything easier. Now, he could look forward to a boring weekend, without any private eye stuff.

Chapter 11
Why Doesn't He Slow Down?

Billy woke up the next morning to the wonderful smell of bacon frying. He knew what that meant. Grandma was fixing their normal Saturday morning breakfast buffet. It was always the Summers's time to talk about the game the night before. It had become a tradition during the football season, and he was glad she was keeping it up, even without Grandpa.

He laid back, putting a pillow over his head, thinking about the game and what kind of mood Gary might be in. Yesterday was a nightmare, and he hoped it wouldn't carry over into today.

After getting dressed, he walked downstairs, seeing Gary at the kitchen table. Gary didn't acknowledge his brother as they sat directly across from each other. It was like they were playing a stupid game of chicken, with one waiting for the other one to say something first. Billy cleared his throat, expecting to get a response from his younger brother. There was none. As he was grabbing a biscuit, Billy finally spoke up. "Hey, Gar, what's happening?"

Gary put a fork of four or five pancakes on his plate. "Not much. I'm just trying to get over last night's game. I wonder what Grandpa would say about the last quarter?"

Billy looked at Grandma. "I'd bet Grandpa would say we gave it our best shot, that's all."

Gary shook his head. "Do you realize how much hell the coaches are going to give us this week? We should have killed Washington; all we needed was that one play." He slammed his glass of orange juice on the table so hard it sent orange droplets flying.

Grandma turned towards the boys, grabbing a dish towel to wipe up the mess without saying a word.

"Hey, I'm sorry about last night, okay? I just lost focus on that one pass. I'll make up for it next Friday. I just had a bad week, that's all."

Gary grabbed a handful of Grandma's homemade little sausages. "It couldn't have been too tough; I mean, you didn't have to go to school or practice, like the rest of us."

Billy started putting raspberry jam on a piece of dark toast. "I'll make all the practices next week, you can bank on it, Gary. I was just tied up working on that paper about Grandpa. Besides, we still lead the conference...that one game won't kill our season. I'll catch three or four touchdowns next week, and everyone will forget about last night."

Grandma spoke up, trying to get the boys off the subject. "Now you all just eat your breakfast before it gets cold. It's Saturday; are you going out to Ray's farm? It's been quite a while since you both worked out there."

Billy swallowed a glass of milk, then wiped his lips with his arm. He turned around to look at his grandmother. "I was planning on it. I've got some tomatoes that really need some work. I might even get Nancy to help me."

"Not me," Gary said. "I'm meeting some guys up in Charlotte around noon."

"What for?" Grandma asked, pulling more toast out of the toaster.

"Willie knows a guy up there that has a complete car that needs a lot of work. I want to look at it and see if he'll sell it to me. I'm sixteen and I deserve a car. I guess no one is going to buy me one like they did for Billy, so I figured between us guys, we can fix it up. What good is a license if I can't drive?"

Billy turned to Gary. "How are you paying for a car?"

Gary put his fork down, looking at his brother. "It's only three hundred dollars. I've been saving for it for a while, and I've got over two hundred already. Willie said he'd lend me the rest. Besides, Willie knows all about engines, and he figures we can get everything we need at Tolbert's junkyard to get it running."

"I'll tell you what, little brother. I've got over four hundred in my savings account. I'll chip in the last hundred for the cause," Billy said, grabbing a biscuit out of a little brown wicker basket.

"That's okay. I'll handle it myself. I don't need any help from you. All my life, you've been the big-shot superstar in the family. You're six-foot-three and people think you look like Robert Redford, with all that blond hair. I'm only five-foot-eight and everybody calls me 'Opie.' You're the best football player ever at Rymont, and I'm only on the team because you're my brother. Girls think you're hot, and they don't even look at me. You got a bad-ass car, and I don't even have a car." He threw his napkin on his plate. "Like Grandpa always said, 'It's time for me to stand up,' and I'm going to do just that."

"Fine, do what you want," Billy said, turning to look at his grandmother. "I'm not hungry. I think I'll just head out to Uncle Ray's." He stood up, grabbing his cell phone off the table, and went out the back door. After getting into the Mustang, he slammed the door closed, muttering out loud, "What a smart ass. All I was trying to do was help him."

Billy turned to back out the driveway, seeing the cooler and his blanket on the back seat. He looked at his watch, realizing it was only 9:45 AM. It was too early to call Nancy, but he really wanted to talk to her. "I'll just give her a ring from the farm," he mumbled, turning onto Old Highway 21.

He noticed how empty the road was, so he gave the Mustang a workout, getting it to seventy miles an hour almost instantly. He glanced at his rearview mirror, spotting a green GMC truck coming up fast. Billy started coasting, expecting to be passed.

"Why doesn't that mother fucker slow down?" Billy hollered.

In an instant, the truck was right on his tail. He felt a thump as the truck hit his left rear bumper. "What the hell is going on?" he screamed, constantly looking in his mirror. The truck slowed down, staying about fifteen feet behind the Mustang. Billy hit the gas, then the truck did the same. The GMC gave the Mustang another push, forcing it to the right.

Billy couldn't stop his car from turning. He yelled out his window at the other driver, "You son of a bitch."

Billy had lost all control of his car. He couldn't stop the Mustang from continuing its big right turn. Seeing a telephone pole coming at him fast, he pulled and pulled on the emergency brake, but it didn't help. Everything seemed like it was in slow motion. The Mustang was starting to wiggle back to the left. He could feel the car going into and over a ditch, still heading for that telephone pole.

He thought he was going to die as he hit his head on the ceiling of his car. The hood flew up, blocking his vision ahead. All he could see were tall weeds flowing by on each side as he tunneled out his path. Then the Mustang bounced two times, hitting something hard before it came to a complete stop. Billy was knocked out.

A few seconds later, he came to. He looked around the inside of his car, seeing glass and weeds everywhere. The broken windshield had been pushed in, lodging itself against his knuckles on the steering wheel. The gear shifter between the seats was also tight up against the caved-in glass. Carefully wiggling his fingers, he finally got free of the broken windshield.

Looking out the broken window over his door, he could see the green truck idling on the highway about twenty yards away. Billy put his arm out the broken window, waving at the truck, just as it took off. A few seconds later, a VW went by but didn't even slow down.

He couldn't get out of the Mustang, and he started to smell gasoline. Thinking the car was ready to explode, he panicked, looking for his cell phone. It was on the floor in front of the passenger seat. He tried move his right leg over, but the pain was unbearable.

"Oh, my God, my leg's broken," he screamed, grabbing his leg with his left hand. The only way to get the phone was to slide it closer. He looked around, hoping to find something to use, when he spotted a jagged V-shaped piece of glass. Using the glass, he slid the phone close enough to reach, so he could call his uncle.

"Uncle Ray, I've been in an accident. I can't get out of my car, and I think it's going to explode. I smell gas. You need to get here fast."

"Jesus, Billy, where are you?"

Billy caught his breath. "I'm out on 21, just west of you. Hurry, Uncle Ray, I'm scared."

"I'll be there in a minute; just hold on, and keep your phone handy."

In less than five minutes Uncle Ray found Billy, driving his truck through the weeds until he got right behind the busted-up Mustang. He ran to the driver's side, pulling as hard as he could to open the door. It was jammed closed, as was the passenger side door. Ray sprinted back to his truck, grabbing a chain out of the back, and wrapped it around his front axle, then attached the other end to the inside handle of the driver's side door on the Mustang. He backed his truck up and the door came off instantly.

Billy tried to get out of the car as soon as he saw the door come off. He leaned out, falling to the ground. He tried to get up, but the pain in his leg was incredible. Uncle Ray pulled him towards the highway, and they both fell to the ground, trying to catch their breath.

Billy was going in and out of consciousness. He could hear Ray calling for an ambulance and then talking to Grandma, saying something about a horse.

"Horse? What's he talking about?" Billy mumbled. Then he passed out again.

Chapter 12
A Horse?

The next day Billy woke up at the Wilson Baptist Hospital in Charlotte. When he opened his eyes, Grandma was looking down at him, patting his hand. The tears on her cheeks glistened in the light streaking in from the windows. Uncle Ray was asleep on a wooden chair next to the bathroom, stretching his legs out onto the base under Billy's bed. His head was tilted back with his mouth open, his snoring penetrating the otherwise silent hospital room.

"He's awake, Ray, he's awake," Grandma hollered, looking down at her grandson.

She bent down, kissing him on his forehead. "You gave us quite a scare yesterday."

Billy shook his head, trying to clear away the cobwebs. "Grandma, what happened? How long have I been here? What time is it?"

"It's Sunday, and it's almost eleven in the morning, son," she replied, wiping away tears. "You've been here since yesterday morning. We've been waiting for you to wake up for over twenty-four hours...Ray, Ray, wake up."

"Is everything okay, Grandma?" Billy asked, getting prepared for a bad answer.

"The doctors said you may have a concussion and or some internal bleeding, they're not sure yet. But you really tore up your leg, breaking it in three spots. They had to put some pins in it. Other than that, you just got a few cuts, mostly on your hands from the windshield." She grabbed his hands, gently rubbing the bandages covering his knuckles.

Ray got up, walking to the other side of Billy's bed. He rubbed his eyes and shook his head. "Hallelujah, he's come to. Well, partner, how are you doing?" He patted his nephew's arm. "Do you know how lucky you are? That was some accident. It looked to me a lot like Steve's, only Steve's truck wasn't tore up near as bad as your fancy Mustang."

Billy looked up at his uncle. "That was no accident, Uncle Ray. Some asshole pushed me off the road and I thought I was going to die. There was this big old telephone pole coming right at me and I couldn't do anything about it. All I could think about was Grandma, Gary, and Nancy. I thought I was a dead man."

Grandma reached over, pushing Billy's pillow down behind his head. "Now, Billy, are you sure about that? Someone pushed you off the road?"

"I'm one hundred percent sure of it, Grandma. This guy in a big GMC pickup came up behind me and bumped me twice. The second time I went flying over the ditch and down into a big field. It knocked me out, then the next thing you know, an ambulance was there. Say, Uncle Ray, how's my car? Is it totaled?"

Ray took a drink out of a Styrofoam cup sitting on Billy's tray. "Man, that's some old coffee." He finished drinking the stale brew, then turned back to Billy. "Yes, your car's totaled. You won't drive that Mustang again."

Billy punched the pillow that was laying next to his left arm. "Damn it. Okay, let's hear it, let's hear the really bad news. Do the doctors think I'll be able to play football again?"

Grandma spoke up. "Who cares about football? All I care about is that you are still alive. Ray took me out there this morning. You just barely missed that telephone pole. You could have been killed...." She started crying again.

Ray gave Granny a minute. "Yes, Billy, you'll be able to play football again. The doctor said you'll have a cast for three months or so, then you can start your rehab. He said there's no reason you can't be good as new by March. But I want to get back to what you just said. Do you think someone really tried to kill you?"

"Hell, yes, he tried to kill me. After he sent me flying over that ditch, he just sat there and watched me. I think he wanted to see if my car would explode."

"Did you know who it was who hit you?" Ray asked.

Billy grimaced from some leg pain. "No, I didn't get a good look at him. But I bet I could pick out that truck if I saw it again. I'll never forget the truck."

Ray leaned over, closer to his nephew. "Billy, I've got to tell you something. The police think you ran off the road on your own, just a teenager going too fast; plus, they found a cooler full of beer in the back seat."

Billy sighed, lowering his shoulders. "So what, they found some beer...big deal. Who would be drinking beer at nine in the morning, anyway? Let them think what they want."

"They took some blood from you, Billy," Ray said. "They told me you had some alcohol in your system, but not enough to charge you with anything."

"So?" Billy looked around the room. "Hey, where's Nancy?"

"She's been here every minute since they brought you up here," Grandma answered. "She had to go home this morning to get cleaned up and get some sleep. The little doll laid next to you all night, Billy."

Billy looked down at his new, white cast. It was so heavy he couldn't move it. The cast went from the top of his leg all the way down to four inches above the ankle. He tried to lift it.

"Hold on, Bud," Uncle Ray said. "Dr. Victor told us not to let you move that leg at all for at least forty eight hours."

"Does that mean I'm going to be here for two more days? I've got things to do, especially homework."

Grandma sat on the chair in front of the window. "I've got news for you. The doctor said you're going to be here for a week so they can watch for internal bleeding or a concussion. Besides, if you're worried about your homework, I'll try to get it from your teachers and you can do it right here. You might as well get used to it. But don't worry, the week will go by fast."

"Shit, some more wonderful news during a wonderful week," Billy said.

Gary came into the room, carrying a white sack and a beverage holder full of coffees. He looked over at Billy, seeing him awake. He put the breakfasts down on a rolling table next to Ray, then moved next to Grandma, looking down at his big brother. "Hey, Billy, how are you doing?"

"I'm not sure, Gary. But one thing I know, you don't have to worry about me blowing any more games this year."

Gary grimaced. "Billy, I feel bad about yesterday…I didn't mean what I said. I don't care about any old football game. Me, and everyone at school, are just worried about you. Besides, think of the jokes in school about my macho brother, the one who hit a horse with his Mustang. You're more famous now than when you caught the winning touchdown against Landon."

Billy opened his mouth, nodding. "Now I remember. I heard Uncle Ray tell someone that I missed the telephone pole, but didn't miss the horse."

Gary looked at Grandma, then Uncle Ray. "No one's told you about the horse yet?"

"He just wokc up, we didn't have a chance," Ray said.

Gary sat down, laughing. "That's right, big brother, you killed the world's biggest horse. It must have been about twice as big as your Mustang, based on the size of the grave they put it in. They buried it right next to where you hit it."

Ray grabbed a cup of coffee, taking a big gulp. "The cops said you hit the horse broadside, like you were trying to go under it. That's why the windshield was pushed in so much. It looked like his legs tore up both sides of your car as he rolled over you, so your doors wouldn't open. And Gary's right, the horse had no brand or markings on it, so the county buried it right there."

Billy twisted his neck. "Man, my neck is killing me. I can hardly move it."

Grandma walked up to Billy, grabbing his hand. "The nurse said you may have some aches and pains for a few days. She said your body went through a major shock hitting that horse. It's a wonder you don't have more broken bones."

Billy sat up, still rubbing his neck. "Has anyone seen my cell phone? I want to call Nancy."

Grandma shook her head. "No, Billy, please don't do that. She just left an hour ago. She didn't get a wink of sleep last night. Let her get some rest."

"Okay, okay, I'll call her in a couple of hours. Oh, Uncle Ray, what does this do to my scholarship at Georgia Tech, do you have any idea?"

Ray walked over to Billy, patting him on his shoulder. "Coach Fatha said he was going to take care of all that. He figured that would be the first question you'd ask when you woke up. Fatha told me he was going to talk to the head coach down there, and tell him you would be fine by next fall. I wouldn't worry about that a bit, Billy."

A couple of hours later, Billy was alone with Grandma. "Grandma, I was thinking, maybe the guy who ran me off the road did the same thing to Grandpa."

She pulled the sheet up under his chin. "I've been wondering about that, too, Billy. I think we need to get the cops involved now."

"I'm not so sure about that; I think we should sleep on it. Have you had any thoughts about filling Uncle Ray in on everything now that I'm laid up?"

"I don't know, Billy, I just don't know."

"Well, just let me know when you decide. You're the one I made the promise to about not telling anyone. Right now, I want to talk to Nancy. Do me a favor? Hand me my phone. It's right over there on that table." Billy pointed to the table now holding empty coffee cups.

She handed him the phone as she turned towards the door. "I need to get some fresh air anyway. You go ahead and talk to Nancy. I think I'll go outside for a little walk. I'll be back in a little bit." She kissed his forehead, then headed out of his room.

He dialed Nancy's number and her mother answered.

"Is that you, Billy?"

"Yeah, it's me, Mrs. Knott."

"My God, Billy, we were so worried about you. It's super just hearing your voice. We've been on pins and needles waiting to hear how you are doing."

"I'm going to be okay. I got a broken leg, that's all. Oh, the doctors think I might have a concussion or some internal bleeding, but overall, I was pretty lucky. Did Nancy tell you I hit a horse?"

"Yes, she did. That's so wild. She said you just missed a telephone pole. I guess it's better to hit a horse than a telephone pole, huh? I'm just glad you'll be all right."

"Is Nancy there?" Billy asked, turning up the volume on his phone.

"She's sleeping, but she told me to wake her up if I heard from you or anyone else at the hospital. Do you want me to do that...I mean, wake her up?"

"I really want to talk to her. Why don't you wake her up and see if she wants to call me back?"

"Sure, Billy, but knowing her, she'll be calling you in about thirty seconds."

She was right. Less than a minute later, his cell phone rang.

"Billy, oh, Billy," Nancy said the second he hit the talk button. She was crying.

"It's okay, baby, I'm fine. It's just a broken leg. Wow, do I ever miss you. Can you come by and see me sometime today?"

She tried to talk between sobs. "Billy, I was so worried…you looked so helpless in that bed. Did they tell you I was there all night? I couldn't sleep, looking at you…you're so important to me."

"So, sweetheart, how soon can you get up here?"

"I'll be there in less than an hour. I love you so much. I'll see you real soon. Bye."

Uncle Ray walked in the room, looking down at his nephew. "Is there anything you need?"

"There is one thing, Uncle Ray. Can you come by later tonight after everyone else is gone? I want to talk to you about something important."

"Sure, Billy, just let me know when you want to talk, I'll be here most of the night, anyway." He patted his nephew's arm. "Look at you, you can't keep your eyes open. What kind of medicine did they give you, anyway?"

"I don't know, it was something called acivan or Ativan or something like that."

Billy turned his groggy head towards the window, watching a few cars go by, as Uncle Ray left. He watched a soft sailboat-shaped white cloud slowly moving over the hospital buildings, heading towards his left. It made him think of the last time he went fishing with Grandpa. They rented a sailboat, but had so much trouble unrolling the sail.

He laid his head back, again feeling the sharp stabbing pain in his gut he felt when they first told him about the killing tree.

He felt the tears starting to build up again as he missed his best friend. Then he went to sleep.

Chapter 13
The Williams Interview

Billy woke up very groggy, feeling someone rubbing his forehead. He knew immediately who it was. Nancy's perfume gave it away. It reminded him of walking into Grandma's flower garden, or the night on the "hill" when Nancy drove him crazy. He opened his eyes, seeing her big, beautiful green eyes loaded with tears.

"What took you so long?" Billy asked, giving her a faint smile, followed by a hug.

"Billy, I was so worried about you. After they called and told me about your accident, I didn't know what to do. I was so scared." She caught a tear falling off the tip of her nose with the top of her hand. "I didn't know if you'd ever wake up. I prayed and prayed that you'd be all right. I held your hand last night for hours hoping God was listening to me. I didn't know what else to do but pray." She kissed his cheek over and over. "Billy, I love you so much."

Ray came back into the room, walking up to Billy and Nancy. "Billy, I talked to Chief Ford. I filled him in on everything that happened yesterday. He told me to tell you not to worry about the beer charges. Oh, and one more thing; he said he was sending a deputy up here to talk to you sometime today."

"Did he say what time the deputy would get here?" Billy asked, looking at the big white clock on the wall over the couch.

Uncle Ray shook his head, patting Billy on the shoulder. "No, he just said today."

Billy turned to Nancy. "How long can you stay, baby?"

"I'm going to stay as long as they let me. I don't know what the visiting hours are, and I really don't care. I'll be here every minute I can."

Ray sat down on a chair next to the bed. "You all don't need to worry about visiting hours. I'm going to talk to the head cheese here this afternoon. I'll take care of it. We'll be able to see Billy whenever we want, you can count on that." He nodded as he picked up the newspaper he had already read twice.

Billy's phone rang. It was Coach Fatha.

"Hey, Billy, how you doing?"

"Oh, hi, Coach. I'm okay. I got a broken leg and a wrecked car." Billy nudged Nancy so he could sit up. "Sorry about the football season. I sure wish I would have stayed home yesterday morning."

"Don't worry about any of that, Billy. The important thing is that you get better so when you get to Georgia Tech next fall you're ready to show them what you got. I'm going to be sure you get on the best rehab program in a couple of months; oh, and when you're back in shape, you're going to be a graduate assistant for me next summer. That way you can keep working out at the school."

Billy took a deep breath, finally finding a big smile. "I don't know how to thank you, Coach. I owe you."

"Huh? You don't owe me a damn thing. No, I owe you; you put our football program on the map. I'll see you soon…bye, Billy."

He laid back, staring at the ceiling. A few minutes later, he was asleep again.

Nancy got up from Billy's bed, brushing her blouse off. "He's out again. Why don't we go downstairs and get something like a sandwich? Come to think of it, I haven't eaten much since Friday night."

They walked to the elevator together, leaving Billy alone with his dreams. An hour later, they headed back to his room, noticing a Rymont deputy leaning against the door frame to Billy's room.

"Well, if it isn't Carl Williams. Here to see Billy?" Ray asked.

"I sure am. Chief Ford sent me up here to talk to him, but he's sleeping. Do you all want me to come back later?"

"Nah, let's wake him up. You came all the way up here from Rymont. Let's just do it," Ray said, walking over to Billy, tapping him on his shoulder. "Billy, wake up."

Billy shook his head, trying to focus on his uncle. "Hi, Uncle Ray."

Ray squeezed a pillow behind Billy, pushing it down his back. "Deputy Williams from Rymont is here. Do you feel like talking to him?"

"Sure, where is he?" Billy asked, looking around the room.

Ray motioned to Carl to come in, who told everyone in the hall to give him some private time with Billy.

After closing the door, Carl sat in the chair closest to the bed. "I need you to stay, Ray; you were at the accident scene."

Ray walked over to the window, picking up another chair to put next to Carl. "Billy, this is Carl Williams from back home. He's a good friend. Chief Ford sent him up here to look into what happened yesterday."

Carl shook Billy's hand as he was pulling a notepad from his shirt pocket. "So, Billy, how are you feeling now?"

"I'm all right. I was lucky, real lucky. All I got was a broken leg. It just puts me behind a little bit on my football career."

"That's too bad, Billy," Carl responded, as he flipped a page in his notebook. "I've enjoyed watching you play this year. You are one hell of a great football player. Do you think you'll be able to play next fall?"

"You bet your ass. They say I'll be as good as new by next spring. Next fall I'm going to Georgia Tech. I've got a full scholarship down there."

"Uh huh; okay, well, let's get to yesterday. Tell me about the whole day, Billy."

"Yesterday…that seems like a week ago. Here goes. I decided to go out to Uncle Ray's farm to check on my acre out there. My tomatoes need a lot of work. After driving on Highway 21 for about ten minutes, I saw this big green GMC truck coming up behind me. I thought he was going to pass me, but he tapped my back bumper, so I slowed down."

Billy took a big breath. "Then he hit me again, knocking me off the road. I was heading for a telephone pole. It all happened so fast. When I went over the ditch, my hood flew up, so all I could see were weeds flying by me. Then I hit a horse, which probably saved my life because it kept me from hitting that telephone pole." He started breathing harder.

"Just take your time, Billy. I've got all night. Start up again whenever you want," Carl said, leaning back in his chair.

A minute later, Billy went back to his story. "I'm okay now. After I hit the horse, I smelled gas. I thought the car was going to explode. Then I called Uncle Ray, who found me and pulled me out of my car by pulling the driver's door off."

The deputy leaned forward. "Did you see the truck after you hit the horse?"

"Yeah, I saw the truck, just sitting on the edge of the road, idling. I waved at the driver, trying to get some help, but he just took off, that son of a bitch."

"Okay; now, how long was it before your uncle got there?"

Billy felt a sharp pain in his leg. He reached down, trying to lift his cast. "Damn it," he moaned, leaning back in his bed. "I'm sorry, where were we? Oh yeah…Uncle Ray got there in a couple of minutes, but I was in so much pain I thought it took forever. He pulled me out of my car and then the ambulance came."

"Let's get back to you driving out there. How fast were you going before the accident?"

"Oh, I don't know, maybe sixty or sixty five. I'm not real sure."

"The investigators say you were going at least eighty when you went off the road. Can that be possible?"

"How would I know? The last thing on my mind was how fast I was going. I thought I was going to die. What difference does it make, anyway?" Billy asked, looking at Williams, then at his uncle.

"We just want to be sure you got hit and just didn't lose control of your car. That's pretty easy to do if you're going too fast. Believe me, going too fast causes a ton of accidents."

Billy opened his mouth in shock. "Are you saying nobody hit me? That's crazy. Do you really think I went out looking for a telephone pole or a horse to hit?" Billy turned his head towards the window, mumbling something about bullshit. "I'll tell you what is really crazy…you keep calling it 'an accident.'" He looked back at Williams. "It was no accident; that prick tried to kill me, plain and simple."

Carl shuffled his chair closer to the bed. "Billy, I believe someone hit you, I've just got to cover all the bases. These are just normal questions I have to ask. Now, getting back to the truck, how can you be sure it was a GMC?"

"I saw the letters on the front of the truck…you know, the insignia. I'm one hundred percent sure it was a big, green GMC."

"Billy, I want you to think real hard. Did you notice anything else about the truck, anything unique to that particular GMC?"

Billy thought for a minute. "Wait a minute…I think it had a front license plate with some kind of a red…no, a Dixie…sure, a Dixie flag on it. I don't know why I didn't think of it before now, but I can see it in my head. Yep, it definitely had a red Dixie flag on a silver-like background."

"Now, we're getting somewhere," Williams said, writing in his notebook. "Do you remember anything else about the truck; or how about the driver? Did you recognize him or her?"

Billy shook his head. "I never got a good look at the driver, but it was a man, not a woman, I'm sure of that."

"A man, huh? Did you see his hair color or what he was wearing?"

"I think he was wearing a cap and some sunglasses. I guess I was panicking and didn't bother to take notes on the asshole's wardrobe."

Deputy Williams looked directly into Billy's eyes. "We checked your car. There weren't any signs of foreign paint on it anywhere. How could anyone hit you and not leave any paint residue?"

"You sound like I'm making all this up. How do I know why there's no paint on my car? Maybe my bumper was all he hit, who knows?"

"I'm just asking. I need to get to the truth. Even if all he hit was your rear bumper, there really should be some paint on that bumper; after all, I would think a GMC trucks sits almost a foot higher off the ground than a Mustang. That part of it is a mystery for me."

Billy turned his back to the window. "Sure, sure. What else do you need?"

"I only have one more question, Billy." He looked down at his notes as he was scratching the side of his face. "Do you know why anyone would want to hurt you?"

Billy gave him a sarcastic "huh." "Well, after I lost the game Friday night, I bet there's a lot of people in Rymont not too fond of me." He grunted, looking out the window. "No, I can't think of anyone out there that wants to hurt me, or kill me; I really can't."

Williams looked at the clock over the sofa, then turned back to Billy. "I heard you are doing some kind of article about your grandfather, and you've been digging up some old criminal cases in Rymont. Is that true?"

"I've been working on a paper for my creative writing class about what it was like when Grandpa was a senior. It's kind of a testimonial to him, but it's also about how kids were different back then, and how they are the same. I wasn't researching anything about any criminal cases or anything like that."

Williams turned a page in his notebook. "Okay, Billy, let me ask you in a different way. Were you interested in any particular event that took place when Steve was a senior?"

"Not really, I just wanted to learn more about my grandfather, that's all."

Carl closed his notebook, sliding his pen over the top of it. "Is there anything else you want to tell me about yesterday, Billy?"

Billy grimaced, shaking his head.

The deputy opened up his wallet, pulling out a business card. "Here's my card. If you think of anything else, just give me a call."

Carl turned to Ray. "Is there anything Billy left out?"

"No, he covered everything, and I believe every word, Carl," Ray answered, putting his chair back to its spot in front of the window, watching Carl shake hands with Billy, then leave.

Billy turned to his uncle. "Uncle Ray, what's with that guy? He sure grilled me, like I did something wrong. Someone pushed me off the road. I didn't do anything wrong or lie about one single thing. I thought you said he was friend of yours."

Ray took a drink of Coke out of a glass on Billy's side table. "Carl was just doing his job. He's just being thorough…he wasn't after you, and I think he believes you. Hey, I've known Carl for a long time, you can trust him. He'll get to the bottom of all this."

Billy raised his right arm up, as it was sore. "I'm not so sure. One thing I found out last week is that you can't trust anyone but family."

"What do you mean?" Ray asked, walking over next to Billy.

"Oh, I don't know. I'm getting tired again. How about getting everyone back in here?"

Ray found the others in the lounge near the hospital entrance, told them Billy was sleepy and needed some rest, and asked them to go back and tell him goodnight.

Nancy sat next to her boyfriend. "Can I call you a few times tonight? Every time I wake up, I think of you, so let's talk some, okay?"

"I'll be here, I'm not going anywhere. What time do you think you'll get here tomorrow?"

Nancy grabbed his hand, holding it between both of hers. "Right after school. I'm not going to cheerleader practice again until you get home. Who cares if I miss a week of it? I sure don't."

Billy kissed Grandma and Nancy goodnight, leaving Ray alone with his nephew.

"Hey, Uncle Ray, how about calling me in the morning? I've got some stuff I want to talk to you about."

"You already told me that once today. It must be damn important. Do you want me to stick around and talk now?"

"Nah, I'm tired. Let's talk tomorrow, Uncle Ray."

"I'll see you then, Billy." Ray grabbed a day-old donut off the table along the wall and walked out of the room.

Billy looked at his right leg, thinking about his accident. He knew it was tied into the Promise somehow, and by God, he was going to find the answers.

Chapter 14
Chief Ford

A nurse woke Billy up at 4:00 AM to give him some pills. She seemed very unhappy as she rolled the side table next to his bed. Looking like she was about seventy, her black and white hair was pulled back into a bun, with a pair of red glasses covering almost her entire face. The wrinkles on her face made Billy think she hadn't smiled in years.

"Just my luck," he mumbled. "If I have to be woken up at four in the morning, why does it have to be another cranky old witch?"

"What'd you say, young man?"

"I was talking to myself about my accident."

"Uh huh."

"What's your name, anyway?" Billy watched her pour water into a white paper cup, spilling a few drops on the tray. "I haven't seen you before."

"I'm Nurse Rawley. It's time for your meds, Mr. Summers. Now, take these pills and drink your water." She handed him a small white container of pills, along with his water.

"How do people stand this? I mean, you all give me pills to help me sleep, then you wake me up every couple of hours to give me more medicine to make me sleepy again. It doesn't make sense to me," he said, grabbing the water, then losing his grip on it and watching it spill on his cast.

"It's not supposed to make sense, young man. It's supposed to make you get better, so you can go home. Besides, if I have to be here this time of the day, why should you get to sleep?" She gave him a faint smile, and another glass of water. "I'm joking. Now you just lay back and get some rest. I'll be back in an hour or so to check on you."

Billy swallowed the pills, then went back to sleep until his phone rang three hours later. He fumbled opening the phone, seeing it was Nancy.

"Hi, Billy, what's happening? Are you feeling better?"

"Nancy, I hate it here. I go to sleep, then they wake me up. Guess why? To give me pills to help me sleep. Isn't that the craziest thing you ever heard? And I hate this crazy bed, it's made for a midget. This isn't fun at all."

"The time will go fast and you'll be home in your own bed real soon. Oh, Billy, I'm going to talk to my mother this morning about missing a couple of days of school so I can spend them with you. I'll let you know this afternoon."

"That would be great. I'm so sick of only having grumpy old nurses to talk to. Tell your mom I was the one asking for you to spend some time up here."

"I will, honey. Listen, I got to go, I'm running late. I'll get up there as soon as I can."

"I'll see you in about what, eight hours?" Billy asked, looking at his watch. "And Nancy, don't let anyone give you any shit about your boyfriend driving his Mustang into a horse. Tell them if they pick on you, I'll find them."

"I'll handle everyone, don't worry. I'll see you about four, love you." She hung up.

He punched in Grandma's cell number. "Grandma, do me a favor. Please stop by Walgreens and see if the college basketball magazines are in yet. I want to see what Georgia Tech's team looks like this year."

"Sure, I've got to get a prescription over there today, anyway. Is there anything else you need?"

"Well, I didn't sleep much last night, and I had a lot of time to think. Do you remember when we talked about going to the police about everything? I think that is what we should do. I want to talk to someone, and I want Ray to sit in on it." He paused for a few seconds. "I keep thinking Gary might get hurt too, now that he's getting a car. What do you think?"

"I guess that's all we can do…we need this to stop. I'll be up there in an hour or so, and we can talk about it more then. Bye, son."

Billy laid back, planning his conversation with Uncle Ray and the police. Maybe they could find out more from the yearbook. "Oh, my God, the yearbook," he screamed out.

He punched in Uncle Ray's number on his phone. "Uncle Ray, can you do me a favor? Where's my car?"

"It's behind Bailey's Garage; you know, where they take junk cars."

"Uncle Ray, Grandpa's yearbook is in the trunk, under the carpet. Do me a favor and stop by Bailey's and grab it for me, will you?"

"Will do, Billy. I'll head over there right now."

"One more thing, Uncle Ray. Do you remember I told you we need to talk today? Do you think you can bring another policeman up here with you as soon as possible, someone you can trust?"

"Billy, you just talked to Carl Williams last night. Why in the world would you want to see another cop?"

"I told Carl about my accident, not everything I found out last week about Grandpa."

"What do you mean?"

"Uncle Ray, I want you to listen to what I tell the cop, then you'll understand."

"If that's what you want, Billy, there's one cop I trust more than anyone else. I'll get Jim Ford to meet us up there."

"Wait a minute, wasn't Chief Ford the one you told about the yearbook? Are you sure we can trust him? I don't know about talking to him."

"Billy, I'd trust Jim Ford with my life. You don't need to worry about him. He's a good guy. I'll get your yearbook and then I'll call Chief Jim, but I can't guarantee he can come up there today. I'll do the best I can."

"Thanks, Uncle Ray. Please call me back after you get the yearbook. See ya."

Billy laid back, turning on the TV. Nothing interested him, so he flipped it off, still thinking about his upcoming conversation with Uncle Ray and Chief Ford as his phone rang.

"Billy, I'm at Bailey's. Your trunk was already open and there's no yearbook. I pulled out all the carpet and looked everywhere, even under the seats. I asked the guy here if anyone was around your car. He said he doesn't know anything. He's a real goober. I can't see how he can protect anything. This place is a joke. Anyway, it ain't here."

"Damn it, I had a feeling it wouldn't be there. Uncle Ray, do you think they've got any video equipment so we can see who took it?'

"Let me ask Goober."

A minute later, Ray got back on the phone. "The jerk just laughed at me when I asked him about any cameras here. He asked me if I thought Rymont was New York City. He's an asshole. Sorry, Billy, but this is a real mom and pop operation."

"They finally got what they wanted, God damn it," Billy screamed, slamming his arm on the bed.

"Settle down, Billy. Who are they?"

"I don't know. All I know is that someone really wanted that yearbook. I bet you it's the same one who broke into our house. Sure, he was looking for that yearbook. See, that's why we need the police. Did you get a chance to talk to Chief Ford about coming up here?"

"I got a hold of him. He's meeting me in the lobby up there in an hour. He acted very understanding on the phone. I told him to keep everything quiet. We'll see you soon, Billy."

Every minute seemed like an hour for Billy as he waited for his visitors. He couldn't keep his eyes off the big white clock on the wall in front of him. He'd glance out the window, then back to the clock, finding it had only moved a minute or two.

A nurse brought him a tray of breakfast, setting it on the rolling table next to his bed. He didn't even look up at her, not wanting to see any more mean old nurses.

"Hi, I'm Nurse Clark. I'll be taking care of you for a while. Listen, I know the food here doesn't look all that great, but it tastes better than it looks."

Billy looked up, seeing a tall redhead with an incredible figure. He couldn't help but notice her smile, and those lips…they were made for kissing, highlighted by shiny red lipstick. "Thanks. I've got to say, you sure are a ray of sunshine, especially compared to all the bossy old nurses I've met so far. There doesn't seem to be a nice one amongst them."

"Oh, don't pay any attention to them. They don't like helping sick people, anyway. Me, I'm different," Nurse Clark replied. "I like to talk to people. I figure if someone is here they are probably not feeling well, and my job is to cheer them up. I've got one motto…I aim to please." She left, giving him a sly smile.

Billy turned on the TV, scanning the sports channels, finding a 1998 UCLA basketball game on ESPN. A couple of minutes later, he heard his uncle's voice out in the hall.

"He's right down here, Jim, in 320."

Billy turned towards the door, watching his uncle and Chief Ford walk into his room.

"Hey, Uncle Ray."

Ray and Ford each grabbed a chair from under the window and sat next to Billy.

Ray spoke up first. "Billy, I brought Jim with me like you asked." He looked over at the chief. "Jim, you know my nephew Billy Summers?"

"Sure, I know this young man; everybody knows Billy, especially during football season." Ford shook Billy's hand, looking at his cast. "Looks like you won't be playing for a while. How's the leg feeling now?"

Billy sat up, putting a pillow behind his head. "It doesn't hurt so much anymore, Chief. They've been keeping me loaded with drugs, so I don't feel it so much, but it sure hurt yesterday."

"So, Billy, what can I do for you?" Jim asked, pulling his chair a little closer to Billy.

"The first thing you can do is close the door. I don't want anyone else hearing our talk."

Ray jumped up. "I'll get it."

Ford watched Ray close the door, then turned back to Billy. "Okay, that's done; so how can I help you, Billy?"

Billy pushed himself up to get to eye level with Ford. "Chief, Uncle Ray said I can trust you. I need someone to hear what is happening in my family and help me find out who wants to hurt us, and it has to be done on the QT."

The chief pulled a notebook out of his briefcase. "Well, Billy, it looks like you found the someone you were looking for. You've got my word, if you want me to keep it quiet, that's the way it will be." He flipped a page on his notebook. "Just tell me your story, I'm all ears."

Billy took a deep breath. "I guess this mess all started the same day we buried Grandpa. After the funeral, Grandma told me she didn't think it was an accident." Billy looked over to his uncle, who opened his mouth in amazement.

Ford took off his hat, putting it on the bedside table. "Billy, I handled that accident myself. Everything pointed to an accident. There wasn't anything at the scene indicating any kind of foul play. Why did she tell you that? Does she have any evidence that it wasn't an accident?"

Billy rubbed his upper lip. "Well, Grandpa told her a week before he died that he had to fix something terrible he did when he was in high school. She asked him what it was, but he said he couldn't tell her. He told her it would be dangerous for our family if he even told us about it. He never did tell her what it was."

Ford laid back in his chair. "Why do you think Steve waited so long to tell her anything about what he did?"

"Grandpa had just found out he had colon cancer. I think he wanted to clear it up before he died. He kept telling us he was going to beat the cancer, but who knows what he really thought?"

"I don't mean to be negative, son, but you haven't told me anything, really. Granny told you it wasn't an accident, but that's just an opinion without any proof."

"Chief, just hear me out, then I think you'll see what I'm getting at. She made me promise not to tell anyone because she was afraid someone may get hurt, so I had to be careful how I talked to anyone. I started asking questions, telling everyone I was working on a paper for school about Grandpa. I think that made someone nervous in Rymont, 'cause look at me now. I think whoever pushed me off the road did the same thing to Grandpa, maybe in the same truck."

Ford lifted his shoulders. "I guess anything is possible, but you've got to have some kind of evidence about either accident. Tell me the rest of what you found out."

Billy pulled out his notes from his billfold. "I found Grandpa's senior yearbook, looking for clues of what he might have done back then. I starting discovering stuff…like there was this thing called a 'Four Raven Promise,' and I know it has something to do with everything. A lot of weird things started happening after I asked people about that Promise." He twisted his neck, rubbing the back of his head.

"Do you need to take a break?" Ford asked.

"No, I'm fine. I found out from the yearbook that Grandpa was one of the Promisers, and there was two guys, a Brad Tillin and a Tim Sanders, who were part of it. I never did find out who the Fourth Promiser was, but I know he or she is still alive. I'm one hundred percent sure the Fourth Promiser has all the answers, including why Grandpa was killed and why someone tried to kill me."

"Spell those names for me," Jim asked, writing them in his notebook.

Billy spelled out Tillin and Sanders's names, then told him everything he'd learned, starting with the death of Brad Tillin, and how he'd found out that Sanders was still alive, and where he lived. He filled him in on the drowning and Niveat, and where she worked. Billy described his conversation with Bob Atlas, as well as his strange talk with Gloria Stillers at the city office. He connected the break in with everything, because of someone looking for the yearbook, and he described every clue that was in that book.

"Billy, I can see where your theories kind of make some sense, but it still boils down to how do we find out what Steve was hiding, and why he chose last week as the time to talk about it.... Wait a second, do you guys want to hear something wild? The day before Steve died, he was looking for me. I was on vacation and Jenny—she's the clerk at the station—took his call."

Ray looked up the chief. "What did he say, did she tell you?"

"She said she told him I was on vacation, but I'd be back the next day. She said she offered to give him the number where I was staying, and he said something that confused her. He told her he had waited so long to talk about something, it could wait another day. When she told me all that, I kind of just shrugged it off, but maybe there's a connection with your story, Billy."

"Maybe he wanted to tell you what he knew, Jim. Maybe that's what led to his death." Ray spread open his arms.

"Who knows? But I'll tell you one thing Billy...you've given me a lot to think about, and I'm ready to get to work on this right away. Is there anything else you want to tell me?"

"That's all I can think of right now, Chief Ford. Last night I told your deputy everything I could remember about what happened Saturday morning."

"I know, he told me."

"So, what do you think?" Billy asked.

"Well, to be perfectly honest with you, almost everything you told me is either hearsay or theories. I wish you had some hard evidence for me, something I could hang my hat on." Ford closed up his notebook, putting it back in his briefcase.

"Chief, please find out about the drowning and the Promise. I hate to say it, but I think Grandpa had something to do with it. I think that is why he was killed. Grandma was right, it was no accident; the boy was murdered. We have to figure all this out before anyone else gets run off the road, like my brother Gary. He's getting his own car, so we're really scared about that."

Ford reached over to Billy, patting him on the shoulder. "Let me see what I can do about all this. You're right, we don't need anyone else hurt." He reached into the pocket on the front of his shirt, pulling out a tan business card. "Now, if you think of anything else, just give me a call, you hear? My cell phone number is on the back."

"Will do, Chief, and thanks for listening. I know I was getting close to figuring everything out. That should help. I'm glad I talked to you. I bet you will figure everything out."

"I'll do my damnedest." He stood up, shaking Billy's hand. "Let's see what we can do. And don't worry, I'll low-key everything. Only me and my deputies will know anything about what you told me. But you've got to do me a favor…just cool it." He grabbed his hat, looking at Billy. "Don't go around saying things about people you can't prove. Like Gloria Stillers. I've known her for years, and she's a straight shooter. You make her sound like she's involved in a murder or a cover up. Listen, you've got to promise me you'll quit talking to folks about all this. Let me do the questioning. You promise to let it rest, and I'll promise to pick it up from here. We got a deal?"

"We got a deal," Billy said, trying to give the chief the best smile he could muster.

Chapter 15
The Answer is the Bottle

Uncle Ray walked Ford out of Billy's room. "Well, Jim, what do you think?"

Ford motioned Ray to follow him down the hall. "Ray, that's a wild story. I guess it won't hurt to ask some questions. The thing that still bothers me is that Steve did try to find me the day before he died. Anyway, I gave Billy my word. Now, you just make sure he keeps his word. No more private eye stuff for Billy, okay?"

"You got it, Jim. Boy, that kid in there's got a lot going on, doesn't he?" Ray patted Ford on the back.

"There's no doubt he believes what he says, and he's got some guts. Now it's up to me to find out what really happened. I'll keep you informed and you can fill in Billy. Maybe that way he won't get hurt again." He shook Ray's hand, turning into the elevator.

Ray anxiously walked back to Billy's room to see what he thought of his talk with the chief. He sat down on the same chair Ford had used. "So, Billy do you feel better now?"

"Yeah, I feel better, Uncle Ray. He seems okay. But he's a hard one to read; I hope he believes me."

"Who knows? I'll tell you one thing, Jim Ford is an honest man." He nodded twice. "He told you he was going to look into what you told him, and he will. I'm betting we'll get some answers within a couple of days. You won't find a better guy to have on your side than Carl Williams."

"Uncle Ray, I just thought of some things I forgot to tell him. I should have told him about the deputy that was at the house after the break in. He kept telling me to quit being a teenybopper cop and how much he got in my face. Oh, and I forgot to tell him about the big black Cadillac that's been following me all week."

"What are you talking about? What Cadillac?"

Billy pushed his bed remote, sitting up straighter. "I didn't want anyone getting upset about it. I thought I'd get the tag number and figure it out, but I never did."

"Figure out what, Billy?"

"I swear to God a black Caddy has been tailing me all week. I don't know who it is or why it's been behind me. Damn, I wish I would have remembered to tell Ford about it."

Ray rubbed his forehead, looking into his hand. "Billy, just get some paper and write down things as you think of them, and I'll get them to Ford. Have Granny get a tablet somewhere...that way you won't forget anything."

"What do you want me to do?" Granny asked, entering Billy's room.

"Hi, Grandma," Billy said, his face lighting up as she walked in. "Me and Uncle Ray were talking about you getting me a writing pad so I can write down stuff I forgot to tell Chief Ford."

Grandma put her purse on a chair, walking over to Billy. "So, Ford did make it up here, huh? Is he going to help us? I want to hear how that went."

"I think it went okay," Billy answered. "At least he acts like he believes me and wants to help. The only problem is that I have no real evidence."

Granny looked at Ray. "Do you know everything now?"

"Yes I do, and I see why Billy didn't tell me, with his promise to you and all. Now we can all work together on figuring things out."

Granny shook her head, looking at her brother-in-law. "God, I hated leaving you out of everything, but I didn't want you hurt. I was scared, Ray. I'm sorry about that."

She turned, looking at her grandson. "I couldn't get you that basketball magazine. The manager said they're not in yet, but he'll hold one for me when they come in. He said they should get there sometime next week."

"Thanks anyway, Grandma." He looked over at his uncle. "Hey, Uncle Ray, do you know Betty Thomas very well?"

"Sure I know her…she was in our class, too. Why do you want to know about her?"

"Oh, it's probably nothing. It's just that she's the last one from Grandpa's senior class that still lives here that I didn't get a chance to talk to. Would you please be sure Ford finds her and talks to her?"

Uncle Ray stood up. "I sure will. I'll be in touch. There are some things I need to do at the farm, so I won't get back up here until tomorrow. Give me a call if you need anything."

"Sure thing, Uncle Ray," Billy answered, watching his uncle leave.

***

An hour later, Ray was almost home when his phone rang.

"Hello, Ray, this is Jim Ford."

"Don't tell me you solved the case already?" Ray asked with a laugh.

"No, not hardly. I just wanted you to know I called the Bradley Hospice. They told me Sanders, or Casey, died last night. Guess he had another stroke, and this one got him. They also said Billy was there last week, talking to Casey. It appears that nephew of yours is being straight with us, after all."

"I told you....oh, shit...."

"Are you okay, Ray?"

"Yeah, I just dropped the goddamn phone, that's all. I told you my nephew was a good kid. So, what's next, Jim? Where do we go from here? Is there anything I can do to help?"

"No, but I'll let you know. I think I'll take Billy's advice and go see that maid tomorrow, then I'll pop in and see Gloria Stillers. I'll keep you updated. Take care, Ray."

Ray hung up, turning onto the gravel road leading to his farmhouse. Stopping at his mailbox, he pulled out a stack of letters and newspapers. "Looks like a shitload of bills in this mess," he muttered, as he pulled his truck next to Billy's tire swing.

After getting inside, he threw the mail on the kitchen table as he passed on the way to his bedroom, where he put on his work clothes and that special hat. He grabbed a beer from the refrigerator and went out the back door towards the barn. Jumping on the tractor, he spent two hours plowing between rows of tomatoes on Billy's acre.

When he had finished, he drove the tractor into the barn and headed into the kitchen through the back door. He grabbed another beer, sitting on his sofa with his feet on the coffee table, sorting his mail. There were two magazines, one newspaper, a few bills, and one letter, which was addressed to him but had no return address. It was mailed two days earlier from Charlotte. He opened it up, finding a single piece of paper inside the envelope.

"Tell Billy the Answer is the Bottle" was all that was written on the paper. Ray scratched his head, wondering what that meant. A bottle? A bottle? What did that mean?

He called Ford, getting his answering machine. He tried again, and this time Jim picked up. "Jim, this is Ray. I'm home. You may want to get over here. I just got something in the mail you ought to check out."

"What do you mean?"

"When I got my mail today, there was a letter in it, addressed to me. There's a piece of paper that just says, 'Tell Billy the Answer is the Bottle.' That's all it says, Jim."

"Listen to me carefully, Ray. Grab the envelope and the letter by the corners, put them down, and don't touch them again until I get there. There may be prints on them. I'll be there in about ten minutes."

Ray put the envelope and letter on an open spot on his kitchen table, waiting for Ford to get there, constantly looking at the small round clock over the stove.

Fifteen minutes later, Jim pounded on Ray's front door, then walked in. "Where is it?"

Ray pointed to the kitchen table. Jim leaned over, reading the note without touching it. He pulled some tweezers out of his pocket, putting the envelope and the letter into separate plastic bags.

"I'll get these over to the lab boys right away," Jim said. "Let's see what the geeks over there can find out. I'm glad you were careful with the letter, Ray. Who knows, maybe this will be the starting point to finding out what happened to Steve Summers."

Ray watched Ford put the two plastic bags into a big paper bag. "How long do you think it will take to get any clues from your lab?"

"I should have an answer by noon tomorrow. I'll make it top priority."

"Oh Jim, after you left the hospital, Billy told me some stuff you should know. First off, a big Cadillac followed him a lot last week. Billy couldn't tell who was driving it, but it really scared him. He also asked me to tell you to talk to Betty Thomas. I guess she's the last one from our class he didn't interview."

Ford turned to look at Ray. "Betty Thomas from the post office?"

"Yeah, but I doubt she knows much. She was kind of a nerd in school, but Billy thinks she's worth talking to. Oh, one more thing...one of your deputies got ugly with him after their house was broken into. I guess he really hassled Billy. He wanted you to know about it."

"Which deputy was that?" Ford asked, opening the front door.

"I'm not sure, but maybe Billy can remember his name."

"Don't worry about it. I'm heading to the office now, I'll find out." Jim turned back to Ray. "I've got to go. You take care." They shook hands, then Ray followed Ford to his squad car.

"You be careful, Jim, you hear?"

Jim started the car, looking back at Ray. "I'll be fine; who's going to hurt me?"

Chapter 16
Let's Check Your Vital Signs

It was hard for Billy to concentrate on anything when he was alone. Grandma had just left, going back to Rymont to do some shopping. He turned on the TV, looking for any sports program worth watching. The only thing he could find was an old bowling tournament that looked like it was taped when Grandma was his age. Both bowlers wore checkered pants and had their name stitched across the back of their shirts. He started surfing the channels again, hoping to find anything to grab his attention, when he heard a voice in the hall.

"Tell her I'll be back in fifteen minutes. I've got to check on one more patient."

Nurse Clark peeked around the corner. "Guess what, Mr. Summers? Tonight's your lucky night. I'm on duty all night." She walked in, smiling. "Now, let's check your vital signs. We've got to make sure you're doing all right, don't we?"

Billy sat up, combing his hair with a few fingers when she turned her head. "Well, hello, Nurse Clark. I'm glad to see you. I was wondering if I was ever going to see you again."

She walked over to the bed, grabbing his right wrist, looking down at her watch. "What do you mean, Mr. Summers? You can't get rid of me so fast. Besides, I've been thinking about you, too. We'll get along just fine. Well, your pulse looks good, now let's check your blood pressure."

She reached across Billy, picking up his left arm, slowly wrapping it with the elastic cuff. Billy wondered why she took his blood pressure that way. She was practically laying on him. It would be so much easier to just walk around the bed and do it from the other side.

But he figured out quickly he liked it this way. Her blouse was unbuttoned at the top, with her breasts rubbing his chest. There was no way he could avoid seeing them. She was wearing a pink half bra that showed almost everything. He lay there, wondering what to do. Should he look away? My God, they were only an inch or two from his face.

"Are you doing okay?" Nurse Clark asked.

Billy cleared his throat. "I couldn't be better," he said, trying not to be too obvious he was loving every minute.

"I'm almost done, Billy, just a minute or two longer."

"That's all right, you take your time. I've got nothing else to do. We want to be sure my blood pressure is okay, right?"

She looked down, watching him gawk at her breasts. She continued to take his pressure for a few more seconds, then unsnapped the cuff, rolling it up and putting it in her jacket pocket.

"Sorry, Billy, but I kept getting weird readings, so I had to take it a second time. Your pressure was a little higher than it was this morning. It's not high enough to be alarming, but it's higher. You must have a lot on your mind, huh?"

Billy nodded. "I'm just glad you're not giving me a bath. That's when my blood pressure would really go nutso."

"So, who do you think is going to give you a bath tonight? Don't worry, I won't take your blood pressure while I give you a bath."

Billy knew she was flirting with him. He raised his eyebrows and nodded. "That'd be okay with me. I like the way you do things. Anytime you need to check my blood pressure, uh, I'll be here."

Nurse Clark didn't say anything. She just gave him a big smile, followed with a wink, then walked out of his room.

Billy punched his bed next to his leg. He must have acted like a crazy teenager in puppy love with his teacher. Why was he so tongue-tied? He needed a few minutes for his insides to settle down from her visit. Shaking his head, he tried to clear some weird thoughts that were hanging on the tip of his brain just as the phone rang. It was Uncle Ray.

"Hey, Billy, how's it going? Is there anything new happening up there?"

"No, there's uh, nothing going on here. In fact, it's kind of getting boring."

"Well, I got some news today. Jim Ford called to check on Tim Sanders at that hospice in Charlotte. Billy, Sanders died last night. It looks like another stroke."

"Damn it, there goes that lead. All I needed was a few minutes with that guy. Goddamn it." He threw a pillow against the wall.

"Don't worry, Billy. Jim's on top of everything. He told me he's going to check on what you told me...you know, about the cop that hassled you, and the car that's been following you. One more thing, he told me two things to tell you; he's going to talk to Betty Thomas, and he said he believes in you."

"That makes me feel a little better. At least someone believes me. Did he say anything else?"

Uncle Ray didn't say anything for a couple of seconds. "Not really. Listen, Billy, I'll see you tomorrow. I've got a lot on my plate tonight. Believe it or not, I've got a dinner date, no pun intended."

"Whoa, Uncle Ray, you tiger, way to go. Hey, let me give you some advice with the ladies; don't wear your umbrella hat, or that 1965 blue suit," Billy said, laughing as loud as Ray's normal laugh.

"Yeah, right, you smart ass. I've got to go, I'll see you later."

Billy hung up from Ray, dialing Nancy's number just as she walked in. "Hi, sweetheart," she said, giving him her prettiest smile.

She looked great, but Billy's mind kept going back to Nurse Clark. Nancy was beautiful, but she looked so young now. Clark was just as hot, but she was a woman, not a girl.

Nancy rubbed Billy's left arm, then pulled his extra pillow out from under his head, leaving her enough space to lay with him.

Billy giggled, causing Nancy to look up at him.

"What's so funny, Billy?"

"Oh, I was just thinking about Uncle Ray. He's got a date tonight…yep, a dinner date. Isn't that something? I mean, a real date. But I took care of him, I gave him some advice."

"So, what did you tell him?"

"I simply told him not to wear his umbrella hat or that beat-up blue suit of his."

"That wasn't very nice. I bet you he loves both that hat and his suit."

Billy giggled again.

Nancy looked up at her hero again. "So, Billy, tell me about today. Did you have much company?"

"Well, let's see. Uncle Ray was up here for a while, followed by Grandma. Oh, I got to talk to Chief Ford this morning. But the best company I had is when you walked in." He turned to look at her. "Say, how did you get here?"

"I used Laura Lee's car. She said I could drive it all week, and next week, too. It's so cool. I don't think you ever saw it, but it's kind of a deep red color, with white racing stripes on the sides. It's really a neat convertible. I felt like a movie star driving it up here with the top down."

"But won't Laura Lee need it?"

Nancy snuggled up to Billy even tighter, running the tips of her fingers over his eyebrows. "Nah, it's her mother's car. They have two cars in the family so they lent one to me. Forget about all that, I want to hear about your talk with Chief Ford."

He leaned his head to the left, trying not to look at her in the eyes. "I've been meaning to talk to you about something. I think Grandpa's accident and mine are tied together somehow. I told Chief Ford everything about both accidents and he's going to check everything out."

"Are you saying someone killed your grandfather and that same person tried to kill you?" she asked, sitting up.

"Nancy, I'm not sure of anything right now. Chief Ford told me he would get back with me after he does some digging. I bet nothing comes of it, but we'll see. Now, tell me about school. What's going on at Rymont High? Has anyone noticed I'm not there?"

She twisted her head, giving him a quizzical look. "If I didn't know better, I'd say you are trying to change the subject. First you tell me that somebody wanted to kill both your grandpa and you, then you ask me about school. I think you're leaving out a lot of stuff, aren't you?"

Billy shook his head. "No, I'm not leaving anything out, at least not anything I know for sure. Right now, everything is just a bunch of theories, and you know as much as I do."

"Swear on our love with nothing crossed?"

He smiled at her, seeing her melt. "I swear. Now, tell me about school, please."

"There's not much to tell you. Everyone is worrying about you, and they're also worried about Friday's game. They think we can't win without you."

He shook his head. "I hope you told them that was a bunch of bullshit."

"I didn't say anything; but Billy, you are our best player."

"So, I'm not the coach. You can bet Coach Fatha has already made some new plays to make up for me not being there. Besides, do you remember how good the team played in the first quarter last week when I was on the bench? I can't see them dropping over and playing dead just because one player is out with a broken leg."

She stared out the window. "Who cares? I sure don't. I don't care if we ever win another game the rest of the year. All I care about is you getting better and getting our lives back to normal. Like going somewhere we can be alone…you know, like out at the 'hill,' or a place like that." She started kissing his neck.

At that moment Nurse Clark walked back in. When Nancy saw her, she sat up, jumping out of Billy's bed, brushing off her blouse.

The nurse smiled as she slid Billy's table away from the bed. "So, what do we got here, Billy? This must be your little honey; either that, or you sure make friends quickly in hospitals."

He shook his head, smiling at both beauties at the same time. "Yeah, she's the one. Nancy, meet Nurse Clark; Nurse Clark, meet Nancy."

Nancy reached across the bed, shaking the nurse's hand. "Sorry about being in bed with Billy. I just missed him so much." She sat down on the chair next to the window, reaching across to her boyfriend, grabbing his hand.

Clark turned, opening the closet behind her, then pulled out a stack of white towels. "That's okay, honey. He seems like a great guy. I guess I'd miss him, too. Now I've got to ask you to leave for a while. Your boyfriend needs a bath, and you can't stay here for that."

"Oh, okay. I need to go to the gift shop anyway. I'll see you in an hour or so, Billy." Nancy gave him a long kiss, a very long one, as if she was marking her territory. She walked out with her head up, giving Billy and Nurse Clark a half-hearted wave.

"She sure is a cutie. Have you all been going together long?" Clark asked, pulling some small bottles out of the cabinet drawer.

"Only a couple of years. She's a good kid. The problem is, next fall I'm going to Georgia Tech, and she'll be staying in state. I'm going to miss her, but life goes on. Both of us will probably end up getting involved with other people; after all, you can't have much of a relationship a couple of states apart." He sat up when she wasn't looking, trying to get as tall as he could.

"Yeah, you never know who you're going to meet down the road. She looks like a keeper, but a good-looking guy like you, especially a jock…why, you'll have girls all over you in college. It's going to be hard to think about her with all that going on, huh?" She put on rubber gloves, then put three folded white towels next to Billy.

"I suppose. Sometimes weird things happen, Nurse Clark."

"Tell me about it. I've been looking for Mr. Right for a long time. Don't be in a hurry, Billy," she said, turning towards the bathroom, returning with a tall white bottle of lotion. "So, have you had a bath since you've been here?"

"Yeah, an old bitchy nurse gave me one yesterday. It was no treat, I'll tell you that."

"Well, I think I can make up for that. Everyone says I give the best baths here." She put a white porcelain pan in the sink next to his bed, filling it halfway with water. "So, tell me, Billy, how old are you?"

"I'm eighteen."

"Heck, you're only five years younger than me. I heard about you. You're that football star from Rymont, aren't you?" She removed his gown, looking him over for a few seconds. "You're not embarrassed with me giving you a bath, are you?"

"I guess a little, but I'll get over it."

"It doesn't look like parts of you mind what I'm doing." She laughed softly. "Now, where were we?" She started rubbing his chest with a washcloth. "Oh, yeah, you want to go to Georgia Tech next year. You know, my brother played baseball there two years ago. All he ever talked about was the parties. He said it was a great party school." She raised an arm to wash under it. "That ought to be a lot of fun for you when you get there."

Billy looked out the window, trying to hide his interest in how the bath was going. "I sure hope so. But the biggest thing I want to concentrate on is getting my leg fixed before the football season starts next fall. I've got to get back in tip-top shape so I don't take a chance on losing my scholarship."

"I bet you want to be a pro football player down the road. I hear that's where the big bucks are." She removed the pillow behind his head in order to scrub his back. "Yeah, you're going to be some catch for a very lucky girl down the road. You know what, I'll try to get to a few of your games down there next fall. I've got a free place to stay at my brother's. Hey, if I get there, maybe I'll give you a call, and we can get together."

"I'd like that, Nurse Clark."

"Good, we got a date in the future, right? Now, let's get one thing straight; I have a first name, it's Vickie…got that?"

"I sure do, Nurse…I mean Vickie."

"Super, now let's get going on this bath. The way I see it, my job is to be sure you're sanitized all over. When I get done, you'll know you had a bath."

Chapter 17
The Party at the Lake

Chief Ford got to his office an hour early the next morning, anxious to start his investigations into all the Summers's adventures. He spotted Carl Williams leaning over the water cooler. "Hey, Carl, who took care of the Summers case last week?"

Williams turned around to his boss, wiping water off his chin. "Which case are you talking about, Chief? Between the old man's accident, the break in, and what just happened to Billy, we're loaded with Summers cases."

"I'm talking about the break-in."

"That wasn't me, Chief…I think it might have been Gunders. I heard him talking about it to someone on the phone the other day. Do you want me to ask him?"

"Don't worry about it. I need to talk to him, anyway; where is he?"

"He's in the back on his computer," Carl responded, pulling his chair out from behind his desk.

Ford walked into the computer room, finding Gunders sitting motionless with his arms crossed, looking at his new computer. "Hey, George, you're not sleeping on the job, are you?"

Gunders laughed. "No, but that doesn't sound like such a bad idea. I was just studying some info about the crime patterns here in Rymont. Did you know there hasn't been a homicide here in over thirty years? That must mean all the officers working here have been top-notch, huh, Chief?"

"I guess we've been real lucky, that's what it says to me. Say, George, let me ask you a question. Did you handle the Summers break-in last week?"

"Yeah, I took care of it," Gunders answered without looking up.

Ford sighed, letting out a big breath. "I heard you were kind of hard on the Summers boy, telling him to quit looking into what his grandfather did in high school. Is that true?"

Gunders turned, looking at Ford. "I just told him he was stirring folks up, and he ought to leave the investigating to us, that's all."

The chief rubbed an eyebrow with his index finger. "So, tell me, George, why did you tell him that?"

"I heard he was snooping around, asking questions about some old cases from at least fifty years ago. It seems to me our job is tough enough without some crazy teenager playing detective." He turned back to the computer. "I didn't browbeat him or anything. I just made it clear that we have to be the ones digging up old cases."

Ford picked up a pencil off the desk. "Okay, George, who was getting stirred up by Billy asking questions?"

"Well, maybe they weren't stirred up. I guess I should have used a different term." Gunders looked back at his boss. "Some lady from Fort Ridge called, complaining about the kid bothering her. She said he was a bigot because she was Hispanic and he didn't show her any respect. But then again, she ended up calling me a racist."

"You didn't catch her name, did you?"

"No, but I'm sure Jenny's got it logged in by now."

Ford looked over Gunders's shoulder at the computer. It was a screen about crimes in Rymont. "Who else was bothered by the Summers boy, George?"

"Let me see…oh, right, even his football coach got involved in looking for stuff on those old cases for him—get this—on our hard drive. I even heard some guys talking about the Summers boy trying to solve cold cases, and they weren't joking. And I know there were a couple more people set back by what he was doing."

"George, just do me a favor. Don't get too hung up on what an eighteen-year-old boy is doing. He just lost his grandfather. All he was doing was writing a school paper in tribute to him, zeroing in on what it was like in high school fifty years ago. Just lay off him, will you?"

"Sure, Chief, I won't bother him anymore. I really wasn't trying to mess with him or hurt him. How's he doing, anyway? I heard he broke his leg pretty good."

"He'll be fine…he's tough. But he's lucky to be alive. You know, he killed that horse instantly? To me it sounded like he hit a brick wall, one full of horse hair. They say he'll be going home at the end of the week." He put his hand on Gunders's shoulder as he stood up. "Thanks, George. I knew you weren't bothering anyone on purpose. You can go back to whatever you were doing."

Ford went back into his office, pulling down the Rymont phone book from the top of his filing cabinet. He flipped the pages, finding Betty Thomas's address and phone number, punching her number into his cell phone. She picked up after the third ring.

"Betty, this is Chief Ford. How you doing, kiddo?"

"Well, Jim, I haven't talked to you in years. How's June doing, and the kids?"

"We're doing just fine, Betty; and you?"

"Oh, I'm just getting used to my new life. Retirement is a lot different than working, I'll tell you that. It's not near as exciting as I thought it would be."

"I bet. Say, Betty, I was wondering if I could come over and see you this morning? I'm working on some old stuff and

I need to ask you a few questions about your high school days."

"Sure, it will be great seeing you again. Do you remember where I live?"

"Do you still live at 118 Washington Street?" Ford asked, peeking at her address in the phone book.

"You've got some memory, Jim. That's right. Do you want to come over now? I was planning on going out to the cemetery and Walgreens, but that can wait."

"I can catch you later, Betty, if you want."

"Nah, that's all right. I haven't had much company lately. It will be nice to see you. I'll just run my errands this afternoon. I'll tell you what I'm going to do; I'm going to make you a pitcher of my world-famous lemonade. When do you think you'll get here?"

"How does thirty minutes sound?"

"I'll be here, along with some great lemonade."

"I'll see you then," Ford answered, going through his little notebook.

Twenty minutes later he hollered to Gunders, telling him he was going over to see Betty Thomas.

When the chief pulled up to Betty's, he noticed her carefully manicured yard. It was like she was waiting for a weed to come up so she could pull it. He rang her doorbell twice. When she opened the door, she had on a big grin, along with the weirdest-looking purple apron he'd ever seen.

"Well, Betty, it's been a long time. How's retirement life treating you?" he asked, laying his briefcase and hat on her entry table.

They both sat down on her couch. It was covered with plastic, crinkling with every movement. "It's all right…I've got a lot more free time now. Everybody told me it would be a big adjustment, and they were right. You know what I miss the most?" she asked, putting both hands on her knees.

"I bet you don't miss getting up so early."

"No, I don't miss that at all. I used to get up at three every morning, just to sort mail. I liked getting home at noon, but I never got used to getting up in the middle of the night. No, what I really miss is the people and hearing about their kin, stuff like that. They were all kind of like a family to me."

"I bet they miss you, too. You worked there for what, thirty years?" Ford asked, trying to avoid moving because of the noise made by the sofa's plastic cover.

"It was thirty three years, and thank God for the memories. But you didn't come over here to see me about my retirement. You said you wanted to ask me some questions, so go ahead, Jim, fire away."

"Betty, as I told you on the phone, I'm checking on some old cases from the fifties. And one case in particular was about some of the kids in your senior class. I was hoping you could help me clear up some stuff."

"I'll try...but give me a second. I made that lemonade, and I want you to try it. I'll be right back." She got up, heading towards the kitchen, talking as she walked. "I hope you like your lemonade a little tart. That's the way everyone I know likes it. But you let me know if you want me to put more sugar in it."

She walked back into the living room, carrying a lemonade pitcher in one hand and two glasses of ice in the other.

"This is great," the chief said, drinking half of the lemonade out of his glass. "It tastes good a little sour. I'll have to tell my wife not to put so much sugar in it." He wiped his lips. "Now, Betty, as I was saying, maybe you can answer some questions about your senior year."

"I'll try, Jim. What do you want to know?"

Ford pulled out his small spiral notebook and a pen from his shirt pocket. "You graduated from Rymont High in 1951, is that right, Betty?"

"I sure did. I'm a Raven through and through. I still got a yearbook around here somewhere, if you want to look at it."

Jim wrote in his notebook, then looked up at her. "No, that's okay. Do you remember your graduation night? I think it was in May."

"Oh yeah, I remember it like it was yesterday. That was a great day." She sighed. "But it was a terrible night."

"Why was it so terrible?"

Betty leaned back, causing a big rumble of plastic. "There was this party at the lake. One of my friends drowned that night…it was awful. We had such a beautiful graduation ceremony. There were only seventeen of us, and I bet you didn't know I was the valedictorian, how about that? My folks were so proud."

"That was really something, but I'm not surprised," Ford said. "You always seemed like the studious type; but can we get back to the drowning?"

She took a big drink of lemonade. "Well, when Brian Kelly drowned, it changed everything. We went from celebrating to watching a classmate die. It was a bad, bad night."

Ford flipped a page in his notebook. "Why don't you tell me everything you can remember about that night?"

She set her glass down on the table. "Well, we all went to Buckley Lake and there was a lot of drinking. Not by me—I never was one for drinking—but I wanted to go with everyone else. Before you knew it, some of the kids were in the lake, and Jim, most of them were completely naked, both boys and girls. That shocked me. Then some things got pretty wild, especially with the group way out in the lake. They—"

The chief cut her off, asking, "Do you remember the names of any of the kids in that wild group?"

"Sure, I do. Tim Sanders was one of them. I never liked him, he always picked on me at school, calling me a prude. Brad Tillin was out there, too. He wasn't much better. His problem was that he was always girl crazy. All he ever talked about was getting into girl's...you know... into their panties."

"And who else was in that group, Betty?"

"Steve Summers, God bless him, was part of it, but I don't think he was with them in the middle of the lake when Brian died. Steve was there in the beginning, but I think he went back to the dock with a girl. I think it was...yes, it was Jessica Stanger."

"This is getting a little confusing, Betty. Can we go back to the group out in the middle of the lake?"

She turned towards Ford, causing the plastic to crackle. "The best I can remember, there were four of them out there and they were drunk, I mean really drunk. Let's see, it was Sanders and Tillin, and of course Brian Kelly. Oh, there was a girl out there; now, let me think, who was that?" She put a finger on the side of her head, just below the temple. "I think it was Gloria Wilson. That's right, it was Gloria. You must know her, she works at the city office, only now she's Gloria Stillers."

"Sure, I know Gloria. But tell me what happened with the group out on that lake?"

"Well, they were going further and further out, and the next thing you know, there was all kinds of screaming. That's when Kelly drowned. He was such a nice kid, and he sure idolized those boys. He was retarded, but he tried so hard to blend in."

"Betty, you said Steve Summers was on the dock. How can you be so sure he wasn't with the kids out in the middle of the lake?"

"No, he was on the dock. I remember because when all the screaming started, he jumped off the dock, trying to get to Brian. It's amazing, Chief...it's been fifty years, but it's still so clear to me...I remember everything about that night. I've always had a real good memory."

"That is remarkable, Betty; so what did that group out in the lake do next?" Ford asked, looking back at his notes.

"Well, they pulled Brian out of the water, but it was too late. They tried to revive him for hours, but he never came back. We all sat there, stunned. The cops got there, asking all of us about what happened. I remember one deputy kept saying he knew it wasn't an accident, but no one spoke up, so it all went away." She raised her shoulders, putting her arms out.

Jim got up, asking where her restroom was. She pointed to a small door by the kitchen.

"That lemonade is working fast, Betty," Ford said. He returned and sat next to her again. "Say, Betty, have you ever heard anything more about the drowning since then?"

"Oh, I've heard some rumors. Somewhere I heard Brian was trying to get overly friendly with Gloria, then Tim got mad and hit him. I even heard he called Tim a name and Tim went crazy in the water. I don't know what to believe. I still think the poor boy drank too much, trying to keep up with the other kids. Besides, he never was much of a swimmer."

Ford flipped another page. "Do you know what happened to the kids in that group since you all graduated?"

Betty thought for a moment, picking up her lemonade glass. "I heard that Brad got killed in Viet Nam, and Tim just disappeared after graduation. Let's see, Gloria is at the city building, and of course Steve just died."

"Is there anyone else still in Rymont from your class?"

"Besides that group, huh? There's Bob Atlas, at the bank, and Ray Summers, he's still out at his farm. I think that's everyone, including me."

"I just have a few more questions, Betty. Have you ever heard of a Four Raven Promise?"

"Sure, Jim. I think Tim was in on it, and Brad, too. Steve must have been part of it, too, if they were. I never knew who the fourth guy was. All I know is they made a promise that after they graduated they would always be looking out for each other."

"Betty, let me ask you; how did you find out about the Promise?"

"Oh, I don't remember. Working so many years at the post office made all of us kind of snoopy, I guess. You know, you hear things. I've known about the Promise for years and years."

Ford turned another page in his notebook. "Now, Betty, I want you to think real hard about my next question. Have you ever heard about anyone in your class using a bottle to do anything wrong? I know that sounds weird, but think about it."

"A bottle? What do you mean, a bottle? That's a strange question. I wish I could help you with that, but I have no idea what that means, or what you are asking."

"I was just wondering if it rang a bell, that's all."

"Like I said Chief, it doesn't register with me. If you think a bottle had anything to do with Brian's drowning, I can assure you it didn't, unless it's because those boys drank so much beer out of bottles down by the lake. I'm sorry, but I can't think of anything that happened that night, or since, that had anything to do with a bottle."

"That's okay. One more thing, then I've got to go. Has anyone ever told you to keep quiet about that night, or threatened you if you said anything to a policeman about the drowning?"

"Heavens no. I haven't talked about any of this to anyone in over twenty years, Jim."

Ford picked up his hat and briefcase, turning towards Betty. "It sure was nice seeing you again, and thanks for the lemonade; it was as good as advertised." He put a business card on her coffee table. "Here's my card. If you can think of anything else about that night, just give me a call, will you?"

Betty got up, leading him to the door. "Chief, if you ever get thirsty, I can always make some more lemonade and we can talk again. Take care of yourself," she said, patting his shoulder, watching him go out to his squad car.

Chapter 18
Someone is Trying to Help Us

Billy woke up Tuesday morning with a monster headache. It hurt so bad he had trouble seeing. Grabbing a half glass of water, he wet his eyes with his fingers. Looking around the hospital room, he noticed Grandma asleep in a chair next to the window. She was curled up, laying on her arm with a blanket covering most of her face.

"Wake up Grandma," Billy said, noticing that it was almost six thirty.

She turned her head towards him, passing on a tiny smile.

"What are you doing here so early?" Billy asked, raising his bed up.

She moved her arm out from under her head, grimacing as she rubbed it, spreading her fingers out. "I did it again. I keep sleeping on that arm and I wake up and it feels like it's dead. It must be a circulation problem."

"But why are you here so early, Grandma?"

"I couldn't sleep last night, so I came over here. I had some real bad dreams."

"What were they?"

"I don't want to talk about them. I'm just thankful you're all right." She stretched her legs out, trying to stand. She got to her feet just as Dr. Victor walked in, then she sat back down.

The doctor pulled Billy's sheet off. "So, how's our football star this morning? Let's just take a look at that leg, shall we? How have you been feeling?" he asked, tapping the bottom of Billy's foot with a small shiny hammer.

"I'm fine, Doc. Do you still think I've got to stay here until Saturday?"

"Maybe not, Billy. All the tests are normal so far, and you've improved a ton since Sunday. Your vital signs all look good, but we need to run some tests tomorrow. If all the scans look okay, and there's no sign of internal bleeding or concussions, I can't see why you can't go home Thursday. But remember, tomorrow's tests will determine that. Have you had any headaches lately?" he asked, looking into Billy's mouth.

"No, none. I'm not sleeping all that good, but no headaches," Billy responded, knowing his head felt like thirty jackhammers were all working away inside of his brain.

Victor patted Billy on the shoulder. "Everything looks good, young man. We'll see you tomorrow after all the tests." He gave Granny a small wave as he left the room.

Billy reached for his phone to call Nancy and tell her what the doctor had said, but there was no answer. He laid back, nodding his head, when Ray walked in.

"Hey, Uncle Ray, we got some good news this morning."

"Oh yeah? I need some good news, what is it?"

"Dr. Victor just left. He told us if some tests turn out okay tomorrow, I can go home Thursday; how about that?"

"That's terrific. I've got some good news for you and Granny too. Want to hear it?" Ray asked, sitting down on the sofa next to Billy's grandmother. He didn't give them time to answer. "Jim Ford called me late last night. He found an eyewitness to the Kelly drowning. He said Steve was not involved in it at all."

Granny started to cry. "I knew it, I just knew it. All that talk about Steve drowning someone was just crazy talk, that's all it was, plain old crazy talk." She pulled a tissue out of her purse, wiping her eyes.

Ray put an arm around Granny, patting her back. "Oh, Billy, have you heard anyone mention anything about a bottle playing a role in anything crazy Steve might have done?"

Billy raised his bed up. "A bottle? No, I didn't hear about any bottle. What does that mean?" He looked at his grandmother. "Does that mean anything to you, Grandma?"

She shook her head.

He turned back to Ray. "How does a bottle tie into anything, Uncle Ray?"

"I have no idea, Billy. All I know is that I got a letter yesterday that was mailed from Charlotte, that had no return address or any signature, that said, 'Tell Billy the answer is the bottle.' Ford's got it now, trying to find some fingerprints." Ray put both arms out, showing his confusion. "My guess is that it's a clue for you, Billy, to help us get to the bottom of everything."

Billy thought for a moment. "It's doesn't mean anything to me. But it does show us one thing…someone is trying to help us. Yes sir, someone knows a lot and wants to help us; maybe it's the Fourth Promiser?

Ray stood up. "You keep thinking about that, Billy; maybe something will come to you. In the meantime, I'm starving." He looked back at Granny. "Want to join me for some breakfast?"

"Hey, Uncle Ray, the big date master, how about telling us how last night went?"

"What happened last night?" Granny asked.

Ray shook his head. "What's the big deal? So I had a date last night. I've had dozens of dates the last couple years, maybe even hundreds. Billy, you make it sound like it was my first date ever."

Billy winked at his uncle. "So, how'd it go?"

"It was a real dud. She looked like she was about seventy. She had more wrinkles than all my hunting dogs put together. When she started talking about a life-long companion, I took her home." He gave them one of his famous belly laughs. "She didn't even get dessert out of me. When the waiter brought the dessert menus, I asked him for the check. She was a crazy one. When I stopped in front of her place, she closed her eyes and puckered up. I just told her, 'No thanks,' and reached over and opened her door. There, now that you got the scoop, I'm going to breakfast. Come on, Granny, I'll buy you whatever you want."

After they left, Billy laid back, giggling about his uncle's date, when Nancy called.

"Why didn't you answer your phone all night, Billy?"

"My battery was dead and I didn't even know it until this morning. Listen, Nancy, the doctor told me I could go home Thursday if I do good on some tests tomorrow."

"Super. I'll be there all day tomorrow and Thursday, too. Mom said I could miss a couple of days...."

His phone went dead again.

Billy's mind was going a mile a minute, trying to remember all the conversations he'd had last week, and if any of them tied to a "bottle" in any way. He was drawing a blank, so he decided to call Coach Fatha again. This time Fatha was receptive, offering to do whatever Billy needed, including looking for any clue to what the word "bottle" might have meant in the fifties. He promised to call Billy the minute he found out anything.

Billy picked up his TV remote, but then decided to pull out all his notes from his billfold, still wondering why anyone would send Uncle Ray a one sentence clue.

An hour later, Grandma and Uncle Ray walked in, walking over to his bed. Grandma grabbed Billy's hand. "Is there anything new, son?" she asked.

"Just this crazy headache; it just won't go away."

"Let me go get a nurse so she can give you something for that."

"No, please don't, Grandma. I want to go home Thursday. I don't want that screwed up because of a little headache. No one needs to know about anything, especially a nurse who will tell Dr. Victor about it. Just give me some Advil, or Tylenol. You must have something in that big old purse of yours."

"I'm sure I do," she answered, going through her oversized handbag. "But this isn't right. They need to know when your head hurts." She handed him two red and white Tylenols from the bottle she found.

Billy swallowed them without any water, then turned to his uncle. "Uncle Ray, have you heard anything new from Chief Ford?"

"I sure haven't, but I'll tell you what I'll do. I got to go by the bank in a little bit. I'll stop in and see Jim at the station and see what's going on."

"That would be great. Maybe he's figured…." Billy went back to sleep.

Chapter 19
The Shoebox Under the Bed

Deputy Gunders peeked around the corner of Ford's office, finding him looking through his notebook. "Boss, still want me to keep looking for something to do with a bottle from the fifties?"

"Yes, sir. You just keep pounding on that computer, maybe you'll get lucky. Did you try Googling bottle crimes in South Carolina?"

"I sure did. Zip, nada, nothing, but I'll keep looking."

"Good," Ford said. "I've got some leads to follow myself. I'm heading out to talk to some folks who may know something. Call me if you figure anything out, George. I'll see you."

***

He decided to start with the maid, driving to Fort Ridge, finding 289 Baymont. He walked up to the front door and punched the doorbell. A middle-aged lady opened the door, wiping flour off her hands.

"Hello, officer, how can I help you?"

"My name is Jim Ford. I'm the police chief in Rymont." He showed her his wallet badge. "Are you Niveat?"

"Heavens no. Niveat isn't here, she bowls every Tuesday. Why are you looking for her? Did she do something wrong?"

"Not that I know of. I'm just checking on some old cases, hoping she could help me."

"To tell you the truth, it wouldn't surprise me if she was involved in something illegal. She's been nothing but a pain for me. I've caught her in so many lies. I guess I should have checked her out more since Cindy died."

Ford put his hand on the doorframe. "You said she bowls every Tuesday. Do you think she's bowling now? And if she is, where's the bowling alley?"

"It's over on Jefferson Street." She walked out far enough to point directions. "Just turn left there at that stop sign, go two blocks and turn right. Then you'll be at the Wolfram Flea Market. Huntington Lanes is right behind the flea market. You can't miss it."

Ford waved at her, getting into his squad car. He easily found Huntington Lanes and pulled opened the heavy glass door. It was a dumpy place, and the whole building smelled of wet, moldy carpet and old cigarettes.

He walked up to the desk, asking the hippy-looking guy behind the counter to page Niveat. The clerk didn't look up…he didn't do anything except continue to read his newspaper.

Jim grabbed his arm, giving it a little twist. "This is official police business. Now, I'm going to ask you one more time; get Niveat Santos up here right now."

This time the clerk did as Jim asked, paging Niveat on his loudspeaker. Niveat appeared a few seconds later.

"This officer here asked me to page you," the clerk said, raising his shoulders and pointing to Ford.

"Are you Niveat?"

She nodded, giving the chief a disgusted look.

"Niveat, let's find a private place to talk. I need to ask you some questions."

"Why you wanted to ask me questions? I don't do nothing wrong. Who are you, anyways?"

"I didn't say you did anything wrong. I'm Jim Ford, the police chief in Rymont, and I want—"

She interrupted him. "If I don't do nothing wrong, go away. This ain't Rymont, it's Fort Ridge." Niveat turned away, heading back to her lane.

Ford grabbed her shoulder. "Listen, you can answer my questions here, or we can take a ride back to Rymont and you can answer them there; it's up to you."

"You can't forced me to do anything, I'm a minority. You can't do nothing to me. But I'll do you a favor and answered a few questions, but not very a lot."

Ford motioned Niveat to follow him to an empty corner of the snack bar.

She sat down at the table next to the wall, putting her hand on top of her fist. "So, what you wanted with me?"

Jim sat next to her, pulling out his notebook. He flipped a page, then looked at her. "I need to ask you about Tim Sanders."

"I don't know no Tim Sanders. There, I answered your question." She stood up, giving him a sour look. "See you."

"Oh, I think you know about Tim Sanders, now sit back down." He looked at his notes. "He changed his name to Casey."

"Okay, I knowed Casey. I wasn't lying, I never knowed any Sanders. Yeah, I hearded of Casey."

Ford moved his chair closer to the table. "Did you know his sister, Cindy Archdale, who lived on Blueberry Avenue here in Fort Ridge?"

"Of course, I knowded her, I was her maid. I worked for that crazy lady for twenty years, so what?" She leaned back in her chair, stretching her arms out, resting them on a metal ledge behind the table.

"Did Cindy ever tell you about her brother?"

"She tolded me he was crazy and not to talked about him to anyone. She's dead now, so I can say what I want. He keeled a kid a long time ago, drownded him."

"What else did she tell you about him?"

"Oh, she said he was a troublemaker ever since he was borned and that he had some kind of a promise with some other boys that they would always taked care of each other."

Ford wrote in his notebook, then looked back at Niveat. "Was that called the Four Raven Promise?"

She stood up, looking at the bowlers, waving at a group on lane sixteen. "I don't know. Old lady Archdale never tolded me what the name of it was."

"Did you ever hear her say anything about a bottle?"

"A bottle? What you mean? The only bottle I ever cared about was the Jell-O one."

"What do you mean, a Jell-O one?"

"Mr. Poleeceman, you can't be that stupid. Her Jell-O bottle had medicine in it that made her mean. When she drank out of the Jell-O bottle, I stayed away from her."

"Oh, you mean a yellow bottle?'

"Yes, like I said, a Jell-O bottle. Don't you understand English?"

"Uh, ah, okay. Niveat, have you ever heard of Steve Summers?"

Niveat thought for a second, then shook her head.

"Okay, how about Gloria Wilson?"

"I think that was Casey's old girlfriend. Mrs. Archdale said she could caused trouble for her brother one day."

"Niveat, do you know anybody who drives a big green GMC truck?"

She twisted her neck, then put a hand behind it. "The only big green truck I sawed was a week ago when some guy started asked me questions, like you are doing. He wouldn't leave until I told him I was going to shooted his fancy truck."

"What did he look like?" Jim asked, leaning closer to her.

"I don't remember. All I know was I didn't like him, and he had a big, green truck. Now you getting done with me? I am in a turmimint."

"Could you pick out the driver of that truck if I brought you some pictures to look at?"

She shook her head three times, then folded her arms in front of her.

"Okay, Niveat, just one more question." He picked up his notebook, flipping some pages. "Do you know about any of Casey's personal stuff or papers about him in Cindy's house?"

She got up, sliding her chair under the table. "There's a box under her bed with stuff in it about heem, a shoebox. She caughted me looking at them and went crazy. She told me to forgeted what I saw."

Ford looked back at his notes. "Do you still have a key to the house?"

"No, the cops got it. Can I go now?"

"Yeah, go back to your bowling, I'm done with you now. Oh, before you go, why do you have such a chip on your shoulder all the time?" He started walking beside her on the way to her lane.

"A cheep; what do you mean, a cheep?"

"Never mind, Niveat." He headed back to his car.

Now he had a good lead. He needed to look under that bed. He drove over to the police station to see Chief Rinken. Rinken was a good friend, and he owed Jim some favors. Now was the time to collect.

Walking into the police station, Ford spotted Rinken in the corner talking to a deputy. "Well, if it isn't Paul Rinken. It's great seeing you do some police business for a change."

"What are you doing here? Not enough crime in Rymont, so you had to come over and borrow some of ours, huh?" Rinken asked. "Jim, what's up? You look serious. What can I help you with?" He motioned for Ford to follow him into his office, closing the door.

Ford sat in the chair in front of Rinken's desk. "Paul, do you remember Cindy Archdale?"

"Sure, she died a week or so ago; why are you interested in her?" He leaned back in his chair with his hands cupped behind his head.

"She had a brother, and I think he was involved in a homicide in Rymont. But he just died. I found out Cindy had a box with some of his stuff under her bed. That might help me close up the case. Is there any way I can get in there and take a peek at it?" Ford scratched his ear, turning away from Paul, hoping for the right answer.

It was silent for a few seconds. Finally, Rinken spoke up. "Jim, I owe you that much. How about the two of us just running over there and taking a look?" Paul opened his middle desk drawer, pulling out a small yellow envelope. "Let's go Jim; but remember, this cleans the slate. I shouldn't be doing this."

Ford put on his hat, following Rinken out of his office. "It more than cleans the slate…now I owe you."

Jim got into Rinken's car, heading over to Blueberry Avenue. Paul opened the front door with a key from the small yellow envelope. After finding Cindy's bedroom, they both got on their knees, looking under the bed.

Ford could see an old picture of a man and a woman in a cracked frame, a rifle, and a white strongbox. He pulled out the strongbox, finding it locked.

"I think this is what you're looking for," Rinken said, pulling a shoebox out and putting it on the edge of the bed. He took off the lid, showing Jim a stack of letters and a few newspaper clippings. They each grabbed a letter.

Chief Ford opened an envelope addressed to Cindy that had no return address. He scanned it, seeing Sander's signature on the bottom. Looking at the envelope again, he noticed a date of August 22, 1954. "These are what I'm after, Paul. Can I ask you for another favor? Can I borrow these? Just for a day or two. I just need to make copies, then I'll return them to you."

"Sure, just watch for anything involving Fort Ridge, okay?"

"You got it, Paul. I'll bring all the originals back by the end of the week, I promise."

After Rinken dropped him off at his car, Ford headed back to his office in Rymont. He was in a hurry to sit down and read all the letters, hoping to find some answers to what had happened in 1951. He flipped on his cruiser's overhead lights, leaving them on until he pulled into his parking spot at the Rymont police station.

When he sat down behind his desk, Jim looked at the shoebox for a few seconds, wondering what he might find. Then he called Jenny into his office.

Jenny had been his lead clerk for over eight years, and he knew he could trust her. She was a beautiful blonde, loaded with energy. Everyone knew she was the one who really ran that office.

She walked in, giving him her incredible smile and her famous twinkle in those emerald green eyes. She sat down in front of his desk, opening one of her patented red steno pads.

"Jenny, I've been meaning to ask you something. Do you remember when Steve Summers called here looking for me that week I was on vacation?"

"Yes, I do. Remember? I told you about all that."

"I know, but let's go over it again."

"He wanted to talk to you, Chief, and only you. I told him you would be back from your vacation the next day and he told me he would call you then, that one more day wouldn't be a problem after waiting so long. That was about the extent of the call."

"Did you tell anyone about the call besides me when I got back?"

She shook her head.

"Did you log it into your book?" Ford asked, fidgeting with his pen.

"Chief, I log in everything, you know that."

"Have you heard anything about the call since?"

Jenny shook her head again. "Not a word, Chief."

"Okay, I'll tell you what...if you remember anything else about the day Mr. Summers called, let me know."

"You got it. Is there anything else you need?"

He picked up the shoebox. "I need some help with a little project, and I want you to handle it very quietly without talking to anyone, or leaving any of this laying around." He grabbed the top letter in the box. "Keep watching my out basket. When you see something like this letter in it, take it, make a copy, and return both sets back to my in basket; got it?"

"I got it; do you want me to take that one and make a copy?"

Ford chuckled. "No, I want you to copy it after I read it and put in the out basket."

She left his office as he pulled out the top letter. It was from June of 1957. He wanted to start with the oldest ones, so he put them in order, with the oldest on the top. Now the top letter was dated August 10, 1951. He could barely make out the post office stamp on the envelope, but it looked like it was mailed from Charlotte. He started reading.

"Sis, I need a big favor. You are the only person in the world I can trust. I'm in a jam and I need three hundred bucks right away. If you can help, get me the money as soon as you get this letter. I don't even feel safe calling you. I know you're not loaded, but I really need your help. I'll explain it all to you later. Send the money to 1132G West Divine Court in Charlotte. I love you, Tim."

Ford lay back in his chair, scratching his head, hoping the rest of the letters had more to say than the first one. The next one was also mailed from Charlotte, again with no return address. He opened the envelope, pulling out a two-page letter. It was not easy to read, making him wonder if it was from her brother.

He flipped the page, seeing Tim's signature. "He must have been drunk when he wrote this one," he mumbled, as he started to translate.

"Cindy, I got the money. Thanks. I owe you. I changed my name, so if anyone asks you, you don't have a brother. My name is Robert Casey now. A friend of mine in the Social Security Office helped me out, that's why I needed the money. I had to change my name because I did something stupid on graduation night. There was this kid named Brian Kelly. Me and some of my friends were out in Lake Buckley and Kelly kept bugging me. I started playing around with him...you know, his private parts. He called me a fag and the other kids heard it, so I went crazy. I pulled him under and he drowned. Everyone was cool about it, saying it was an accident.

Please don't tell anyone what I did. There's only two or three people in the whole world who know what I did that night, and I need to keep it that way. I'd give anything if I could go back and change everything. I have to live with it for the rest of my life. Please forgive me for all that. I just had to tell you. Sis, I will always love you, Tim.

P.S. Here's your money back."

The chief put the letter down, shaking his head. A kid had to lose his life for calling this scumbag a name. At least now there was no doubt…the drowning was not an accident, and Tim Sanders was the killer. He put that letter in his out basket, unfolding the next one. It was typed, with Sanders's signature on the bottom. It almost looked like a business letter, and it was dated September 12, 1951. It read:

"Cindy, I wanted you to know everything is going great for me. I got a decent job with a big construction company. It's hard work, but it pays good. The only thing that still bothers me is how much I miss Rymont. I had some real good friends there. I don't know if I ever told you, but I was in a club called the Four Raven Promise. Our promise was to always try to help each other.

One of the other Promisers got into a big jam a couple of weeks ago, killing some guy in a liquor store with a vodka bottle. Have you heard anything about that? If you do, how about sending me the info? You've got my address now. I sure wish I could see you. Maybe someday we can meet up again, when everything is safe for me. One more thing…I haven't had a drink in over a month. Isn't that great? Well, I've got to go, I love you, Tim."

Ford called Carl Williams into his office. "Carl, do me a favor…run me a printout of all liquor store homicides in the entire Charlotte area in August of 1951. I need to know if anyone was killed by getting hit over the head with a vodka bottle."

"Will do, Chief. Do you think that's what Ray Summers's letter was all about?"

"It could be, Carl, just check it out." Ford got up and walked to the window, looking out but not really seeing anything. Maybe that's what Steve Summers was hiding…maybe it wasn't the drowning after all. He sat down, pulling the next letter off the stack. It was dated January 17,

1955. This one was written in pencil, with a lot of smudges on it. He had to read it slowly.

"Cindy, I've been thinking about you a lot lately. How was your Christmas? Mine was great. I found a new friend, someone who cares about me. We had a wonderful holiday together. He makes my life worth living again. I hope you get to meet him one day. Maybe that surprises you, but he's my soul mate.

Have you heard anything about the drowning or the liquor store mess? I still keep in touch with a couple of the Promisers, but I haven't heard much lately. I guess everything has totally died down. That's good, huh? Oh, guess what? Chuck and I are going to Mexico on an eight-day vacation. I'll be sending you some pictures. I hope I can see you soon. Love, Tim."

Jenny walked in with the second set, laying it on his desk and grabbing the last letter from his out basket.

Ford stretched out his arms, yawning. "Jenny, how about getting me a strong cup of coffee? It looks like I'll need it tonight."

Gunders knocked on Ford's door. "Hey, Chief, I just got the report on the Ray Summers letter." He held up a piece of paper. "The only fingerprints were on the envelope, most of them smudged. I'd bet they are all from the post office. The letter itself only had one thumb print on it, and it was from Ray Summers."

"I'm not surprised. Thanks, George. Did Carl tell you about the liquor store thing?"

Gunders nodded, starting to close Ford's door. "Yep, I'm already working on that one, too."

Two minutes later, Jenny walked back in, delivering the next set. "Hey, you're getting behind," she said with a smile.

"Now your out basket is empty. I didn't think you could keep up with me."

"I'll have another one for you in a minute, Jenny. There's a lot to digest here."

Jenny put both hands on the front of his desk. "What time do you think we'll be done? I don't care, but I got to let Jackson know something because of dinner."

Ford looked at his watch. "It's a little after five. I'll go faster, and we should be done, say, about six or so; how does that sound?"

"That's fine, Chief," she responded, leaving his office.

Ford picked up the next letter, dated February 12, 1956.

"Hi. How are you? Nothing new here. I just wanted you to know I'm still alive. Sometimes I think everyone is watching me. I hate living like this. I'm alone again, Chuck left me. I had a hard time at first, but I'm getting used to it. I wish I could go back and be Tim Sanders again, and have some fun. Cindy, I really miss Gloria. I think about her a lot. I'm going crazy living like this. I still haven't had any liquor, but I tried some drugs. They made me feel better for a while, until I lost my job. Those assholes said I wasn't dependable. They're the crazy ones. I'm just me, and if they don't like it, the hell with them. It's just that I'm not sure who I am or what I'm doing. I'm really getting mixed up about everything. Well, I'm getting tired, so I got to go. I love you so much, Tim."

"This nut case has gone totally wacko," Ford said, loud enough for the whole office to hear.

He grabbed the next one. It was thicker than the others. Pulling out three pages written on what looked like a kid's school tablet, he began to read the February 17, 1965 letter.

"Cindy, happy birthday. The big 3-0. I wish I could be there for you. Maybe I'll get over there and see you next weekend. It's time for me to stop worrying about the drowning. It's been over fourteen years. I guess I've suffered enough. Do you think Bruce would mind if I stopped by? I got my life straightened out now.

By the way, is there anything new in Rymont? I haven't heard a word about anything, or anyone from down there. Oh well, no news is good news. I still wonder what happened with that liquor store thing in Georgia.

Cindy, I decided to give my life to Jesus. When I think of all the things I've done, there is no way I am worthy of His forgiveness, but I'm trying to make it up to Him. I don't have a job, but I don't need one. I even sold my house and gave all that to the church. That's where I live now, at the church's mission. They don't charge me for nothing. Finally, I'm content. It's a blessed life for me, because of God.

My prayer is that one day you find the peace I have found. It's too bad it took me so long to figure it out. Do you realize how great my world would have been if I had found God when I was young? Just think about it. I know I wouldn't have drowned that kid if Jesus was in my life. That would have made everything so much easier, not having to hide all the time.

I wish I could change so many things from my past, but I can't. All I can do is make it up to God by honoring Him and asking for His forgiveness. God is the only answer, Cindy, for all of us. If He can save me, He can save you, too. All you have to do is ask Him for His forgiveness. He'll be there for you.

Well, I have to go now. I've got morning bible study to go to. Cindy, I love you, and God loves you, too. Just ask Him. Tim."

That was a head-scratching letter, Ford thought. Now he knew the liquor store murder was in Georgia and it involved one of the Promisers.

Carl opened the door a crack, leaning in. "See you tomorrow, Chief."

"Did you run that printout?"

"That computer is so slow today, but it should be printed out by the time I get here in the morning."

"That's great. Oh, I'll have another twist for you in this crazy case tomorrow, too. You go ahead and go home. By the way, who's on tonight?" Ford asked, hoping it was Gunders and not Sean, the new trainee.

"It's Sean's turn, Chief."

"Uh, okay. I'll talk to you tomorrow," Ford said, watching his deputy leave.

There were three more letters to read and copy. He was hoping they would tell him more about the liquor store killing, or the identity of the Fourth Promiser. But they didn't tell him anything new, just the ravings of a crazy man.

Jenny finished copying everything at 6:15 and left.

Ford put the original letters back into the shoebox, then put the copies, as well as everything else about the case, into his briefcase, then headed out to his car.

As Ford pulled up to his house, waiting for the garage door to open, he picked up his cell phone. "Carl, do me a favor; call Gunders and tell him I want to see both of you at seven sharp in the morning. I've got some new leads I want you to check on."

"I'll do it, Chief; good night."

Ford reread every letter while he was eating dinner, hoping to find a clue he might have missed. He didn't find anything.

Chapter 20
He Recognized the Driver

The next morning Chief Ford brought Carl and George into his office, filling them in on the interviews he'd had the day before with Betty Thomas and Niveat. He also gave them a sketch of what was said in the letters he had retrieved from under Cindy Archdale's bed, including the few details about the Georgia killing.

"Now listen up; I want all of your efforts today to be focused on any liquor store murders in Georgia in August of 1951," Ford said. "Look for a murder with someone getting hit over the head with a bottle. Pull out all stops on this. If we find out who was involved there, we'll probably find out who killed Steve Summers, and tried to kill his grandson. Put everything else on hold…we're just working on this case. I don't care if we have to work all day and all night."

"Carl, you start with Georgia. Call the state police over there. Gunders, I want you to use that fancy computer of yours and see what you can find. Start with Googling unsolved Georgia liquor store murders from 1951."

The deputies left his office, talking to each other, while Ford reopened his briefcase, watching a piece of paper fall out. He bent down and picked it up as Carl walked back in.

"Chief, do you know anybody over in Georgia that could help me get started?"

"Start with Detective Nell with the Atlanta Police Department, the big office downtown. She's a woman, but she's damn good. Her first name is Linda. Oh, and Carl, I've got a little work to wrap up here, then I'll be going over to the city office to talk to someone. If you find out anything, give me a call."

Ford left ten minutes later, heading to see his old friend in the utilities office. After getting to the city building, he found Gloria Stillers at her desk, going through her purse. "What'd you lose this time?" he asked, sitting down on the chair next to her desk.

"Why, if it isn't Jim Ford. How are you, Jim? And how's June and those beautiful babies of yours?"

"Everybody's great at our house…well, almost." He yawned. "Excuse me, Gloria, I haven't gotten much sleep lately. I think June might be coming down with a case of bronchitis; she's been coughing a lot at night."

"Oh, wow. I got that last year, that can be tough. You know, I miss seeing June. Please tell her to stop by sometime when she feels better and we can have lunch, like we used to."

"I'll do just that, Gloria. So tell me, how's your tribe doing?"

"It's been a little hectic for us, Jim. We had our third grandbaby this week, and Mattie's the prettiest little baby girl I've ever seen. Oh, my husband gave me a big surprise. It's looks like we're going to Aruba for our anniversary next month…it's our fortieth. Can you believe it? Forty years, isn't that something? Oh, listen to me ramble. Now, I know you didn't come up here to ask me about my vacation, and I bet you don't need your electric turned on. So, what can I do for you?"

"I just wondered if an old friend can buy you a cup of coffee downstairs?"

"Sure you can. Are you wanting to go downstairs right now?"

"Yeah, I've got some things to ask you…you know, just some police business."

She grabbed her purse, following him to the elevator.

They went downstairs to the city cafeteria, finding an empty table next to the emergency exit. Sitting across from each other, Ford could tell Gloria was nervous, constantly turning her Styrofoam cup in a circle, creating little typhoons of the hot coffee to look at.

"Gloria, you seem uptight. I just want to ask you some questions about when you were in high school; no big deal."

"What's all this about high school? That Summers boy was asking me about that just last week. Why is everyone so interested in what happened fifty years ago?" she asked, still turning the coffee mug.

"I'm not interested in anything from back then, except what happened on graduation night at that lake party."

"You mean the drowning?"

Ford scratched his right temple, looking at Gloria. "Yeah, let's start there."

She teetered back on her chair. "Okay, well, there was a bunch of us kids swimming out at the lake. A kid named Brian Kelly was way out by himself and wasn't a very good swimmer, so, uh, he drowned before anyone could save him. I think it was so loud…I mean, we were having a big party, it was so loud that no one could hear him screaming. It was terrible."

Jim cleared his throat. "Let me ask you, Gloria; were you very close to him when he died?"

She looked away. "Like I told you, he was way out in the lake by himself."

"So, even if he was by himself, how far away was that from you?"

Gloria looked down at her coffee, swirling it again. "Oh, I don't know, Jim. I guess I was about fifty or sixty feet away from him when he went under."

Jim looked at his notes. "Okay, did you hear Kelly call Tim Sanders a name?" he asked without looking up.

She was silent for a moment. "That was fifty years ago; I can't remember stuff from yesterday, Jim."

The chief raised his shoulders, looking into her eyes. "What if I told you I have a witness who said you were only a few feet from Kelly when he drowned? And that same witness says Sanders pulled him under water after Kelly called him a fag?"

Gloria picked at her fingernails on one hand with the other hand. She looked up at Ford, then quickly looked back down at her hands again. "That may have happened. Why are you asking me about all this? Why don't you ask Tim?"

"I wish I could. The problem is, he just died in a hospice up in Charlotte."

She was quiet as tears built in the corners of her eyes, and one darted down her left cheek. She tried to find something in the cafeteria to focus on. "Jim, I did see Tim kill Brian. What you told me happened exactly as you said. I've been so afraid all these years of Tim doing something crazy if I told anyone. It's kind of funny…he told me a thousand times how much he loved me, but since that happened, I've been awfully afraid of him."

"Gloria, I know you didn't have anything to do with the drowning, but you should have gone to the police back then. Anyway, let's put that behind us. I really came here to ask you about some other things, okay?"

"I'll do the best I can, Jim."

He looked at his notes again. "All right, have you ever heard of the Four Raven Promise?"

"Sure, that was a promise Tim made with Steve Summers and a Brad Tillin and someone else that they'd always watch out for each other."

"You don't know who that someone else is?"

"I have no idea."

"Do you know anyone in Rymont who drives a big green GMC truck?"

"No…I don't recall anyone driving a green GMC, but I can check with the girls on the second floor in the DMV department if you want. Maybe they can find out about all that."

"That's okay, I'm still waiting for that info from Columbia. I just wondered if you knew anyone who drove one, saving me some time." He turned over a page in his notebook. "Gloria, now I want you to think hard about something. Have you ever heard of one of your classmates hitting a liquor store clerk over the head with a vodka bottle in Georgia the summer after your graduation?"

She tilted her head towards Ford, lowering her eyebrows. "Of course not. Jim, let me ask you a question. I'm not in any trouble, am I?"

He grabbed her hand. "No, Gloria, you're not in any trouble, but if you think of anything else about what I asked you, give me a call, will you? And thanks for the answers. You're still okay in my book."

She nodded as he handed her one of his business cards.

He stood up and bent over, giving her a kiss on the cheek.

She gave him the best smile she could as she watched him leave the cafeteria.

***

Ford drove back to the station and found Carl waiting for him at the front door.

"Chief, I got some information on the liquor store killing; am I good or what?"

"Yeah, you're good; now what you got?" Ford asked him as they walked into Ford's office.

"Well, that Nell woman in Atlanta called back, You're right, she's super. Anyway, there was a murder at a liquor store in Morton City, Georgia on August 5, 1951. Chief, Morton City is a little hole in the wall eight miles from the South Carolina line. I guess the clerk died an hour or so after someone hit him over the head with a vodka bottle. He never regained consciousness, so he couldn't identify his killer."

Ford sat down, laying back in his brown leather chair. "Carl, check on the legal drinking age in South Carolina and Georgia in 1951. And while you're at it, find out what day of the week that was and if there were any 'dry' days in Rymont back then. Oh, what's Gunders doing? Did you fill him in on everything?"

"He's checking on some old files in the basement about either the drowning or the liquor store thing. And yes, I covered everything with him."

"Great job, Carl; now get George up here."

Carl left and five minutes later, Gunders walked in, carrying a big box of papers.

"What do you got there?" Ford asked, watching Gunders strain to put the overstuffed container on the open table next to the chief's desk.

"Oh, these are some old papers from the fifties. I figured I'd go through them looking for anything on the drowning or the liquor clerk murder."

Ford stood up, looking down in the big box. "I'll tell you what, George, forget the drowning, just concentrate on the murder in Georgia. And do me a favor; separate out the cases from 1951 and bring those cases back to me before I leave today."

"Sure, but that might take a while," Gunders answered, carrying out his box.

Carl knocked on the door window, then walked in. "Chief, I got that info for you. The drinking age in both Georgia and South Carolina was twenty one in 1951, August 5 fell on a Sunday, and that was a 'dry' day in Rymont, but not in Morton City."

"That's what I thought you'd find. Sure, it fits. A kid who wanted booze on a Sunday in Rymont just needed a fake ID and a car to drive eight miles into Georgia to get it. Thanks, Carl."

Carl left, then Ford called Ray Summers, asking him what was the most popular booze the kids drank his senior year and what Steve drank. Ray told him beer was the popular drink back then, but that Steve liked both beer and vodka.

Ford asked him if he had thought of anyone yet who could be the Fourth Promiser. Ray said he'd like to see a yearbook, in that he still hadn't found his. The chief told him he knew where he could get one, and he'd bring it up to the hospital in about an hour.

It was 5:00 PM. Both Carl and George were getting ready to go home. Gunders walked into Ford's office, putting a smaller box of papers on his desk. "This is all the paperwork for all the cases in 1951, but there isn't anything about a liquor store killing in Georgia."

"Thanks, George. Have a good night. I'll see you tomorrow," Jim said, filling George's box with all of his papers on the Summers case.

Carl walked in, sitting on the chair in front of the chief's desk, loosening his tie. He put his legs out straight. "It's been a long day, huh, Chief?"

"You can say that again, and I've still got to go see Betty Thomas to get her yearbook, then hit Fort Ridge to return Sanders's letters. After all that, I have to go the hospital and see Ray and Billy Summers. Oh well, after all this is over, I'm taking some time off, I'll tell you that."

"Well, I'm hitting it, Chief. I'm beat. I got to get home because Kristy's got a special meal planned tonight. I'll see you in the morning."

Ford grabbed the box, along with his briefcase, anxious to go see Betty Thomas. He was getting tired and he didn't want to waste any time on anything. He parked in front of her place, walked up the sidewalk, and rang her doorbell. No one answered. Looking around the right side of the house, he spotted her pulling weeds from the flowerbed next to the garage.

She looked up when he came around the corner. "Hey, Jim, back so soon? You must have really liked my lemonade, huh?"

"Uh huh, it was really good; but what I really need is to borrow that yearbook from your senior year. Do you think you can find it? I'm kind of in a hurry."

"Sure, Jim, I'll get it. Want a quick glass of lemonade before you go?"

"No, I have to take a rain check on that. I just need your yearbook, if you don't mind."

She went inside, leaving him on the sidewalk. He knew if he went in, he'd be stuck for a while; and besides, he couldn't take any more of that crazy plastic sofa covering. He started tapping a shoe on the sidewalk just as she walked out with the yearbook.

"Here you go, Chief; now please, take care of it for me." She halfway handed it to Ford, then pulled it back. "You know, there's a note in there from my dad. I think it's on the inside of the back cover. I wouldn't want to lose that. Only two kids even signed my book, but Dad made up for them." She put a couple of fingers over her mouth. "Oh, please, don't look at the pictures of me, they're awful. I never did take a good picture, you know."

Ford stood there with his hand out, waiting for her special book. "I won't Betty, I promise. Now I've got to go."

He looked at the yearbook she was holding against her chest. "Betty, I can get a copy of that from someone else if you prefer."

She opened her mouth, like she'd forgotten she even had the book. "Look at me, would you? Here I am hogging this old yearbook when you came all the way over here to borrow it. I'm so sorry." She finally handed it to him. "Now, you take your time bringing it back if you need it a while."

"I'll get it back to you by the end of the week, Betty. Thanks so much...you take care." He turned, heading towards his cruiser. As he opened the door, he looked back at her. She hadn't even said goodbye; she was just worried about her prized high school possession. "I'll take care of this like it was my own, I promise. Oh, and Betty, I'll be back soon...I love your lemonade."

He'd found the magic words. She smiled, waving goodbye to both a friend and a book. Ford pulled out of her driveway mumbling about Betty. "Wow, she's something. No wonder no one signed her goddamn yearbook. And her lemonade sucks, too."

Ford stopped at the Ame's Miracle gas station at the Highway 21 intersection to buy a Coke and fill up with gas, heading to Fort Ridge to take the Sanders letters back to Paul Rinken. The road was quiet...it was like he owned the road. After driving a few miles, he looked in the rearview mirror, seeing a truck closing on him fast.

He coasted for a mile or two, constantly looking in his mirror. "Slow down, Bub. I don't have time for this. Okay, you want to ignore me? Let's see how you like a big fat speeding ticket." Ford said to the guy in the GMC, as he watched him in his rearview mirror.

A minute later the truck was only a few yards behind him. Ford could see now that it was a green GMC, and it wasn't slowing down. Ford looked in the mirror again, then felt the hair on his neck stand up as he recognized the front license plate. It was a bright red rebel flag on a silver background. "Oh, my God, that's the truck…the truck that hit Billy," the chief hollered.

He flipped on his flashing lights and pushed up the siren button, in hopes the truck would stop. The GMC went by him like he was standing still. "I'm going to get that son of a bitch," Ford screamed. He hit the gas, trying to catch the truck. He caught up with the GMC two miles later as the truck slowed down, coming to a stop in the right lane.

Ford pulled onto the shoulder next to the idling truck. He turned to get out of the police car, and saw a shotgun resting on the open passenger window frame. Ford pulled his gun out of its holster in a panic, recognizing the driver, and shouting "What the hell...?"

There was a blast. The chief was shot in the head.

***

The driver of the truck ran to Ford, finding him slumped against the passenger door with part of his head blown off. He opened the door, put Ford's cruiser in neutral, then got back into his truck, pulling it behind the squad car. He pushed the car off the shoulder, sending it down a steep hill. It careened towards the woods, picking up speed as it rocketed towards a tree, hitting it so hard the hood bent in half.

The killer took a five gallon gas can off his truck and ran down to the destroyed squad car, emptying some of it on the hood and a gallon or two on the chief's dead body. He pulled a handkerchief out of his pocket, igniting it with his lighter, and threw it on Ford's chest. Black, billowing flames sharply lifted up towards the heavens. The whole thing took less than two minutes. No one saw anything. Chief Ford was dead, the killer was gone, and all the evidence was destroyed.

Chapter 21
Those Poor Babies

Billy had a busy day. Nancy and Gary got to the hospital before breakfast, with Granny getting there an hour later. Gary was excited about getting his reworked Buick to Rymont, and everyone was getting tired of hearing, especially the nurses, about how hot his car was going to be after he finished it.

Billy was getting frustrated as the day slowly sputtered by. He was anxious to get the tests over with so he could go home. "This is getting boring now," he told Nancy.

She walked over next to him, chewing on an old doughnut. "Oh, Billy, there was this kid in school yesterday with a cast on his leg, too. The bottom of it looked kind of like a boot. He walked funny, but he didn't need any crutches. Maybe you could ask Dr. Victor if you can get one of those?"

Billy raised his shoulders, as if to say, "Who knows?"

He turned towards the door, hearing someone talking in the hall. "Right down there, the one on the right."

Coach Fatha leaned in, making sure he was at the right room. He waved at Granny and Nancy, then walked up to Billy, patting him on his shoulder. "So, how's the Rymont flash doing today?"

"I'm doing okay. At least they say I can go home Thursday if tomorrow's tests come out all right. Coach, I'm really getting tired of all this. Why did all this have to happen to me? I mean why do I have all the bad luck?"

Fatha sat down close to Billy. "I'd say you've got a lot to be thankful for. In fact, I think you are a very lucky young man. Just think of it; you hit a horse that saved you from hitting a big old telephone pole that would probably have killed you. God gave you an incredible amount of athletic ability, enough to get a full scholarship from one of the best colleges in the country. Your granny is a wonderful mom, your girlfriend is the sweetest person on earth, and just look around at all the flowers from Rymont. No, your world isn't so bad; at least it's better than that horse buried next to the highway," he said, snickering.

"Well, that sure puts things in perspective, Coach Fatha," Granny said. "Now, I see why your players think so much of you. That was some pep talk. It kind of made me forget about my arthritis some. In fact, do you think you can draw some plays up for me for Friday night, and find me a uniform? I'm fired up."

Billy nodded, chuckling. "Grandma's right. I got to quit feeling sorry for myself. So, tell me, Coach, what's new?"

"I came by to give you an update on a few things."

"Excuse me, Billy," Granny said, standing up. "But it's after six and Nancy and I are going to find Gary and head back home. Besides, you got some company now so you don't need us just sitting here. We're all beat, son."

Granny and Nancy kissed their hero goodnight and thanked Coach Fatha for his help before they went out the door.

"I said I came by to give you an update on some stuff," Fatha said, pouring himself a glass of water from a blue plastic pitcher that was sitting on a table next to the bathroom door. "First off, I'm still working on finding out what the word 'bottle' means in Rymont. I've tried every angle I can think of and can't find a thing, but don't give up on me.

Secondly, I talked to the AD down at Georgia Tech. Nothing has changed with those folks…they're still looking forward to getting you up there."

"Thanks so much. I'll make you proud when I get there, I promise."

"I know you will, Billy. One more thing…I want to officially invite you to the game Friday night against Jefferson; that is, if you are out of here. I'm saving a special spot near the bench for you. I want you to see firsthand some new plays we put together, and our fired-up team wanting to make you proud."

For the first time in days, Billy was beaming. "You have no idea how great that sounds. I'll be there, count on it. No tests will keep me away from that."

Fatha looked down at his feet. "Billy, there's one more thing. I wanted to apologize to you about the time I was rude to you when you came to me for help. Can I just say it was a very bad day that day, and leave it at that? I am here for you now, and will be forever for anything you need."

"Hey, I've had my share of bad days lately. No big deal. You're a good friend and you've always been there for me. One bad day won't change that."

They talked for a half hour, then heard Uncle Ray walking down the hall. His old work shoes made a noise that everyone could recognize. It was as if one shoe had a clicker under it and one didn't. Ray walked in whistling, spotting Coach Fatha. "What are you guys up to, devising some new plays for Friday's game?"

Fatha stood up, looking down at Billy. "No, I just wanted to come by and see my superstar. Now, you take care, Billy, I got to go. I left my wife at Hazelton Mill Mall with a credit card." He laughed. "That's more dangerous than a three hundred pound defensive end heading right at our quarterback. Remember two things Billy; I'm saving you spot at the game, and I'll always be here for you, for anything."

"Thanks, Coach Fatha."

The coach nodded and left.

"He's a hell of a guy, that Coach Fatha," Ray said. "Oh, Billy, have you heard from Chief Ford?"

"No, should I have heard from him?"

Ray sat at the foot of Billy's bed. "He called me and said he'd be up here to give us some news, and he sure sounded excited."

Billy and Ray talked for over an hour, with Ray constantly looking at his watch. "I wonder where Jim is? Maybe I should call him." He punched in the number, getting no answer. He called the station and the new deputy had no idea where Ford was.

Ray called the chief's home again, but again there was no answer. He decided to call Carl Williams at home.

"Carl, this is Ray."

"How are you doing, Ray?" Carl asked, obviously eating something.

"I'm fine. Do you have any idea where Jim is?"

"You sound so serious, Ray, is everything all right?"

"Yeah, I'm just wondering how to get in touch with Ford, that's all. He was supposed to meet me and Billy up here at the hospital over an hour ago. I guess we're just anxious to hear what he found out today, that's all."

"I bet he's going to tell you that we figured out what the 'bottle' clue meant. A clerk at a liquor store just over the line in Georgia got hit over the head with a vodka bottle and died in August of '51. And catch this…we have proof one of the four Promisers was involved."

"Now I really can't wait to talk to him. I bet you're right, I bet that's what he's going to tell us when he gets here. Listen, Carl, if you hear from him, tell him I'm up here, will you?"

"You bet, Ray. I'll see if I can find him tonight, too. Bye now."

Ray turned to Billy, shocked at what he'd just heard. "Billy, Carl said they found out the 'bottle' clue was about a killing in Georgia in '51, right after graduation. Somebody hit a liquor store clerk over the head with a vodka bottle, and a Promiser was involved. I think that's why he's coming up here…but where the hell is he?"

Billy bent down, trying to scratch his broken leg through his cast. It was pointless. He looked back at his uncle. "Uncle Ray, they're not saying they think Grandpa had anything to do with that, are they?"

Ray shook his head. "I doubt it. It sounds like they're still figuring things out. Maybe Jim will fill us in tonight." He looked at his watch again. "Man, it's past eight. I think I'm going to run down to his place. Say Billy, if he gets here while I'm gone, just give me a call, okay?"

"Sure, Uncle Ray." Ray left just as Nurse Clark came in.

"Well, hello there, Mr. Summers." Her hair was pulled back, making her look even younger. She sat down in the chair by the window, giving him that sly smile again. He could tell it was going to be a wild night.

They talked for over twenty minutes, with her rattling off one hospital story after another. She mesmerized him with her sweetness. Finally, she slapped her knees with both hands and got up, pulling the blood pressure wrap out of her pocket. She walked all the way around the bed to the right side. "Time to check your vital signs, Mr. Summers," she whispered as she started to lay across him.

Billy noticed her blouse was unbuttoned at the top again, like she was teasing him. He looked down, seeing her half-covered breasts, and began to get excited again. It was almost show time. He decided to get bold, so he put his right hand between his face and her breasts, like he had to sneeze. She didn't do anything as he touched her, moving his knuckles around just enough to make it obvious what he was doing. He continued to rub her breasts.

"I can't seem to get a good reading, Billy, just bear with me."

His cell phone rang. They both looked at it, sitting on the rolling table on the other side of the bed.

"Don't you want to get that?" she asked, looking down at him.

"No, that's okay, it's been ringing all day. I'll just give it a rest. You just go ahead and finish. I'll call whoever it was back."

He pulled his hand off her breast, sliding it down the side of the bed, touching her left hip. Now what was he going to do? He slowly moved his hand down her hip to the bottom of her skirt, feeling the top of her knee highs.

Nurse Clark looked down at him, smiling. "I finally got a good reading. I'm sorry it took so long," she said, pulling away from him as his hand fell to the side.

"It didn't seem like it took so long to me. Maybe you ought to check it again." He gave her a pleading smile.

"I'll tell you what...I've got to check on some other patients, but with you having all those tests tomorrow, I better check your pressure a lot tonight, don't you think?"

"That sounds like a good idea to me, Nurse Clark," he said, watching her walk out the door.

"I was right, she wants me," Billy said at half-volume. He turned and picked up his phone, seeing that Uncle Ray had called him twice.

"What's up, Uncle Ray?"

"Billy, Jim Ford is dead."

Billy shook his head. "What? Uncle Ray, did you...what? Oh, my God, what happened?"

"Well, it looks like he hit a tree, just like Steve. Carl just called me and told me Jim's car exploded, and he died instantly. Billy, he was burnt up. I can't believe it. I guess it happened about two hours ago. The state police are already there. It's terrible, just terrible."

Billy could see Grandma trying to get through on his line. "Uncle Ray, I got to go. Grandma's calling me. I'll get right back to you after I talk to her. Bye."

"Billy, did you hear about Chief Ford?" Grandma asked with a panicky voice.

"Yeah, Uncle Ray just called. I'm in shock, Grandma, just in shock."

"My God, poor June, and those kids," Grandma said. "They had two little ones, you know. Billy, this is all a nightmare…it's got to stop. I got to go, I want to see if there's anything on TV about Jim. I'll get back to you as soon as I can. Love you."

Billy turned his TV on, hoping to find any news about Ford. He flipped the channels looking for anything about the accident. Finally, he found a local Charlotte news update.

"Now, back to the tragic accident outside Rymont tonight. Art Anagnostu is at the scene. Art, what's the latest?"

"Jada, Jim Ford, the chief of police in Rymont, was killed tonight just outside of Fort Ridge. He apparently lost control of his car and hit a tree, killing him instantly. You can see what remains of his squad car being towed away. The South Carolina State Police are at the scene, trying to figure out what happened. We hope to have more details of this tragic accident on *Eight on Your Side Eyewitness News at Ten.*"

Billy sat back in his bed, staring out the window. How could all this be happening? What could be worth two people dying, plus someone trying to kill him? Could all this really be tied to a murder some fifty years ago? It didn't make any sense.

He went to sleep an hour later, then woke up to Nurse Clark taking his blood pressure again. She was rubbing up against him, but he wasn't interested. He knew he would regret not taking advantage of her gyrations, but he just couldn't.

After a couple of minutes of no response from him, she looked down. "Billy, are you okay? You don't seem to be yourself tonight. Is there something wrong?"

He rubbed both eyes, trying to focus on the nurse. "Yeah, I got some bad news tonight. Chief Ford from Rymont was coming up here to see me about my accident. He was trying to help me. Well, he died tonight in a bad car wreck."

"I'm sorry, Billy…I'll leave you alone. Do you think you'll need a pill to help you sleep? Or how about just someone to talk to?" She got off his chest, buttoning the top of her blouse.

He gave her the best smile he could muster. "I think I'll probably need both tonight."

Clark left, returning almost instantly with two pills and a paper cup filled with water. "Here, now take these and I'll check on you later. Again, I'm sorry about what happened to your friend."

"Thanks. Hey, it's not your fault. You're the best thing that's happened to me since I got here. Don't forget to come back for our talk."

He woke up the next morning at 8:45. He didn't remember any more blood pressure shows overnight. Maybe he'd turned her off with his problems.

Ten minutes later, a grumpy old nurse came into his room to give him a bath. He turned to look around her. "Are you the only nurse on duty now?"

"Of course not. There's three or four more nurses just on this floor. We all came in at eight this morning." She pulled a tall stack of white towels out of his closet. "Today's shift day, so you're stuck with me every morning for a while." She pulled back his sheets, starting his bath.

"So, does that mean whoever worked yesterday and last night is not working today?"

"You got me, all I know is my schedule. I don't keep up with anyone else." She scrubbed his arms with a washcloth that felt like it was made out of sandpaper.

She finished his bath without any more conversation, then Dr. Victor walked in.

"This is the big day, Mr. Summers. We're going to start your tests in an hour or so, and they'll take most of the day," Victor said, as he listened to Billy's chest. "We'll be taking pictures of your skull, your leg, and your abdomen. If there's no sign of problems, you'll be going home tomorrow morning, if that's okay with you."

"That sounds awesome."

Victor wrote on a clipboard, then smiled at Billy. "Now you rest; this will be a long day for you. I'll see you this afternoon."

Billy was taken aback by how quiet it was, like there was a directive from the hospital that everyone had to be silent. It gave him time to think—about Chief Ford, Nurse Clark, and the liquor store killing. He laid there with his thoughts for over an hour until Gary and Nancy walked in.

Nancy sat next to Billy on his bed, then slid down next to him, starting to cry.

Billy patted her back. "What's wrong, baby?"

"It's Chief Ford. It kept me up all night. My God, Billy, what is happening?" she asked, her face glistening with tears.

"I wish I knew," Billy responded. "I was hoping I'd wake up this morning and find out it was all a bad dream. Ford was just trying to help me, and look what happened."

"Grandma is really broken up about Chief Ford," Gary said, looking out the window. "She's over with June Ford now. They've been friends for a long time. She told me to tell you she'd get up here today if she can."

"Gary, do you want to go with me downstairs to grab a cup of coffee?" Nancy asked.

Gary got up without answering, following Nancy towards the elevator.

Billy looked around for his phone, finally finding it under his sheet, and called Fatha. They talked about Chief Ford for over ten minutes, then Billy filled him in on what they found out about the bottle killing in Georgia, getting an offer from his coach to see what he could find out about it.

Ten minutes later, Uncle Ray called.

"Is there anything new down in Rymont?" Billy asked his uncle.

"Carl said the state police will be taking a statement from me, and then maybe you. I've got a feeling they don't think it was an accident. They got most of the background from Carl and Gunders, starting with Steve's accident. Anyway, I'll keep you informed as things happen. I've got to go. Take care."

Billy looked at his phone. "I've got to see how Grandma is doing."

She picked up on the second ring. "Oh, Billy, it's awful. Poor June, she's such a mess. Jim was the love of her life. And the babies, those poor babies. Billy, you should see all the people here, it's amazing…but so sad. Such a young man, and such a good man; it's so sad."

"Grandma, I don't know what to say. Please tell Mrs. Ford how sorry I am, and how much I liked Chief Ford, will you? He was really trying to help me. I hope they get to the bottom of this fast. Are you hearing anything?"

"A couple of state troopers are here. I heard one of them say there were some fresh skid marks on the road that weren't from the chief's car. They also said their lab was going through Ford's car with a fine tooth comb, but based on what I saw on TV this morning, I can't imagine them finding anything in that big pile of metal."

A thin black man pushed a wheelchair next to Billy's bed, bending over to lock the front wheel brakes.

"Grandma, it looks like they're starting the tests, I'll call you back later. Love you."

"It's time for an MRI," the wheelchair driver said, lifting Billy into his new Hot Wheels.

Chapter 22
Take Him First

Billy looked around the MRI waiting room for something to focus on. He noticed a little girl wearing a green turban, sitting in a wheelchair covered with small flower stickers. She was clutching a rag doll that had a bright yellow braided ponytail. The girl was whispering to her doll when she looked up, noticing Billy staring at her. She turned away, looking back at her doll, making an effort not to make eye contact.

"What a beautiful doll; where'd you get her?" Billy asked, slowly moving his wheelchair closer to the little girl.

"My grandma gave her to me when I first got here." She patted the doll's arm, raising her head up with obvious pride for owning such a wonderful possession.

Billy reached over, rubbing the doll's head. "So, you just got here today, huh?"

"No, silly, I said my first day here. That was over five months ago. I got here when I was six, but I'm seven now."

Billy paused, trying to collect his thoughts. "So, what's your name?"

She stared at the door to the lab. "I'm Leslie; what's your name?"

"My name is Billy."

"Are they going to fix your broken leg?" she asked, looking down at his cast.

"Oh no, they can't fix anything here. They're just going to take a picture of it, and one of my head too, just to see if I'm okay."

She lifted up her head covering, pointing to a spot behind her ear on her beautiful bald head. "They're going to take a new picture of this, too. And my daddy says they might fix it when they take my pictures. I got cancer and I sure hope he's right. But I've had so many pictures taken, and it never gets better. Maybe today's the day."

Billy took a deep breath, blowing air out slowly. "I sure hope so, Leslie. I'll tell you what I'll do. If I go in there before you," he said, pointing to the door ahead of him, "I'll tell them to be sure they make this the day you get better, okay?"

"That would be great," she said, looking at her special doll.

A nurse opened the door, looking at a chart. "Leslie, honey, are you ready to let us take some more pictures?"

"No, Nurse Smalls; can you take him first?" she asked, pointing at Billy.

"Sure we can, sweetheart. We'll come out and get you in a few minutes," the nurse replied with a puzzled look on her face.

Billy winked at Leslie as he was wheeled through the double doors into a well-lit hallway.

"Mr. Summers, why did she want you to go first?" Nurse Smalls asked.

Billy turned his head towards the nurse. "Oh, we're just friends. She wanted me to tell everybody back here to take a good picture of her and fix her cancer."

"That would be a miracle for that wonderful little girl. Yes, that would be a miracle," she replied, lifting Billy out his wheelchair when they got to the inner waiting room.

After he finished his test, they wheeled him back through the waiting area. The little girl was still there.

"Did you tell them?" she asked, her eyes getting bigger.

"I sure did, Leslie, and I'm going to say a prayer for you today. Hey, good luck in there. They did a nice job taking pictures of my leg…maybe today's the day for you, too, Leslie."

Billy was still thinking about his new precious friend when he got back to his room. He realized he really didn't have any problems compared to little Leslie.

He picked up his phone, seeing Uncle Ray's number.

Billy called him back. "Uncle Ray, I see you called while I was getting an MRI; so what's new?"

Ray cleared his throat, started to talk, then cleared his throat again. "Sorry, Billy, but I got a sore throat somewhere. Anyway, I just got done talking to the state police. They're all over this big time. You should see this place, there must be fifty cops here."

"So, what did you tell them?" Billy asked, sitting up in his bed.

"I told a Captain…let me see…oh yeah, a Captain Hank Glade everything, from when Steve died to what you found out."

"Do you think he believed you?"

Ray cleared his throat again. "It's hard to say. Glade was very tight-lipped. He did say he would try to get up there and see you himself. Listen, Billy, I'm going to wander around the station and see what else I can find out this morning. By the way, Carl Williams wants you to call him when you can. Listen, I've got to go."

Billy punched in Carl's number.

***

"Deputy Williams here."

"Carl, this is Billy Summers. My Uncle Ray told me to call you."

"I'll have to call you back. I'm at the station and it's getting crazy here. No, I have no comment," Billy heard Carl tell someone. "I'll catch you in an hour or so. No time now, sorry."

"Are you talking to me, Carl?" Billy asked.

"No, Billy, I'm sorry, I'm trying to get past all these reporters. I can't even remember why I wanted to talk to you. I'll call you back when I think of it. This is nuts, bye."

Carl battled the reporters all the way to his car when he spotted Ray Summers standing behind a group of state troopers. He motioned to Ray to get into his car. They drove carefully through the mob of newspaper and TV people, heading out onto North Main Street.

"Wow, that sure was something, Carl," Ray said, shaking his head.

Carl took in a deep breath, raising his shoulders. "Ray, you have no idea how wild it is back there. I can't even get to my desk. All they want from me and Deputy Gunders is what we know, then they told us to stay out of their way. I've never seen anything like it. They really remind me of the Keystone Cops."

"Have they figured anything out yet?" Ray asked, lighting a cigarette.

"Well, Ray, I'll tell you what. They sure don't think it was an accident. It's a homicide case now, at least that's what they're calling it. But, of course, they don't share anything with me or Gunders, so it's hard to tell what they're doing. Hey, let's get a cup of coffee; is McDonalds okay?"

They stopped at the McDonalds by the interstate. After getting their coffee, they found an empty table next to the kids' playground.

Carl sipped his coffee, looking up at Ray. "Ray, do you want to hear something? A couple of nights ago I watching an old 'Andy Griffith' rerun. It was the one where the state police came into Mayberry looking for an escaped convict.

They took over Andy's office, just like they took over our office, telling Andy and Barney to stay out of their way, just go find some jaywalkers or chicken thieves. Eventually, Andy and Barney solved the case." He nodded, turning his coffee stirrer as he added sugar.

"What are you saying, Carl?"

Carl scratched his chin, putting down his coffee. "That's what we ought to do…you, me, and Billy. Let's solve this on our own. The hell with the state troopers. You pick Billy's mind, I'll listen down at the station, and we'll solve this together; what do you think?"

"Just tell me what to do and I'll do it. It can't hurt to have some of us local yocals doing our own investigation. Say, is there anything new about the bottle thing?"

"No, but I think we're getting close. It's hard to do anything with everybody only thinking about Chief's accident; or as I heard them call it today, 'the Chief's murder.'"

They talked for over an hour, then headed back to the circus. Carl fought the crowd at the station, finally getting into his office, while Ray drove back to the hospital to see Billy.

***

When Ray walked into Billy's room, he found Gary, Granny, and Nancy eating a pizza. He looked around the room. "Is Billy getting tested?"

"Yeah," Gary said, between bites. "Want some pizza, Uncle Ray? We've got extra."

"No thanks. Hey, where's Billy's phone?" Ray asked.

"It's over on the table next to his bed, under that tray," Nancy said, pointing to the table. Ray found the phone, checking for missed calls. The only call was from Coach Fatha. He called him back, using Billy's phone.

"Hello, Billy," Fatha said.

"No, this is Ray, he's down getting a test done. I'm just calling you back for him."

"Ray, I got into the files from the Georgia killing. I found out an investigator believed the clerk was bludgeoned with a vodka bottle on a downward swing, hitting the guy above his ear. According to the investigator's theory, that means whoever did it was either a very short man or a woman. And my bet is that it was a female."

Ray thought for a second. "That means we've been pissing up the wrong tree all along. Why didn't we think of that?" He looked at Granny, raising his eyebrows. "So, it's possible that Steve was part of it, but some girl did the killing. Maybe that's what he was hiding all these years."

"Do you think we should take this to the police, Ray?" Fatha asked.

"Damn right I do; I'm going to get this to Carl right now," Ray said, hanging up.

Granny put down her slice of pizza and wiped her lips, looking at Ray. "Did I hear what I thought I heard? Does Fatha think Steve's secret was about protecting someone who killed somebody?"

"He just said that a cop in Georgia thought a short man or a woman killed that liquor clerk in Georgia in 1951. I want to tell Carl about that right away." He picked up Billy's phone again. "Carl, I've got some news."

"So do I, I've got some scoop for you, Ray. I just heard a trooper say they found shotgun pellets and some glass from Ford's windshield on the road where he went off the road. Do you know what that means? If they're right, he was killed long before he hit that tree. And that's not everything. The police lab thinks Ford's car was doused with gasoline before it exploded. Isn't that something?"

"Oh, my God. Man, I hope they get that son of a bitch fast," Ray said, looking at the other three.

"Me, too, Ray. So, what did you find out?"

"I just talked to Fatha. He did some digging on that Georgia case. He says the killer was either a short man or a woman, based on how the bottle struck that clerk. That means Steve didn't do it, but maybe he knew who did. It sounds to me like it might have been a girl he was with."

"Wow; listen to me Ray, I think we should zero in on who he was dating after graduation. Do you remember any of his girlfriends, say in August of 1951?"

"He was playing the field back then, even dating some juniors."

"Is Billy there?" Carl asked.

"No, he's still getting some tests done so he can be cleared to go home tomorrow."

"Ray, when he gets back, ask him if he knows about Steve's girlfriends right after graduation. After all, he talked to almost everyone still alive who knew Steve back then. In the meantime, I'm going to find a yearbook somewhere. I'll let you know what I find out. I'll call you when I hear anything else."

Thirty minutes later, Billy got back. A nurse helped him into his bed as he looked around. "So, what's new?"

"Oh, I think there's a lot that's new; what do you think, Granny?" Ray asked, picking up a piece of pepperoni pizza from the box sitting on the sofa.

"There sure is. Ray, you tell him," Granny said. "You talked to everyone."

Ray walked over and sat on a chair next to Billy. He told him about the shotgun pellets, the piece of glass from the cruiser, the gas that was poured on Ford's death car, and the likelihood of a short person killing the liquor clerk in Georgia. He finished by asking Billy if he could guess who Steve might have been dating that August, based on what he'd found out.

Billy looked at his grandma, then back to his uncle. "Wow, I asked for something new, and I guess I got it. It sounds like we might have found out what Grandpa was hiding. Well, if I get a yearbook, it shouldn't be too hard to find out who Grandpa was dating. After all, there were only what, eight or nine girls in his class?"

"It's not that easy," Granny said, standing up, pulling her grey sweater down. "I didn't go to Rymont, and he married me. Besides, Ray said Steve dated some juniors that year, after he broke up with Kaylee what's her name."

Ray stood up. "I bet Carl can get a yearbook. I'll see what I can dig up, too. I'll see you all later."

Granny reached down for her cane, almost falling. Gary caught her, helping her stand back up. She patted Gary on his arm. "Gary, I'm getting tired. These old bones ain't what they used to be. Do you think there's a place to get some sleep, like a waiting area with some soft chairs?"

"Come on, Grandma, I'll help you find a place to rest," Gary said. "Want to come, Nancy?"

"Sure, I need to walk around a little bit, anyway." She waved at Billy, who was barely awake.

Twenty minutes later, Dr. Victor woke Billy up, tapping him on his shoulder. "Hey, young man, how's the leg feeling today?"

Billy opened his eyes, shaking his head to clear his brain. He ran his fingers through his blond hair. "Hi, Doc; do you got any word on those tests yet?"

"I sure do. I reviewed everything. You can go home tomorrow. I'll check you out about nine in the morning. What do you think of that?"

"That's so cool. That means I can go to the game Friday night. Now, what about walking?"

Victor patted Billy's cast. "You're going to have to be on crutches for about twelve weeks. Then we'll take that cast off, but you'll still need those crutches a couple more weeks after that. Then, you should be able to start a rehab program for that leg."

"Doc, my girlfriend said she saw someone in school with a cast that had a heel on the bottom. Do you think I can get one of those?"

"That's a different injury. When you see someone wearing what is called a boot cast, it's because their fracture isn't affected by putting weight on the leg. Your break needs to heal up and down, so you need crutches. Just let them do the work. I know it sounds like a long time before you heal, but it will go fast.

"One more thing; tomorrow you'll get an exercise packet that will tell you what to exercise and when," the doctor added, looking down at his beeper. "The bottom line is, you can exercise any part of your body right away…except your leg." His beeper went off again. He peeked at it, hitting a button. "The packet will tell you everything you need to know, just follow it." He patted Billy on his shoulder, then left.

Billy picked up his phone, calling Nancy. "Babe, the doctor just came by. I can go home tomorrow."

The Summers clan was back in Billy's room in five minutes, giddy about getting him home. The world seemed brighter for the family as they talked and laughed for over an hour. Then they all hugged Billy goodnight and went back to Rymont.

Billy dozed off until he felt someone shaking his right arm. He looked over, seeing a familiar face smiling down at him.

"Mr. Summers, do you remember me? I'm Nurse Smalls. I was with you for one of your scans this morning. Remember, you had an MRI?"

Billy nodded.

"Well, I just wanted to come by and give you some news," she continued. "Do you remember that little girl in the waiting room in a wheelchair?"

"You mean Leslie? Sure, I remember her. What a cutie. Is she okay?"

"I thought you'd like to know that for the first time, we saw some remission of her tumor. I mean, it was incredible. The doctors couldn't believe it. I've been crying all day." She wiped the tears from her eyes. "Leslie asked me to tell you thanks for telling them to fix her when they took her picture."

Billy felt a warmth running up and down his body. He struggled to get any words out. "So... uh... do you think she'll be okay now?"

Nurse Smalls raised her eyebrows and her shoulders. "Only God knows, but I'll tell you one thing; it looks a lot more promising for Leslie today than it did yesterday."

"Wow, that's great. How about doing me a big favor?"

"Sure, just name it."

He picked up a piece of paper off his tray, along with a pen, writing his name and cell number down. "How about giving her my number? I'd love to talk to her tonight."

"I'll take it down to her right now." She stood up, wiping a tear off the end of her nose. "I can't explain what happened today, Mr. Summers, but I'm so grateful you took the time to talk to Leslie. Who knows, maybe cheering her up was all she needed to start getting better." She kissed Billy on his cheek and walked out.

A few minutes later, Billy's new best friend called. Leslie was so excited she had trouble catching her breath. They talked for over an hour. It was the greatest hour of the whole week for Billy Summers. He smiled, then dozed off.

A nurse came in to take his blood pressure. Even before he opened his eyes, he knew it wasn't Nurse Clark, as his left arm was being wrapped on the left side of the bed.

"Hello, I don't remember you," Billy said as he studied her.

She was a short, fat redhead with pimples all over her face. She looked at him without any expression. "That's because I was off for a few days. Don't worry, I don't bite. I'm Nurse Custer—you know, like the Indian fighter—and I'll be taking care of you tonight."

"What happened to Nurse Clark?"

"She's off till Saturday. She left me a message that you were a good patient and to take good care of you. She even left this note for you." She pulled a small, pink envelope out of her jacket pocket, handing it to him.

He immediately recognized the scent on the envelope. It was the same perfume she wore when she did those special blood pressure tests. "Thanks, I'll read it later."

Nurse Custer wrote something on a clipboard. "I don't care when you read it, that's your business. My business is making sure you leave here healthy tomorrow." She put two fingers on the inside of his right wrist as she looked at her watch. "Your pulse is fine. Call me if you need me, I'll be around."

"Another witch," Billy mumbled as he opened the little envelope. Pulling out a hand-written note, he once again felt the excitement of Clark's perfume as he started to read.

Hey, Billy. I'm going to miss you. You were fun. I sure hope I get to see you again. Give me a call anytime at 555-0445 (home), or 789-7775 (cell). I would love to hear from you. Vickie Ann Clark (the world's best blood pressure taker).

"Wow, I guess she really was interested," Billy said, punching in her cell number.

"Hello," Nurse Clark quietly and softly answered.

"Guess who this is? It's Billy Summers. I just got your note."

"Well, hello. How's my favorite patient of all time doing? I'm so glad you called. I hear you're getting out soon. When you do, do you think we can get together?"

"I'd like that. It'll be hard for me to get around for a while, with this cast and all, but I'd like to see you, too," he responded nervously.

"How about if I email you my schedule? That way you can see when I'm off."

He gave her his email address. "Oh, Nurse Clark—?"

She interrupted him. "What do you mean, Nurse Clark? I've got a first name, you know. Call me Vickie. Listen, Billy, once you get home you'll still need to have your vitals checked. Maybe when you get a chance, you can come over to my place so I can check you out."

"That sounds good to me, Nurse…I mean Vickie. I'm anxious to see you again."

"That goes for me, too, Tiger. Don't forget to call me. Take care; bye bye."

Chapter 23
The Black Caddy

It was Thursday morning, and Billy was going home.

Billy woke up and looked around the room, noticing Grandma and Gary reading newspapers on the sofa under the big white clock. "Gary, you got off school again, huh?"

Gary lowered the paper, nodding at his brother. "Yep, this isn't a bad program after all. The only thing is, I still got to go to football practices, but they're getting to be more and more fun with all the plays the coaches are putting in. We're really going to surprise Jefferson High tomorrow night. Are you going to the game?"

"You bet your ass…I wouldn't miss it for the world. What do I use to get there? Am I going to get crutches, or what?" Billy asked, looking at Grandma.

Granny put down her newspaper. "We got you a neat wheelchair. Gary wanted to get an electric one, but it was too much money. You'll like the one we bought, and we found some crutches, too. Everything's at home."

Billy got his release papers and his rehab packet from a nurse an hour later, followed by an attendant with a wheelchair.

"It's time to go home, Mr. Summers. Are you ready?" the attendant asked.

"I was ready Sunday. Let's do it."

Ten minutes later, they all packed into Granny's car, along with Billy's clothes and over a dozen flower arrangements. After getting on the interstate, Uncle Ray called on Billy's phone.

"Billy, what time are you getting out of there?"

"We're on the road now. We ought to get home in about a half hour or so."

"Great. I'm over at the station with Carl. He got a yearbook from Gloria Stillers. So, hurry home and we'll look at the pictures together. It shouldn't take too long to figure out who Steve was dating. Hell, between the senior class and the junior class, there couldn't have been more than twenty girls. I'll see you there."

When they pulled into their driveway, Uncle Ray and Carl Williams were on the front porch talking. They helped Billy out of the car, getting him into his new wheelchair then into the living room.

Ray handed him the yearbook as Billy pulled his list from his billfold.

Granny grabbed Nancy's hand. "It looks like you boys got some detective work to do. Nancy and I want to do some girl talking, anyway. We'll be out in the kitchen."

Billy opened up the yearbook on his lap. "What do you think, should we concentrate on the junior class first?"

Carl shook his head. "Let's finish up the seniors before we look at the juniors."

Without answering, Billy opened the yearbook to the senior page, putting his folded list in the crease. There were nine girls in that class. Looking at his list, he realized that three of them were dead. "There's only six girls from Grandpa's class still alive." He read off their names.

"Let's see," Ray said. "Kaylee Jones left town right after graduation."

"And I bet you miss her, don't you, Uncle Ray?" Billy asked.

"Not at all. Let's get back to that list. Okay, Betty Thomas just retired from the post office, but she was a nerd, not someone who would try to buy liquor on a Sunday with a fake ID. Jessica Stanger…let's see, she moved to Ohio right after graduation. Gloria Wilson, she's Gloria Stiller now. She was Sanders's girl. Hey, Carl, what did Ford say about her?"

"He said she knew about the drowning, but not the Georgia killing, and he believed her."

"Let's see, that's four. What were the names of the other two, Billy?" Ray asked.

"Beverly Mason and Jean Penn."

"Beverly Mason, Beverly…. Sure, that was Bob Atlas's wife. She died years ago, Billy. You must have forgotten to cross her name off." Ray thought for a moment. "Jean Penn…I remember her. She was a smart one, but she went with Bill Watson for years. Oh yeah, they got married later that year, but that was up in Minnesota. They weren't around that August."

Billy sighed, taking a deep breath. "Well, I guess that's it. Either Grandpa was dating someone from another school or a junior."

"How many girls were in the junior class?" Ray asked.

"Let's see," Billy said, turning the page to that class. "There were one, two, six, twelve girls. They must have had a population explosion that year."

"Let me look, I might know some of them," Ray said, studying each photo. Everyone waited to see what he remembered about the girls, but he didn't recall anything about any of them.

Carl stood up, picking up his hat. "I don't know about the rest of you, but I'm starting with the juniors. Billy, make me a list of all the junior girls and I'll start checking them out at the station."

"That sounds like a plan," Ray said. "And I'll give Gary a list and see what he can find out on Billy's computer, and he can send Fatha the list to check, too. Maybe one of us will get lucky and find something." Ray went upstairs, returning a couple of minutes later.

Both Carl and Uncle Ray left, leaving Billy alone. He closed the yearbook, sitting quietly for a few minutes until Grandma and Nancy walked back into the living room.

"It sure is quiet in here," Grandma said. "I guess that means you men folk have finished everything?"

"Yeah, we're done talking. But, you know what? I'm really getting antsy. I just can't sit around here and wait for things to happen. Do you think there's any chance I can get out some?"

Granny raised her shoulders, extending her arms out. "I don't see why not. Why don't you and Nancy use my car and go for a ride? Oh, by the way, your new crutches are in the entry closet, if you need them."

"Why don't we take Granny up on her offer, Billy?" Nancy asked.

"Okay, baby, let's go."

Gary came downstairs, telling Billy he had sent the list of junior girls to Fatha. "Man, you have got a ton of emails, Billy. You better plan a full day just to read them."

Billy's mind flashed back to Nurse Clark. "It won't take me long to get through them, Gary. Just do me a favor and don't pay attention to any of them. I'll clean them up tonight sometime."

Finally, Billy and Nancy left. He was getting his life back to normal, going wherever he wanted, and he was alone with his girlfriend.

Nancy backed out of the driveway, turning the corner onto Elm Street. Billy noticed a line of cars turning the corner behind them. One car caught his eye. "Oh, my God, Nancy, there's that asshole in that car again. Son of a bitch."

"Where?" Nancy asked, trying to see the car in her rearview mirror. "I don't see anything. What is it?"

Billy turned, looking out the back window. "It's three cars behind us, that damn black Cadillac I told you about. Let's see who's driving it, Nancy. Slow down and see if he follows us. I want to get his plate number."

They turned off Elm onto a side street. The black car slowed down and the driver looked at them, then sped up, not taking their bait to turn off Elm Street.

"Hurry, Nancy, get back on Elm. He couldn't have gone too far."

They drove up and down all the main streets in Rymont looking for the mystery car. When they pulled onto Wausota Drive, Billy spotted a black Cadillac parked in front of Norma's Craft Shop. They slowed down to look at the car, noticing a South Carolina plate.

"That could be the car, Nancy. Just park in that spot right there," Billy shouted, pointing to a parking spot in front of the insurance office, two spaces ahead. They waited for almost an hour, constantly looking back at the car.

Finally, a distinguished-looking lady with white hair came out of the craft store, heading towards the Caddy. She was wearing a blue blazer over a white ruffled blouse. She stood at the driver's door, fumbling in her purse, obviously looking for her keys.

"Hurry, Nancy, hurry. She's getting in her car; go out and stop her. She's fixing to leave."

Nancy ran back to the car just before the woman closed her door. "Hi, excuse me...my name is Nancy." She pointed to Billy. "My boyfriend is in that car, right up there." She held her breast, trying to catch her breath. "Could you please come talk to him?"

"What? You want me to talk to your boyfriend? You two aren't having an argument or anything? I don't want to get involved if you are."

Nancy shook her head. "No, no, nothing like that. Billy just loves old cars, and when he saw yours, he told me to stop and wait for the owner to come out so he could talk to him. This is your car, right?"

"Yes, she's mine. She's an '82; ain't she something? That's because I take care of her. She's like an old friend," the older lady answered, patting the Caddy's dashboard. "Anyway, since your boyfriend likes old cars, that makes him a good guy. What's his name, honey?" She got out of her car, starting to walk towards Billy.

"He's Billy."

When they got to Billy, Nancy leaned on the roof of Granny's car. "Billy, this lady owns that black car. I told her you really like old cars and you wanted to find out about hers."

"Hi, I'm Billy Summers." He put his hand out the window and shook her hand. "You must be Norma, right?"

"You're right. I'm Norma Yorkshire, and that's my shop over there." She pointed to the craft store.

"Well, Norma, I really do love old cars. My grandfather had a car like yours once, and your Caddy brings back a lot of memories, especially since yours looks so sharp."

"Thanks. I take a lot of pride in how it looks. Do you know it's got over two hundred thousand miles on it? Now I just take it to work with me and park in front of my store so it's safe."

"Norma, you remind me of someone I used to know; did you teach out at the high school?"

"Oh no, Kirk and I are transplants. We moved here from Alabama eight years ago. I work on my crafts while he plays golf and fiddles with his big green truck. I guess you could call us a couple of fixer-up crackers. I fix up antiques and he fixes up his GMC." She looked down at Billy's cast. "Say, you're not that football player who hit that horse last week, are you?"

"That's me. I'm okay now, just a broken leg," Billy answered, patting his cast.

"Well, I got to go, Billy. It's been nice talking to you. Bye now."

"Another dead end, Nancy, but she sure was nice, wasn't she?"

Nancy put the keys in the ignition, then stopped. "I don't know about that, Billy…I mean, about her being a dead end. Did you hear her talk about her husband's green truck, and that it was a GMC?"

"I can't believe they have anything to do with anything. What did she say…she's only been here, what, eight years? What could she have to do with something that happened fifty years ago? I doubt if she is much older than that, Nancy."

"She said she's only been here a few years. At least, that's what she said, but anyone can say anything. I think you ought to have Carl check her and her husband out."

"You're right, Nancy. How did you get so smart? I'll tell Carl about them."

They pulled out of the parking spot just as Billy's phone rang.

"Well, hello, Tiger. I heard you got discharged this morning. Hey, I was wondering if you got the email about my schedule," Nurse Clark asked with a soft, sexy voice.

"I'm not sure. Uh, I haven't checked yet," Billy answered nervously.

"You sound preoccupied. Are you with that honey of yours?"

"Yeah, that's right." Billy could feel sweat pouring down one cheek.

"I still want to get together. If you do, just say yes somehow."

"Yes, that would be great."

"Okay, I'll call you back tomorrow. Bye, Tiger."

Billy hung up, looking at Nancy, who had a confused look. "So, who was that, Billy?"

"Oh, uh, that was just one of the nurses at the hospital wanting to know if I was all right. I gave her my cell number because, uh, she promised she'd tell me about a website she found about rehabbing broken bones. I think her name was Barbara, or something like that."

"They sure liked you at that hospital, Billy. You ought to send that floor some flowers, or a thank you card, or something."

"You're right. They were nice to me. Maybe I'll do just that…I'll send them some flowers." He waited a second, then looked at Nancy, seeing that she'd bought his bullshit story. "Let's head back to the house."

Nancy and Billy got home ten minutes later.

***

Uncle Ray was alone on the front porch. "You two weren't gone very long; did you miss me already? What did you end…? Hold on, Billy, let me grab this call."

It was Coach Fatha.

"Coach, how you doing? Did you find out anything?" Ray asked.

"Ray, I've checked out six of them already, and one really interests me. Listen, grab the yearbook and get everyone together and turn on the speaker phone, will you?"

"Sure, just give me a minute." He found Granny and brought her out to the porch, between Billy and Nancy. "Okay, I got the book, and everyone can hear you on speaker, Frank."

"I told you one girl interests me. Anybody there heard of Suzy Blakely?"

"Hold on a second." Ray opened the yearbook to the junior class, finding Suzy almost instantly. "She does look familiar, Coach. Steve might have dated her some, but I'm not sure."

"Could she have been in the picture that August?" Fatha asked.

"Maybe, but remember now, it's been fifty years. Tell us why she interests you so much?"

"Suzy Blakely—that's Suzy with a Z—was arrested in 1954. She was charged with DWI and vehicular homicide. She killed a pedestrian and spent three years in prison. Maybe there's no connection to the Georgia killing, but it's worth looking into. Oh, get this…she had a half bottle of vodka in the car when she was arrested."

"Let me see her picture," Granny said, grabbing the yearbook. "I remember her. Steve told me about her right after we got married. She was on trial down in Columbia. He even went down there to see her, and we had a big argument over her. I couldn't understand how he could go see an old girlfriend for any reason. Yeah, that's the girl." She handed the yearbook back to Ray.

Ray scratched the side of his face. "Did you hear that, Coach?"

"I heard most of it. It looks like we might have a good lead, huh?"

Billy reached down, grabbing his cast. "Damn these cramps…uh…I was going to ask, Coach, did you find out where she's at now?"

"I sure did. Her name is Suzy Thompson now. Her husband is Jeff Thompson. Does that name ring a bell for anyone?"

"Do you mean Jeff Thompson, the guy who just ran for governor?" Ray asked.

"Bingo. The mayor of Shelbeville, that Jeff Thompson. I wonder if he knows about what his wife did for fun in the fifties? And I wonder how his opponent in the election didn't know that?" Fatha asked, chuckling. "You all take care. I'll keep checking the other girls, too."

Ray picked up the phone, looking to be sure it was still on speaker. "I'm calling Carl; you all listen up. Carl, this is Ray. I got you on speaker phone along with Granny, Billy, and

Nancy. We just got some info from Coach Fatha about the junior girls in the yearbook. Steve was dating a girl in the summer of 1951 named Suzy Blakely—that's Suzy with a Z. Anyway, she went to jail in 1954 for drunk driving and killing a pedestrian. Granny remembered Steve getting involved in the trial. And catch this, Carl...she's Suzy Thompson now. Her husband's name is Jeff Thompson; you know, the mayor of Shelbeville."

"You mean the guy who ran for governor last year?"

Ray nodded his head. "I sure do, Carl."

"Man, I got to think about this one. I better be careful. It sure sounds like a ticket to the unemployment line if I don't handle this right. I'll see what I can find out about her and you can bet it will be done very quietly. I think we all need to keep Suzy to ourselves for a day or two. I've got a connection in Shelbeville. I'll see if I can reach him in the morning. Take care, you all."

"Listen up, you all. Carl's right," Ray said. "Let's keep this quiet. Granny, see if you can remember anything else about the trial. In the meantime, we'll just have to wait and see what Fatha or Carl find out." He walked down the steps, heading to his truck. "I'll see you all later."

Nancy had to go to cheerleader practice, and everyone else left except Billy and his grandmother. They sat on the porch for over an hour, talking about Suzy and the trial. Billy thought it was cool how she was still jealous because Grandpa had gone down to Columbia to support Suzy.

Gary went out and got a pizza for the three of them. They had a quiet night together talking about Grandpa and Suzy.

Chapter 24
The Gin Party

Billy woke up Friday morning, wondering if anyone had found out anything more about Suzy Thompson. He put on his robe, found his crutches, then hobbled down the stairs to the kitchen. Granny was sitting at the table, reading the newspaper.

"Hey, Grandma, I didn't hear you get up. You couldn't sleep either, huh?"

"No, I had a tough night. I racked my brains all night trying to remember all that crazy stuff about that Suzy Blakely. Hey, how come you're up so early?" She stood up, walking to the refrigerator to grab a bottle of orange juice.

"It's probably because I went to bed at eight last night, Grandma. Say, you didn't hear anything more about that Suzy girl, did you?"

"Not a word. I think it might take a few days to find out about her. Anyway, here's the paper, Billy. Why don't you read it while I fix you some breakfast? What do you want? How about some cereal, or some ham and eggs?"

Billy was pre-occupied. "Just surprise me."

"Take a look at the article about tonight's game. They even mention you."

"Wow, I want to see that." Billy found the story on the second page. "No way, Grandma. They think we can't win without me? They don't know Coach Fatha very well, I guess. I bet we beat Jefferson tonight."

Billy looked at the clock on the microwave…it was almost eight. It wasn't too early to call Carl. He got a hold of him on the first ring, asking him what was new about the mayor's wife Suzy. Carl told him he had a good friend who was a cop over in Shelbeville, but he was on vacation, and Carl would call him back on Monday.

Billy also told Carl to check into the background of Norma at the craft store, explaining that her husband had a green GMC and she drove a big black Cadillac. Carl told Billy he'd get back to him when he found out anything. Then he hung up.

"There's really a lot going on, Billy," Granny said. "I can't wait until everything settles down and we can get back to our boring, quiet life. Listen, I heard you say something about a Norma at the craft store. Is that Norma Yorkshire?"

"It sure is," Billy said, gulping down a big glass of tomato juice. "Do you know her?"

"She's the lady who helped me make that big flower arrangement I got for your grandfather's grave; you know, the artificial one. She's really a wonderful lady. I can't believe she needs to be checked out by the cops. There's no way she can be involved in anything, Billy."

"I found out her husband has a green GMC, that's all. I'm sure it's nothing."

She handed him a plate with two eggs and three pieces of ham, with a very dark English muffin. "Does that muffin look cooked enough, Billy?"

"It looks perfect; and it didn't set off the fire alarm, Grandma. You're getting better."

After finishing breakfast, he stood up, grabbing his crutches. "I think I'm going out to the living room to watch a little TV, and maybe study the yearbook some more."

Just after noon, Uncle Ray popped his head around the front door, seeing Billy watching a wrestling match on TV. "Billy, do you want to get out? How about if I buy you lunch and then we'll drive out to the farm? There's something out there I want to show you. Besides, you need some good old-fashioned clean farm air."

Billy grabbed his crutches from next to the sofa. "Sure, Uncle Ray, let's go."

When they got into Ray's truck, Ray asked, "So, Billy, where do you want to go for lunch?"

Billy thought for a minute. "Let's go to Uncle Woody's over by the interstate. I thought about one of those greasy pork tenderloin sandwiches every time I got that awful hospital food."

Ray turned his truck onto Highway 21. "Billy, we'll be coming up to where Jim Ford died in about three or four miles. Are you sure you want to go this way?"

"Yeah, I think so, Uncle Ray."

Ray stopped the truck where Ford had gone over the embankment. There were big black skid marks near the edge of the road, but none of them pointed toward where Ford's car had gone. It was easy to see the path of Jim's car, as the weeds were down all the way to the death tree. The tree was missing most of its bark, and the whole area showed the signs of a fire.

Billy turned to Ray, shaking his head. "Uncle Ray, I'm not real hungry anymore. Why don't we just go out to the farm?"

Ray nodded. "I agree. It took away my appetite, too."

Billy didn't answer. Fifteen minutes later they got to Ray's place. "Wait until you see your tomatoes," Ray said, pulling up next to the swing tree. He got Billy's crutches, helping him walk to his crop. There wasn't a weed in sight. The plants were all staked and popping full of dark red treasures.

Billy hobbled up to his plants, marveling at their color. "This is awesome, Uncle Ray. How did you get them to grow so fast? And I don't see a single weed anywhere."

Ray picked an oversized tomato off a big bush, taking a bite out of it. Juice and seeds rolled down the front of his shirt. "I just decided that you had enough going on, and you don't need to worry about any of this. You know, there's a ton of tomatoes here. Your grandma better get her canning jars out. I bet she'll teach Nancy a thing or two about canning, and that girl will catch on quick. You got yourself some great filly there. Like I always said, when God made her, he hit the cute button three times instead of once like the rest of us. You better hold onto that one, she's a keeper."

Billy rested his arms on the top of his crutches. "Damn right she's a keeper, and I will hold onto her forever. In fact, I've been meaning to tell you that she's going to Georgia Tech with me next fall. She just told me that last night."

"I thought you said she couldn't afford to go out of state?"

Billy nodded. "Her dad refinanced his house, and she said she'll find a job down there, so we maybe can live together. We'll share expenses, so it will be easy."

"Do I hear wedding bells starting to warm up?"

Billy got into Ray's truck by himself. "I sure hope so, Uncle Ray; I sure do."

Ray took Billy home, helping him get on the couch, where he slept until he felt a tap on his shoulder just after six.

"Now Billy, I let you sleep as long as I could," Grandma whispered in his ear. "We need to get ready for the game. It starts in less than an hour. Nancy called and said she'd meet us there, so I'm driving. Now let's get it in gear, young man."

Billy looked at his watch. "Oh my God, Grandma. Why didn't you wake me up?" He pulled himself up, looking around. "Grandma, you've got to help me. How about getting me a pair of jeans and my Rymont sweater? Oh, I want to wear those new sneakers; you know, the ones with the blue stripes. I think they're under the kitchen table."

Granny drove him to the stadium, parking as close as she could to the football field. Instantly, the car was surrounded by Rymont students. When she opened the trunk, big teenage hands grabbed Billy's wheelchair. Granny stood back as his friends took over, getting him into his fancy chariot.

"They sure love Billy," Granny said to the boy pushing the wheelchair, who turned around and nodded at her.

Billy was wheeled to the end of the Rymont bench, followed by a group of twenty to thirty kids walking closely behind their superstar. All of his teammates surrounded him. Coach Fatha came up to him, patting him on his shoulder. "Billy, this game is for you…yes, for you. All the guys want you to know that. Every one of them has dedicated tonight to you."

Granny heard everything. She was bursting with tears as she grabbed Billy's hand, noticing a tear forming in one of his eyes, too.

"Ladies and gentlemen, welcome to Rymont High's Raven Stadium," the voice boomed over the loud speakers. "Please stand as the Rymont High award-winning marching band plays our national anthem." Two players helped Billy to his feet and they all watched and listened as the band play the Star Spangled Banner.

"Please remain standing," the announcer said. "All of the Rymont family lost a great Raven this week. Jim Ford, our chief of police, died in an accident while protecting us. Please say a prayer for June Ford and the entire Ford family. He will truly be missed. Jim was a very special man, a special policeman, and a special neighbor, who only wanted all of us to be safe. Please join all Rymont Ravens in a moment of silence to honor Jim Ford."

The stadium was quiet for fifteen seconds, until the announcer broke the silence. "Ladies and gentlemen, we have the honor of having a true Raven with us tonight. Undoubtedly, he is the best football player ever to put on a Raven uniform. He, too, recently had an accident, so you won't see him play for Rymont tonight, or the rest of the season. However, I'm sure you'll hear about all of his touchdowns at Georgia Tech next year. Please direct your attention to the end of the Raven bench and put your hands together, welcoming a true champion, a true Raven. Ladies and gentlemen, please help all of us at Rymont High welcome back Mr. Billy Summers."

The crowd stood, cheering for over three minutes. Billy turned, waving at the crowd, not believing what he was seeing. Almost everyone was waving a small white flag that had "Billy #81" across it.

Granny was crying when Coach Fatha walked over and put his arms around Billy. Nancy hugged him, her face loaded with tears. It was as if the entire Raven nation was thanking Billy for all the great plays he'd made on that field. It was a spectacular Rymont moment. Billy wasn't thinking about anything except how great the moment was. He didn't even notice Nurse Clark, just three rows behind him, crying, too.

It was the most important game of the year. If they won, they would be conference champions for the very first time. The smallest school in the county could finally call itself a champion with a victory.

Rymont played their best game of the year, even without Billy. Every time a Raven teammate scored, he'd come up to Billy and say, "That was for you, Billy." Rymont won 58-10, the most lopsided game in their history.

After the game, they wheeled Billy into the locker room. Coach Fatha brought the entire team together to circle around him and Billy. "I'm so proud of each one of you. You didn't have your star on the field with you, but he was there. I heard all week that you were dedicating this game to him." He held a football over his head. "So, I want to present this game ball to our leader, our champion, Billy Summers." Fatha held out the ball, handing it to Billy.

Billy looked at the team as two teammates helped him stand up. "Man, you guys were great tonight. I am so proud of you, and so proud of our school. You showed everyone what teamwork really means. I will never forget you all, or tonight. Thanks."

After they were done congratulating Billy, they wheeled him out of the locker room, where Nancy was waiting.

"What a great night, huh Billy? Guess what…you made it happen. The whole school's been talking about how great we were going to play in honor of you." She bent down and kissed him. "But your night isn't over. We're going to my house for the party of all parties. My folks are out of town, so I invited the whole team to come over. You're going to have a blast."

"That sounds great, Nancy; I need some fun."

Nancy looked around at the parking lot. "Just wait here. I'll find Granny and let her know what's happening, then I'll get Laura Lee's car around to pick you up."

In a couple of minutes, Nancy was back, loading Billy into the fancy convertible, heading out of the parking lot. She started talking to him, then looked in the rearview mirror. "What is that?"

"Nancy, what are you talking about? What's in the rearview mirror?"

"Billy, I think your friend is back. That big black car is behind us again."

Billy turned around, seeing his nemesis. "That's him, that son of a bitch. Nancy, don't go too fast. I don't want to lose him. Let's see how far he follows us. Let's get his tag number."

The black Caddy tailed them all the way to her house. As they pulled into the driveway, they both watched as the car went by, going so fast neither Billy or Nancy got a look at the driver.

"Did you get his license plate number?" Billy asked.

"No, it was too dark."

Billy slammed his fist on the dashboard. "Who is that guy, and what does he want?"

Nancy lifted her shoulders, indicating she had no idea. "Billy, let's go in. We've got some surprises for you, so you better like them."

She helped him get in the front door, then flipped on a light. Instantly, kids came at them from all directions. Billy looked around, noticing posters of him on every wall. Within thirty minutes, the house was full of teammates, coaches, cheerleaders, and even some teachers. It was Billy's special night. At least for a while, he forgot about the murders, his grandfather, and everything he'd been through the last two weeks. He wasn't even thinking about Nurse Clark.

When Billy woke up Saturday morning, he looked around, not recognizing anything. There were strange pictures on the walls, and a concrete floor. He had slept on a flowered sofa with a red satin pillow that was frayed on each end. It looked like he was in someone's basement. Three small windows were near the ceiling, all covered with green and white striped mini-curtains dangling from white, dusty curtain rods.

He tried to stand up, but he couldn't find his crutches. He hopped to the end of the sofa, then slumped back down to where he had slept. He rubbed his eyes, looking around the room again. There were kids everywhere, most of them football players. He reached over, yanking on the jacket of Rick Gall, the team's best defensive back.

"What do you want? Let me sleep," Rick whined. Billy pulled on his coat again. This time Gall looked at Billy. "Why do you keep waking me up, Billy? My head feels like it's three times its normal size."

"Rick, where are we?"

"We're at Nancy's house; now go back to sleep."

"But how did I get in this room?"

"Why don't you just go to sleep? You passed out about the time you got down here. I mean, you were out before you hit the bottom step."

"What do you mean 'passed out'? Was I drinking last night?"

Rick laughed as he grabbed his head with both hands, obviously in pain. "Didn't you know the punch was full of gin? After the teachers left, they kept spiking it, and you kept drinking it. You were the hit of the party. You even danced a lot…or maybe I should call it hopped a lot. You were something. But I bet you're feeling pretty shitty right now; I know I am."

"Yeah, I don't feel so good. By the way, what time is it?" He looked at his bare wrist. "And where's my watch?"

"It's pushing noon, and your watch is probably upstairs," Gall answered. "Okay, let's go up there and see what's going on." He wrapped his arms around Billy's shoulders, pulling him up the stairs to the kitchen.

Billy stopped, looking around at the kids all over the house. He spotted his watch next to his crutches, and his cell phone on the floor next to the dishwasher. He picked up the phone, looking for messages. There were nine calls from Grandma.

He called her back. "Grandma, can you come and get me? I'm still at Nancy's."

"Billy, where have you been? I've been trying to call you all morning. Your phone keeps ringing and ringing. What happened? Why haven't you called me back? We've got to go to Jim Ford's funeral this afternoon."

"Just come and get me. I'll explain everything to you when you get here. Please hurry, Grandma, I feel sick."

When she got to Nancy's house, Billy was waiting for her on the driveway, leaning on one crutch. Nancy came out, grabbing his arm. "Billy, are you all right? I've been looking all over for you. Where did you sleep?"

"I woke up in your basement. What happened last night? Rick Gall said I got drunk , but I don't remember anything."

"They kept adding booze to the punch. My dad had at least eight big bottles of gin, and now they're all empty. Anyway, I'm sorry how it turned out. It was supposed to be a party about you, and it turned into a drunken mess." She put an arm around him, hugging him so hard he almost lost his balance.

"That's okay, Nancy." He got into Granny's car, then rolled down the window. "I don't feel so good…I'm going home for a while. Maybe I'll see you at the funeral."

Chapter 25
IRWY

The Summers were amazed when they pulled into the parking lot at the Sherman Pace Funeral Home. There were about fifty police cruisers, along with twenty state trooper motorcycles, lined up, all pointing in the same direction, as if they were choreographed. After they parked their car in the cemetery line, Gary pulled Billy's wheelchair out of the trunk and lifted him into his two-wheeled chariot.

Billy looked up at his grandmother. "Where's Uncle Ray? Shouldn't we wait for him?"

She pulled some tissues out of her purse, handing a wad to each of her grandsons. "He said he'd meet us here; just watch for him."

Finally, Billy spotted Uncle Ray walking towards them, wearing that same blue suit. The four of them went into the funeral parlor together, seeing Jim Ford's brown maple casket up front, along with a blown-up picture of the chief. Billy motioned to Gary to wheel him up front so he could see June Ford. Billy hugged her after waiting in line behind four other mourners.

"Mrs. Ford, I just want you to know how great your husband was to me. When no one listened, he was there. I'm so sorry about what happened. I think he was super. I will never forget him...I'm so sorry."

June wiped her eyes with a tissue, then leaned down to pat Billy on his cheek. "Billy, Jim didn't know you very well, but just the other night he told me you were a fighter with a lot of guts. He really liked you, and I know he respected you." She put her hand over his, then turned away to talk to someone else.

The service lasted two hours. The pallbearers were all policeman, straining as they walked by with the casket, even though everyone knew Ford's body was only a pile of ashes.

When they got to the grave, there were two lines of policemen, creating a walkway for everyone to walk through. Billy saw June get out of her limo with her kids, and it looked like her legs were made out of rubber. He wished he could lend her his wheelchair as two cops helped her to the front row under the funeral tent.

After the graveside service, Billy looked over at all the cars parked alongside the road. Then he saw it…the black Cadillac, about twenty cars away. This was his chance; all he had to do was wait and see who got into it.

Carl Williams was a few yards behind Billy. "Hey, Billy, how are you doing?"

Billy turned around, trying to locate Carl. "Oh, I don't know…I really don't know. It's a tough day for all of us, Carl."

"That it is. Jim was one hell of a guy. There's not many better than the chief," Carl said, patting Billy on his arm.

Billy let out a big sigh. "Carl, are you going to the ceremony at the high school?"

"Yeah, I'm going; maybe I'll see you there?" Carl answered as he turned and walked away, heading towards June Ford.

Billy turned around to check on the black car. It was gone. "Shit, I almost had him."

"What did you say?" his grandmother asked.

Billy shook his head. "I said shit, why him? Why did this have to happen to him?"

Uncle Ray walked over to Billy, bent down, and whispered in his ear. "Billy, I got another letter this morning."

Billy swallowed hard, watching Ray stand up. "What'd it say?"

Ray bent down again. "It was just like the other one. It had no return address or signature, and it was mailed from Charlotte. I got it in a plastic bag in my truck."

"But Uncle Ray, what did it say?"

"It only had four letters, 'IRWY.' I know you know what that means, but what the hell kind of a clue is that?"

"I think I know," Billy answered, pulling a piece of paper out of his billfold. He remembered where he'd seen those four letters. He turned to his uncle. "Do you think you can get Carl and Fatha over to our house after Chief Ford's ceremony, say about four? I think your letter just might tell us who killed that liquor clerk."

"I'm sure I can round them up. But tell me, how will 'IRWY' lead us anywhere? How can that mean anything?"

Billy looked at the little paper before he put it back in his wallet. "Like I said, I think those four letters will give us the name of the girl with Grandpa that night. I've got a yearbook at the house and my list. I think that's all we need."

"Is it Suzy Thompson?" Ray asked, leaning closer to Billy.

"No, it's not Suzy Thompson."

***

After the memorial service, Uncle Ray pulled up in front of the Summers's house, followed by Fatha and Deputy Williams. Billy was sitting in the kitchen, watching out the window, his heart bouncing with excitement, wanting to share what he knew. As the other three walked in, they each got a chair from around the Saturday buffet table, waiting for Billy's news.

"I think we found out who did the Georgia killing," Billy said, looking around at the other three.

"What are you talking about, Billy?" Carl wondered, pulling a notepad out of his front coat pocket.

"Uncle Ray has something to show you, don't you?" Billy asked, looking at his uncle.

"I sure do. I got this in the mail today." He pulled a plastic freezer bag out of his pocket, setting it on the center of the table, along with a second bag, containing the envelope.

Everyone leaned in, trying to get a good look at what Ray had brought to the meeting.

Ray pulled back, trying to give the rest of them more room. "See, it's like the first letter; it was mailed from Charlotte, and there's no return address or signature. I put them in plastic bags thinking Carl could get them checked out for prints. But I'll bet you the only prints except for mine are on the envelope, just like the 'bottle' clue."

Carl reached out, motioning to Ray to hand him the bags. "Can I see them? Huh, 'IRWY.' Does that mean anything to anyone?" He looked around the table.

"Oh, yeah, it means something, all right. It stands for 'I really want you.' That was a saying we had in high school," Ray replied. "When a girl or guy wanted to tell someone they liked them, they flashed those four letters. Some girls even had necklaces with 'IRWY' on them so when they saw a guy they liked, they just lifted up their necklace. It was a big deal back then."

"So, how does that help us find the girl who hit the liquor clerk?" Fatha asked.

"I'm kind of nervous right now," Billy answered. "So bear with me. When I had Grandpa's yearbook, there was only one girl who wrote that in there, and that was…let me check my list…her name was Jessica Stanger."

"What does that prove?" Fatha asked. "So she liked Steve; how does that make her the person we're looking for?"

Billy sat back in his chair. "Listen, whoever is sending these clues wants us to find the killer. I think it's the Fourth Promiser. That's probably the only person on earth who knows Stanger wrote that in his yearbook. Don't you see? Somebody is trying to point us to all the answers without getting involved himself. Besides, I remember hearing she had a big crush on Grandpa, and she'd do anything for a drink. It all fits. She had to be the one with him on that Sunday."

"But Billy, didn't you say before that she left town right after graduation, going up to Ohio or Minnesota or someplace like that?" Ray asked.

Billy sighed, releasing a long breath. "Somebody told me she went up north after graduation. I thought they meant in May or June, but maybe she didn't leave until August…who knows? Or maybe she left because of what happened in Georgia."

"How do you spell her name, Billy?" Carl asked, pen in hand, ready to write.

"It's Jessica Stanger. You spell it S-T-A-N-G-E-R."

"And she was in the Rymont class of 1951, right?"

Billy nodded. "That's right. Do you think you can do a check on her on a Saturday?"

Carl stood up, looking at Billy. "Crime doesn't follow a calendar. Of course I can find out everything about Miss Jessica Stanger on a Saturday. I've got a phone and I bet you I'll have her story in less than an hour." He walked out the back door, heading to his squad car.

Fatha stood up, too. "I can do some tricks on your computer, Billy; just get me signed on."

"Gary can do that. He's probably in his room upstairs."

Billy kept looking out the kitchen window over the sink, watching Carl in his car. Every minute seemed like it took an hour. Finally, after twenty minutes, Carl got out of his cruiser, walking back towards the back door. His face was as white as the stitched doilies on the table they all surrounded.

Carl walked into the kitchen shaking his head, then slumped on the chair he had just left. "Where's Fatha?"

"He's upstairs on the computer," Billy answered. "Do you want us to get him?"

"Oh, yeah, you need to get him," Carl responded, grimacing as he sat down.

Less than one minute later, Fatha walked back into the kitchen. The other three stared at Carl, waiting to hear what he had found out.

"Do I have everyone's word you won't tell anyone—and I mean anyone, hear?—what I'm going to tell you until I have time to digest all this and figure it out?" Carl asked, looking at the other three one by one, getting a promise from each of them.

"Well, here it is, guys. A lot of what Billy said is right. Jessica Stanger did move to Ohio, in September of 1951. She got married up there in 1960, and divorced in 1969. She got remarried in 1972 in Charlotte. She has two sons, Tommy and George. Her husband died in 1988, and his name was Ken…." He took a deep breath. "His name was Ken Gunders."

There was dead silence in the room. Everyone was looking at each other, waiting for anyone to say something.

Finally, Ray spoke up. "That son of a bitch. That son of a bitch. I'll bet you that's what Steve was covering up, sure it was. Jessica Stanger killed that clerk, and George knew it. He's been protecting his mama the whole time. And I'll bet you Gunders figured Steve was going to spill the beans to Chief Ford when he called the office. Sure, George couldn't let that happen. It looks to me like Steve's call looking for Ford started everything."

Carl nodded. "That's sounds logical to me. He even had to murder Jim because he had all the evidence in his car. Do you know what? I think I might have been next to get pushed off the road. Oh, my God, the whole time he was acting like he wanted to help us find the killer, and he was just waiting for the right time to kill off anyone who knew anything. That son of a bitch."

"What can we do?" Billy asked. "Why don't we go to that captain, what's his name…Glade?"

"There's no way Glade will listen to any one of us without some evidence," Carl said. "What do we have? Just a big theory that Gunders's mother lives in Charlotte and likes to drink and may have liked Steve. That's nothing. Everything we know is just circumstantial."

"We've got the notes…won't that help?" Ray wondered.

Carl shook his head. "That's not anything, either. We don't even know who sent them, we are guessing as to what they mean, and there's no fingerprints on them. No, we've got to think this out carefully. I think we're all pretty sure what really happened, but we got to get some real evidence, anything to get Glade to believe us. Besides, I don't want to go to Glade with Gunders around. If he kills people who are getting close to figuring out what his mother did, just think what he might do to us or our families if we accuse him of all the murders."

Fatha looked puzzled. "What do you mean?"

"I mean if George Gunders is really the killer and he gets wind that any of us have put the pieces back in the puzzle, he'll come looking for us or our families in a heartbeat. He's already killed two people, and almost killed Billy, to protect his mother…he'll come after all of us, too. That's why I made you promise to keep this to yourself."

"So, what do we do, Carl?" Ray asked.

Carl stood up. "Here's what you do. You go about your lives as normal and give me some time to figure out an answer. I've got more police books at home than anyone in South Carolina, I bet. Let me do some digging. And don't say anything to anyone, not even your family, until I get back with you all. That has to be our Four Raven Promise, to keep this quiet. I think I might find something from one of my books at home, so all I want any of you to do is to not say a word about any of this to anyone, got it?"

They all agreed, so he went out the back door.

Chapter 26
We've Got a Lot on Our Plate

Carl got home and started going through his police books, looking for anything that might give him an idea on how to get Gunders. He stayed up all night, looking for the magic answer. At 6:10 the next morning, he stretched back, looking up. On the top shelf of his book rack was an old manual given to him by an instructor at the police academy called *Families, Bullies, and Mafia Interrogations*.

He put his feet out onto his coffee table, hoping to find anything that would help with the Summers case. One chapter talked about getting confessions from numerous suspects from the same family, and a later section described how to get criminal bullies arrested, despite all witnesses being afraid to talk to anyone. He read both chapters twice.

"Wow, here it is; an old book I hadn't read for at least fifteen years, and it lays everything out perfectly." He kissed the book. "I've got to call Ray."

"Ray, I didn't wake you up, did I?"

"Hell no, I'm a farmer, remember?"

"Listen, Ray. I think I figured a possible way out of this thing. Do you think you can get Fatha and Billy over to your place in an hour?"

"Wouldn't it be better for all of us to meet at Billy's? I mean, it's a hell of a lot closer for everyone."

"No; now listen, we've got too many people involved in this case already. I don't want anyone else hearing anything or guessing why there's so many cars at Granny's place this early on a Sunday morning. Besides, your farm is so remote, none of us have to worry about anything. No, let's meet there."

"You got it, Carl, I'll see you in an hour."

Forty minutes later, Carl pulled up to Ray's farmhouse. He walked into the living room, spotting Coach Fatha sitting on the couch with Billy next to him, his leg on top of a small blue travel pillow on a chair next to him.

"Hey guys, thanks for coming. I know it's early on a Sunday, but I figured out some stuff this morning."

Ray came out of the kitchen, carrying a pot of coffee and four cups, all of which were different in color and size. He set them down on the coffee table, pulling a handful of spoons out of his back pocket. "So, what's up, Carl?" he asked, sitting on the sofa next to Billy.

Carl sat on a green recliner next to the sofa with his reference book on his lap. "Listen guys, I've been reading all night. I was really having trouble finding anything that would help us until I pulled out this old police book about six this morning." He held his book up.

"This is called *Families, Bullies, and Mafia Interrogations*. It's an old book I've had for probably…over twenty years." He opened the book up to a chapter that had a bookmark in it. "Listen to this; here is a chapter devoted to interrogating a family suspected of committing numerous crimes. The key is to interview all of them at different locations, but at the same time. That way they can't warn each other of the investigation, and they can be played against each other. That's what we need Glade to do."

"So, how do you think we can get Captain Glade to listen to any of us? They already think we are just a bunch of hicks." Ray turned to look at Fatha and Billy.

"I worked all that out this morning, too," Carl answered. "There's a chapter in this wonderful book that gave me a great idea. It describes how a group of people can expose a bully who continually breaks the law and threatens everyone not to talk or he will kill them."

"That sounds a lot like our situation, huh?" Fatha asked.

Carl took a sip out of his blue coffee cup. "It sure does; the key is to get Glade to meet with us. This book tells us what to do after we get that meeting. We have to make sure Glade thinks we've got evidence about a crime and we will share it only if he meets with us in private and checks out what we say."

"But how are we going to get him to meet us?" Ray asked.

"Don't worry about that. I'll get a meeting set up with him today; that is, if he's working on a Sunday, and I bet he is, with the pressure he must be feeling. Before I do that, I'm going to make copies of some of these chapters to give to him. But listen, we've got to make it clear to him that our cooperation is based on him keeping everything confidential, and following our plan to the letter. We have to stand firm on that, and we definitely have to work together."

Ray put his coffee cup on the table, looking at Carl. "So, Carl, what do you think he'll say when you ask him to meet with us?"

"Oh, he's going to say we can't withhold evidence, and will probably threaten us. If he does, let me handle it."

"That sounds like it might work, Carl," Fatha said. "What do you think, Ray?"

Ray's eyes got big as he shrugged his shoulders. "It's worth a try; we've got to do something."

Carl stood up, looking at Billy. "Okay then, I'm going to see if I can find Captain Glade this morning. I'll tell him you all want to meet him privately today and you have some evidence about Ford's killing. Oh, one other thing; when we talk to him, we have to be in control. Don't let him intimidate you. I'm going to get started, every minute counts." He turned towards the door, then looked back. "Does anybody know where we can meet up with him that's completely hidden?"

It was quiet for second, until Fatha snapped his fingers. "Carl, I've got a key to the school. I can get into a classroom, a very private classroom, and no one—I mean no one—is around Rymont High on a Sunday."

"That's great," Carl replied, patting Fatha on the back. "Now, don't talk about this to anyone. Oh, and Ray, follow me out to my car and I'll give you the 'bottle' note. I just got it back from the lab. You can keep it with the other one, in case we do meet up with Glade this afternoon. And guys, we've got to pull this off." He pushed so hard on the screen door that when it closed, it shook the whole porch. He was anxious to get started.

Carl stopped by Walgreens and made a copies of the chapters he wanted to give Glade. He folded them up and put them in his shirt pocket. Ten minutes later, he pulled into the police station. It was hard to find a parking spot, especially for a Sunday. The station was alive with activity. There were about fifteen state cop cars, and six or so motorcycles scattered everywhere.

He parked behind the station and walked in the back door, heading for his office. He put his hat on the inside door knob and his briefcase on his desk. Walking back out into the hall, he stopped the first state cop he saw. "Is Captain Glade in yet?"

The trooper stopped and turned around, looking at Carl. "In yet?" He chuckled. "In yet? We don't take Sundays off, like you local yocals do. Captain Glade was here before you even thought about getting up. Yeah, he's here."

Carl wanted to slap the jerk trooper as hard as he could, knowing he was up all night working on the case. "Okay, smart ass, where is he?"

"My, aren't we getting touchy? I bet you think you're a bad ass. Well, you're not, Mr. Rymont Redneck. Glade is up front in your chief's old office, and he's busy, very busy. You don't need to bother him. Just tell me what you want, and I'll get it to him. We've got a ton on our plate, so we don't have time for any local chit chat."

"So do I, buddy; I've got a lot on my plate, too. But I can spare some of my precious time to talk to your high and mighty captain about Chief Ford's accident. Now, you just go up there and tell him I'm waiting in my office, and if he can find the time for a lowly Rymont deputy, I might just have some information he could find helpful. Tell him I'll be waiting right here, in my office. Oh, and one more thing…you're a very lucky cop. I've got a lot going on, or else you and I just might need to talk in private out back; you got that, Mr. Bigshot?"

The trooper stood there in disbelief, giving Carl a look that said, "you stupid hillbilly." Then he headed towards the big office.

Carl sat back in his chair, cupping his hands behind his head. Ten minutes later, Glade was standing in the doorway to his office.

"I hear you want to talk to me, Williams. This better be good. I've got a lot of irons in the fire right now."

"I think you really want to come in, Captain, I've got some news for you that you want to hear, and you better close the door."

Glade sighed as he closed the door, then sat in a white metal folding chair in front of Carl's desk. "All right, you got my attention. So tell me, what earth shattering news are you going to share with me today? Don't tell me you got a cat down from someone's tree and you think it will solve the Ford case. I better listen good, huh?"

Carl took a breath, trying to fight back his anger. "I know you're a captain and I'm a measly little deputy from Hooterville, but that doesn't mean I can't help you with this case. In fact, I'll bet you when all this is over, you just might be thankful you walked into this office."

Glade lowered his head, acting bored. "I'm still listening; get to the point."

"Okay, Captain, I've got some information that might help you tie up some loose ends to this case, but I don't want it to be front page news. Even though we're a bunch of hick cops here, we still know how to investigate without leaking everything to anyone."

Glade twisted his neck, constantly looking at Carl. "I never said you were a bunch of hicks. We've just got the resources to get to the truth, and maybe you don't. So, once again, what have you found out that will help me with this case?"

"Some local people have some theories on what happened last week with the chief, and I think you may want to hear them out."

The captain shook his head, getting madder by the second. "Hear them out? What do you mean, hear them out? You're a deputy, act like one; go get them and bring them in. Then I'll listen to your local people. Being a witness isn't optional, you know that."

"Captain, they're really nervous, but they're serious about helping you solve this case. They told me they wanted to meet with you—and only you—this morning. I don't think they'll open up individually, but they will as a group, all three of them."

"What are you talking about, all three of them?" Glade raised his voice. "Why can't I have my men interview them one at a time?"

Carl put his index finger in front of his mouth. "Nothing will happen if any of this gets out. We have to keep it quiet. Anyway, they know a lot about this town, and what goes on here. They told me they had something big to tell you, but if this thing gets blown up, they won't say a word to anyone, and they mean it."

Glade ran his fingers through his black hair. "This is all crazy. Is this how you do things in Rymont? I don't have time for games. I can subpoena their asses in a minute if I want, and you know that."

Carl nodded, putting his hands out, with the palms up. "Sure you can, but wouldn't it be better just to take an hour and listen to them? They just might really have something that will help you solve this case. It looks to me like you really don't have much choice."

It was silent for a few moments, then Glade shuffled his feet, looking up at Carl. "All right, you win; I'll meet up with your amateur detectives."

"Just you alone?"

Glade nodded. "But Deputy Williams, this better be good. I don't want to waste any time on some barbershop bullshit."

Carl chuckled. "These guys don't bullshit. How soon can we get going?"

Glade looked at his watch. "Give me fifteen minutes," he answered, standing up. "Then we can go wherever the hell they're at. Where are they, anyway?"

"I've got to call them when we get in my car, then they'll tell me where to meet them."

Glade left Carl's office, shaking his head.

Carl got up and closed the door, then called Ray. "Hey, he's coming with me in about fifteen minutes. Get everyone over to the school and I'll call you from the car and find out exactly where to meet."

Twenty minutes later, Glade walked back into Carl's office, carrying a brown and white leather briefcase, with a hat under his arm. "Let's go Williams. I can't wait to see what this is all about. Maybe we'll get some news on a moonshiner, or some jaywalker; or how about a trespassing problem? Wow, wouldn't that be great?"

Carl led Glade out to his car. He pulled out of the parking area, picking up his cell phone. "Ray, this is Carl. I've done what you asked, I've got Captain Glade here with me. Where do you all want to meet us?"

Ray told him they were waiting in classroom 2B, next to the gym at the high school. Ten minutes later, Carl pulled into a parking spot next to Fatha's Murano. There was no one in sight. The gym blocked anyone from even seeing their cars. Fatha had picked the perfect spot.

Glade got out of the car, looking around at the school buildings. "Why does this have to be so secluded? I wonder what big, bad secrets I'm going to hear about today?"

They walked into the classroom, seeing a large table up front with six chairs around it. In front of the table was a large black chalkboard on wheels, filled with x's and o's and big block letters that said, "How good are we?" and "Stop #39!" It was obvious this was Coach Fatha's classroom.

Billy, Ray, and Fatha were all sitting at the table, talking. When Carl opened the door, they watched Carl put his hat on a chair next to the wall, as Glade followed him into the classroom.

"Hey guys, this Captain Glade. He's with the state police. He's leading the investigation into Chief Ford's death. I did as you all said; I brought the top guy to see you all by himself." He glanced back at Glade. "Just have a seat, Captain, and we'll get started."

Glade shook hands with all three of them, then pulled up a chair next to Coach Fatha. He put his briefcase on the table and opened it. He looked over at Billy. "You must be that kid that had that horse accident. You know, I've been meaning to talk to you."

Billy raised his shoulders, looking at the captain. "First off, it wasn't an accident, and secondly, I just got out of the hospital, and you could've come up there to talk to me at any time. But the way it has turned out, this is better, because you're going to hear from all of us."

Glade pulled a pen out of his shirt pocket after getting a yellow legal pad from his briefcase. "So, why am I here? What's so damned important that I have to meet you all here, and not at the station?"

"We've got a story to tell you, and we want to tell it to you in private. You'll understand why we're handling it this way when we're done." Ray leaned back in his chair. "We think—no, we know—what we're going to tell you will help catch Jim Ford's and my brother's killer, as well as who tried to kill Billy. But there's a catch."

Glade wrote something on his legal pad. "I'm listening."

Fatha cleared his throat, grabbing Glade's attention. "Here's what we got. We want you to interrogate a woman and her two sons. She lives up in Charlotte, and one of her boys lives there, too. The other son lives right here in Rymont."

The captain looked up from his notes. "I can't bring people in without a good reason…not just because a group of citizens asks me to."

"Just hear us out," Ray replied. "We'll be glad to tell you everything we know, provided you give us your word you'll handle some things the way we want."

Captain Glade turned his head as if he couldn't hear. "Let me get this straight…you want me to do an investigation your way if I want to get any evidence from you about Chief Ford's death. Is that what you are saying?"

"That about sums it up, sir," Fatha answered.

Glade let out a loud "huh," then shook his head twice. "Do you know I can run you all in for obstructing justice and concealing evidence? Do you all realize that?"

"Yes, sir," Fatha said. "We're aware of that, and I guess we'll have to just take that chance. We have to handle everything this way, that's all there is to it."

"Listen, I agreed to talk to you, but you are not going to run my investigation in this case, is that clear?" Glade asked.

"Captain, can I see you for a minute outside?" Carl asked.

Glade got up, pushing his chair back so hard he knocked it over. He looked at the other three, then followed Carl out the door.

"Captain, I don't want to tell you what to do, but what harm does it do to just listen to them?" Carl asked. "Humor them a little. All they want is for you to take an interest in what they tell you. Just listen to them…I think it may help solve this case. That's all I want, to solve this case. That's why I brought you here."

Captain Glade lit a cigarette, slowly exhaling the smoke towards Carl. He thought for a few seconds, then stomped the butt out on the sidewalk. "All right, I'll listen, but this better be good; they better convince me there's some credibility in what they say."

They walked back into the classroom and sat down. Everyone was quiet for a few seconds, then Glade spoke up. "Okay, okay, you all win. I'll listen to what you say, and I'll talk to who you want, as long as you can convince me they are really suspects."

"That means you'll talk to that lady and her sons?" Ray asked.

"Yes, I'll talk to them; but again, you have to convince me they are bona fide suspects in this case before I'll do anything."

"Oh, Captain, we want you to talk to them one at a time at the same time. Can you do that, too?" Ray asked.

"Yes, anything to get this over with. So, who wants to start giving me something, anything I can use?"

"I will," Billy answered. "I guess I kind of started all this." He leaned forward, looking at Glade. "After my grandfather's funeral, my grandma told me she didn't think he died by accident. You see, Grandpa told her a week before he died that he did something terrible in high school and he had to make it right."

"What was that?" Glade asked.

"He never told her what it was, he just said he was going to fix it. The day before he was killed, he tried to get in touch with Chief Ford at the police station. But Ford was on vacation, so Grandpa didn't tell anyone what his secret was."

Glade looked up from what he was writing, staring at Billy. "So, who do you think killed your grandpa, and what did it have to do with Ford's death?"

"I know who killed my grandfather, and I know who tried to kill me, and I'll bet that asshole killed Chief Ford, too."

Uncle Ray spoke up. "It's a long story, Captain. Billy found out a lot when he was looking for what his grandpa was hiding. He told everyone he was working on a story for school about Steve, but he was really digging, trying to find out who might have wanted to kill Steve. Based on all the stuff Billy found out, we figured out that the killer was George Gunders."

Chapter 27
Keep Going, Billy

Glade wrote something on his pad, then shook his head. "You better be sure, making a statement like that. Everyone has rights, and one of those rights is that people can't just make claims about a crime without real evidence. Plus, you better have something concrete to go after a cop, and I mean concrete."

"Just let Billy finish, Captain; you'll see why we're right."

Glade rubbed his chin, then looked at Billy. "Okay, go ahead, Billy."

Billy took a deep breath, raising his shoulders. "When I was looking into Grandpa's past, I found out there was a murder in Rymont on graduation night in 1951. A kid named Brian Kelly was killed by a Tim Sanders, making it look like an accidental drowning. I first thought that was what Grandpa was hiding…that maybe he'd killed Kelly. But then we found out Sanders did it, based on a letter he wrote to his sister."

Glade flipped the page on his legal pad, writing a few sentences on a fresh page. "Okay, so now we know who drowned that Kelly kid. So what? I thought I came here to find out some hot scoop about Jim Ford's murder. Are you saying there's a connection?"

"Yes, I am, Captain," Billy answered. "The connections are those letters Sanders wrote to his sister. That's how we found out about another murder. A liquor store clerk got hit over the head with a vodka bottle and bled to death in Georgia in August of 1951. We believe George Gunders's mother did it, with Grandpa in the car. That's what Grandpa was really hiding and wanted to clear up, not the drowning.

"Grandpa called Chief Ford, who was on vacation, to tell him about the liquor store murder. Gunders got wind of the phone call and killed Grandpa, then he shot Ford, because he was getting close to figuring out that Gunders was protecting his mother. He tried to run me off the road after I started snooping around about what Grandpa did in 1951 that he was ashamed of. He wanted to kill me and make it look like an accident, like what happened to Grandpa."

Captain Glade stopped writing, then turned to look at Billy. "Carl told me some details about all three accidents. Why don't you tell me about yours?"

"I was pushed off the road by a guy in a big green GMC truck that had a rebel flag on the front license plate—"

Glade interrupted him. "A rebel flag, are you sure? It wasn't just something with a lot of red on it, was it?"

"No, no, Captain. He had a front license plate with a red rebel flag on it with a silver background. It was all metal."

"Gotcha; keep going, Billy."

"Anyway, the truck hit the back of my car and the next thing I knew, I was heading for a light pole, but I ending up hitting a horse instead. That's how I got this broken leg." He lifted his new cast up enough for the captain to see it.

Glade turned to Carl. "I don't remember anything about a green GMC truck." He looked through some papers in his briefcase.

"Yeah, I told you about it, Captain," Carl answered. "We think it was driven by George Gunders. In fact, I bet you can find that truck at one of the Gunders's places right now."

Glade sat back in his chair, tilting his head. "Carl, do you have the addresses of all three Gunders?"

Carl pulled two papers from his shirt pocket, finding the paper with the Gunders's information, and handed it to Glade, who picked his phone off his belt. He called a Deputy Skiles, telling him to send unmarked cars to the three addresses he gave him, along with a description of the truck.

"See, you've got my interest," Glade said, putting his phone on the table in front of him. "Keep going, Billy."

Billy took a deep breath, trying to digest what Glade had just told his deputy. "Well okay. We figured out that a Jessica Stanger, who is now Jessica Gunders, was with Grandpa in Georgia when the liquor clerk was killed. The clerk was hit with a bottle in such a way that it had to be done by a woman or a very short man. My grandpa was as tall as me, so we think Jessica did it, and that's what Grandpa was hiding, just knowing what she did. Now her son, Deputy Gunders, is trying to protect her by killing anyone getting close to finding out that she hit that liquor store guy. See, Captain, it all fits."

"Not real tight, it doesn't," Glade answered. "At least, not yet. What proof do you have that this Stanger girl was the one who killed the clerk? You can't say she did it just because she was shorter than Steve Summers."

"It had to be her," Uncle Ray said. "You see, Steve was my twin brother, and I knew who he went out with, and she was one of his favorite drinking buddies. They both were very heavy drinkers back then, and they drank vodka. The clerk was hit over the head with a vodka bottle."

"So, are you saying Summers saw the whole thing and that's what he wanted to tell Ford?"

"Yes and no, Captain," Billy answered. "Grandpa didn't know about it until after she came out of the liquor store. So, he didn't see it happen, but he didn't tell anyone, either. That right there was what he wanted to fix by calling Jim Ford the day before he died, and Gunders probably heard about the phone call. I mean, it came into the police station where he works."

"One thing keeps bugging me. If Steve Summers wanted to clear up something he did in high school, what took him fifty years to decide to do that?"

It was silent for a few moments. Uncle Ray finally spoke up. "Steve found out just last month that he had a bad colon cancer. I think he wanted to make his life right by confessing to what he knew happened that night in Georgia. Steve wouldn't hurt anyone. At the same time, he wanted to protect his family, and he knew Deputy Gunders could be dangerous. I think that's why he waited until now to talk about it, with the cancer and all. Doesn't that make sense?"

Glade wrote something on his legal pad, then looked up, scanning the four of them. "Listen, guys, that's not evidence. What you have told me so far is that Gunders killed Summers because of a murder committed by Gunders's mother in 1951, and Summers wanted to tell Chief Ford about it. The only other thing you got was that two kids liked vodka, and because a vodka bottle was the murder weapon, it had to be them. That's not evidence, that's guesswork." He shook his head. "You all had better get me some hard evidence if you want my help."

"There's more, a lot more," Fatha said. "Gunders was hassling me because I was trying to help Billy with his paper about Steve. Don't you see? Why would Gunders care about any of that unless he knew Steve was with his mother when she killed that guy?"

"And he badgered me, too," Billy added. "Our house got broken into, and I'm sure someone was looking for Grandpa's yearbook because it had some clues in it, clues that got me started on all this. Anyway, Gunders was at our house after the break in. He got in my face because I'd been asking questions. Why would he get so uptight about my digging unless he wanted to scare me so I'd stop looking about what happened in 1951?"

"Okay, I hate to tell you guys this, but I'm still not impressed with your theories," Glade said, looking around the table. "So, what else you all got that might impress me?"

"Captain, I'm not sure if this helps, but someone's been tailing me a lot over the last couple of weeks," Billy said. "Almost everywhere I've gone, a big black Cadillac has been right behind me. Whoever it was made no secret they were following me."

"So, what do you think that was all about?" Glade asked.

Billy sighed. "Well, I'm not sure, but I'll tell you one thing; no Caddy ever followed me before all this happened."

"Sorry, Billy, but that doesn't mean much unless we know who followed you and why," Glade said.

"There's one more thing nobody mentioned, Captain," Carl offered. "We found out from Sanders's sister's letters that one of the four Promisers were involved in the liquor store murder."

Glade put his notebook down. "What is a four Promiser?"

"The four Promisers were in Steve's yearbook; Billy found out about that. It was a club four seniors in our class made to always protect each other," Ray added. "We know Steve was one, Sanders and a guy named Tillin were in it, too, but they're both dead. We don't know who the fourth Promiser is, but we think he's the one who sent me the two clues to keep us on track. Who else would know about everything, except Gunders and the fourth Promiser?"

"This is getting more twisted every second," Glade said. "You guys are making it hard for me to follow. Tell me about the clues."

"They're right here," Ray said, pulling the two letters from a large brown envelope that was sitting on the table in front of him. He handed them to Glade.

The captain looked at both letters through the plastic coverings. "This is it? There sure isn't much here to tell me anything. What do they mean?"

They all looked at each other for a few seconds until Billy finally spoke up. "The 'bottle' clue was just to direct us away from the drowning and towards the Georgia killing. Chief Ford figured out, with the help of those letters, that 'bottle' meant the bottle that killed that guy in Georgia." Billy pointed to the "IRWY" clue. "And 'IRWY' was mailed to Uncle Ray to tell us who the killer was."

"I'm confused; what does 'IRWY' mean?" Glade asked.

"It was a saying they had back in the '50s," Billy answered. "It means 'I really want you,' and I swear, Grandpa's yearbook had a girl, just one girl, who wrote that. It was Jessica Stanger, who is now Jessica Gunders. Whoever mailed that clue must have known that was in that yearbook; that's why we think it was sent by the fourth Promiser."

Glade shook his head, laying down his pen. "I can see where you think all this points to Jessica Gunders, and then to her son George, but it's still only hearsay. I need more than that to bring anyone in. People have rights, guys, and while your story makes some sense to me, I can't question people based on what you just told me. I have to have some real evidence. The only physical evidence you've given me are two letters that don't mean anything to anyone except you all. I really want to help you, but give me something I can use. And you keep referring to some letters a guy wrote to his sister, but I understand they went up in flames with Ford. So, once again, I still don't have any real physical evidence on anything, just your guesses."

No one said anything, they just looked at each other. It was so quiet, they could hear each other breathe. They sat there for over five minutes as they watched Glade read through his notes. Then they all jumped when Glade's phone rang.

"Glade here…Oh…which one?...That's the brother…Did you see anything?... Be specific…Good…Describe the plate to me again…No one saw anything, right?...Listen, I'll call you back in a couple of minutes, Skiles."

The captain sighed, then wrote on his legal pad. Everyone was looking at each other, waiting to hear about the phone call.

They didn't have to wait long. Captain Glade looked up at the other four, then back to his notes. "Well, it looks like we finally got some evidence. Catch this; it seems Mr. Tommy Gunders up in Charlotte owns a green GMC truck. One of my men just saw it parked in front of his house. It's got some damage to the front end; and one more thing…there's a rebel flag on the front license plate, with a silver background. I guess your story isn't so wild, after all."

"Yes!" Ray shouted as he slammed his fist on the table.

Glade finished writing, then balanced his cell phone on his shoulder, holding it with the side of his head after he punched in a number. "This will show you I keep my word that if you give me something to work with, I'll follow up…Skiles, I want you to pick up all three Gunders. You've got their addresses. Listen, Skiles, you know George, he can be a handful. I don't know about the other two, but I think we should treat all of them like they're armed and dangerous. And don't let one or two cops pick them up. Send four or five officers to get each one of them, especially George."

Glade looked at his notes again. "Skiles, I want all of them picked up at the same time…you coordinate that. Oh, let's interrogate them at three different spots. Let's see, use the Charlotte office for Mom, the sheriff's office for Tommy. I want to avoid any local mess, so take George over to the Fort Ridge police station. Keep the press out of this…let's keep a lid on it. I'll be heading over to the Rymont Police Station. Call me if you need me."

"Wow," Ray said. "You don't waste no time, Captain. I'm glad you're on our side."

Glade scratched the top of his head. "And I'm glad you're all on my side, too. I know I'm going to be glad I met up with you today. In the meantime, Carl and I have a lot of work to do." He looked over at Ray, Fatha, and Billy. "I sure hope you guys are right about everything."

Captain Glade closed his fancy briefcase, then shook everyone's hands, heading out of the classroom with Carl. He turned back, looking at the threesome still sitting at the table. "I don't want any of you talking to anyone about any of this, got it?"

They all nodded, watching him open the door.

Glade turned back, looking at them again. "Billy, I think you'd make a great cop one day. None of this would be happening without your stubbornness and your intuition. Your family should be very proud of you. I know I am."

Carl and the captain drove back to the station. Carl pulled the copies he'd made from his reference book out of his pocket, handing them to Glade.

"What's this?"

Chapter 28
Officers Taking Fire

"Last night I went through some police books I have at the house. I found a reference manual I got at the academy that explained how to handle families with more than one felon and how to get confessions from them. There's another case about a bunch of people afraid to talk about a bully that's killing people. Just do me a favor and take a look at it. It's scary how similar the cases on those copies are to this one."

"Uh huh," Glade said, folding the copies in half and putting them in his pocket.

"Not much excitement there," Carl said under his breath as he pulled into the station.

"I'll look at it later, Carl; there's no time to read anything right now. We've got work to do."

Captain Glade spotted Deputy Skiles as soon as he walked into the police station. "Hey, Skiles, let's go over everything about this case. But before we do, you need to clear out my office, and get a man outside my door. I don't give a shit what they say, you keep the press away from us. In fact, clear out the entire office expect for cops, right away."

In less than five minutes, the noise in the Rymont Police Station was cut in half. Glade motioned to Skiles and Carl to follow him into his office, then closed the door.

Carl looked around, as it was the first time he had been in Chief Ford's old office since he was killed. It looked different now, with maps, flipcharts, and an extra row of chairs filling all the previously open areas.

Glade sat down behind the desk, while the other two grabbed a seat from the front row of neatly spaced brown folding chairs. "Skiles, we need to get the lead guys on speaker phone. Who did you pick to head up the three interviews, anyway?"

Skiles pulled out a small notebook from his back pocket. "Bob Antrum has the mother. He should be there any minute, but I haven't heard anything yet. Willie Akers has Tommy…that's George's brother. He lives about two miles from Mom in Charlotte. Willie just checked in; he just got to Tommy's house. I'm taking the lead on George, and my team should just about be at his place. I'm leaving here in a minute, heading over there."

Glade nodded. "And how many men are at each location?"

Skiles looked at his notebook again. "Antrum has four, counting himself, as does Akers. I sent five men over to pick up George. When I get there, that will make six."

"Officers taking fire," boomed over the station's loudspeaker.

Glade jumped up, opening the door. He leaned out his office, screaming, "What the hell is going on?"

A state cop screamed back from across the room. "We've got a firefight at 333 Tropicana, Captain."

"That's George Gunders's place," Carl said.

Glade grabbed his hat off the desk. "Let's go, guys. Listen, Skiles, I want every available man on the road now, and I mean now. Carl, how far away is Gunders's place?"

"It's only about ten minutes from here. Let's take my car, I know a shortcut."

They ran out to Carl's cruiser, Carl flipped on the lights and siren, and they squealed out.

"Get me someone at the scene," Glade told Skiles.

Skiles handed the phone to Glade. "It's Ben Thoms, sir."

"Ben, this is Glade. What's going on there?"

"Captain, there are five of us here." He gasped. "We pulled up to pick up Gunders, and before we knew it, he started shooting. It's like he knew we were coming. He's been firing ever since…it sounds like a shotgun." Thoms caught his breath. "Julian Beverly was hit, but he's okay. It's just a shoulder wound. He's in my car now. We got an ambulance coming."

"Thoms, do you got anybody covering the back so the son of a bitch can't get away?"

"Walters is back there. He had to go around two houses to get there. Captain, Gunders is nuts. It's like he built himself a fortress," Thoms said, still breathing fast. "I'll call you back."

The captain turned to Carl. "Carl, does Gunders have any kids or a wife in there?"

"No, he's single, Captain."

"Do you think he's got a gas mask?" Glade asked Carl.

"I wouldn't put it past him. He's probably got an arsenal in there. He told me once if anyone came after him, he'd have some real surprises waiting for them."

They cut in and out of back roads, giving Glade a tour of some old Rymont neighborhoods.

Glade called Thoms. "What's the latest? We're only a minute or two away," he said, looking at Carl, who nodded.

"Captain, I think Gunders got shot. Joelle thinks she got him. Anyway, he stopped firing a minute or two ago. What do you want me to do?"

"Get on the bullhorn. Give him ten seconds to come out, and if he doesn't, they shoot his place full of gas, got it?"

"Aye, aye, Captain."

Carl pulled his car behind the fourth state police car in front of 333 Tropicana. Four cops were behind the first car, all with their guns drawn, watching smoke billowing out of every window. They ran up to the lead car, finding Sergeant Thoms.

"Thoms, how many cylinders did you shoot in there?" Glade asked, catching his breath.

"Six, Captain. And we haven't heard anything for a while. No coughing, no shooting, nothing. Six cans going into such a little house would bring anyone out, unless they had some special gas masks."

Glade grabbed the bullhorn. "Gunders, this is Captain Hank Glade. You need to come out at once, with your hands in the air. We've got the place surrounded. Listen, it's not worth dying over. We've got over twenty cops here, and there's more on the way. Let's end this thing right now."

There was no response from the house.

"Okay, men, get your masks on. Oh, and Skiles, get Carl one."

Glade picked up the bullhorn again. "Gunders, this is your last chance, time's up. Come out immediately or we're coming in."

The captain waved to start the attack. They all ran up to the front door, three on one side, and four on the other. Thoms kicked the front door in, encountering less than three feet of visibility. The captain motioned directions to all the officers as they spread out in the house. Carl went into the living room, finding two rifles and a shotgun on the sofa, but no George Gunders. He had escaped.

"Oh, my God," someone screamed from behind the house, their voice muffled by a gasmask.

Everyone ran to where the voice came from. On a concrete slab just outside the back door lay the body of Officer Walters, shot in the chest and in the head. They stood there in silence, looking at their fallen brother, as they removed their masks.

"Listen up, men…we are going to get that son of a bitch; he's a dead man," Skiles said, wiping his forehead with his left arm.

"Captain, look over there," Thoms hollered, pointing at a blood trail that went from the rear of the house to the tree line at the back of the property.

They followed the blood through the trees to an opening on Bollings Avenue, seeing the last spot near some fresh tire tracks. The grass next to the tire tracks showed signs of a vehicle parked there for a long time.

Glade pulled off his hat, rubbing the top of his head. "That scumbag had an escape plan, sure he did. He knew we were getting close and all he had to do was run through the woods to his car and take off, that asshole."

He turned to Skiles. "I want someone calling every clinic, every hospital, and every doctor within fifty miles. This guy can't go far with all the blood he's lost. Oh, and get someone to watch his mother's and brother's houses. He might be heading their way. I want an APB on this prick right away. And let's get a couple of cops to guard the Summers place."

Carl walked up to Glade. "Do you think he'd really go after one of them?"

"You bet your ass. I bet he'd love to get his hands on Billy. Gunders is a nut case; he probably blames Billy for everything. I mean, it was all quiet for him until Billy started sniffing around. No, we better protect Billy…do you know where he's at?"

"I think he's home, but I'll find out," Carl answered, opening his cell phone.

Skiles walked up to Glade and Carl, putting his cell phone on his belt. "Listen, guys, I just heard from Akers. We've got both the mother and the brother in custody. They're being grilled right now."

Glade slapped his hands together. "Good, now tell Thoms to handle everything here. Be sure to get the coroner here fast for Walters, and check on Julian. We need to get back to the station. I've got something to do I hate doing...I got to call a cop's widow." His voice cracked. "Skiles, I want this guy, and I mean today, got it?"

"I've got it, Captain."

Chapter 29
Now He Can Rest

Glade and Skiles followed Carl to his car, heading back to the Rymont police station. When they pulled out, the captain turned to Skiles in the back seat. "I want to move on this fast. When I get done talking to Walter's wife, I want you to get Antrum and Akers on the phone. I want to find out all we can from Gunders's mother and his brother, especially what kind of car that asshole drives."

"10-4, Captain."

Glade looked at Carl. "Carl, I'm going to need your help on this, too. Check with all the locals to see if anyone knows anything, especially about his car. Do you have any idea?"

Carl shook his head, chewing on his lip. "I've racked my brain trying to remember, but I don't think I ever saw him drive anything but his squad car."

When they got back, Glade closed his office door, making that terrible phone call, while Skiles was getting the two lead officers on a speaker phone. Glade opened his office door and motioned for Skiles and Carl to join him, watching the two of them sit in the front row.

"Boys, you've heard about Sammy Walters by now, I assume?" Glade asked Akers and Antrum. Their silence indicated they knew. "We've got to get this shithead. I need to know what kind of car George Gunders drives. His family should know that. Don't let up on this for a minute, you hear?"

"10-4," Akers answered, followed by Antrum.

"Now, Antrum, you need to zero in on the Georgia case with Mom. I've got a feeling she'll open up fast; she's been carrying that murder with her for over fifty years. Don't forget to tell her we've got a source, a 'Four Raven Promiser,'—write that down—who knows all about the killing. She'll know what that means.

"Get her to crack…we need her to lead us to her son. Remember, she's looking at a lot of years in prison, plus she needs to know we got George on a murder charge. Don't tell her George is still on the run…let her think we got him. Press her hard; I need to know what kind of car he drives and who his friends are. Any questions, Antrum?"

"No sir, I've got it."

"Akers, get the brother to open up. The key with him is that we have a witness who can identify his truck, and we know that truck was used in two murders and one attempted murder. Make him think he's a prime suspect in everything. Play up the years he's going to spend in prison. And don't forget to find out what you can about George's car from him, too. You know what to do?"

"Yes, sir, I'm clear on everything."

"Go get em, guys. I just got done talking to a widow because of this guy. I want answers in less than hour. Now, show me what you can do."

After the meeting was over, Glade was alone in his office with Carl. "Deputy Williams, you're okay. Talk about learning a big lesson. I should have used you the minute I got here. I'd still be beating my head against the wall trying to find Ford's killer without your help, and the help of your buddies at that school."

"Oh, I don't know about that, Captain…you're pretty good. I reckon you would have found the answers eventually.

Me and the boys just gave you a push, that's all." Carl stood up. "Captain, if it's all right with you, I'd like to go over and see the Summers. They need someone to make them feel everything will be all right."

"You do that, Carl. Don't worry, I'll give you a call if anything breaks. You go see Billy and his family, and give them my best."

"Will do, Captain," Carl said, heading towards the door, glancing back to see Glade pull out the folded copies that he'd given him in the cruiser.

***

Carl walked into the Summers home, quickly spotted by Granny. She walked up to him, giving him a big hug.

"Thank you, Carl," she said. "Thank you."

"It's not over yet, Granny. Did Billy fill you in on everything I told him this afternoon?"

"He sure did. The only thing we're worried about now is that George Gunders is still out there somewhere, but I sure feel safer with you here; plus, those cops at the front and back doors make it a lot easier, too."

Gary came downstairs, sitting next to Billy as their grandmother got into her rocker by the window after grabbing her quilt off the couch.

Carl sat on one arm of Grandpa's old brown recliner. "Here's what we got, folks. Gunders's mother is being questioned in Charlotte. I'm betting she admits to the Georgia killing tonight. Tommy is George's brother, and he's being interviewed in Charlotte, too. George got away, but I wouldn't worry about him too much. He got shot up pretty good, based on all the blood at his place. Hell, he might even be dead by now. Captain Glade thinks we'll have all this wrapped up in a couple of hours."

"Well, the best thing for me is knowing Steve can rest now, and what he wanted to get off his chest finally came out," Granny said.

"Amen to that," Gary added.

Nancy came into the living room from the kitchen, laying her sweater on the back of the sofa. "Hey, what's happening? Why is there a cop at the back door?"

"There's one at the front door, too. George Gunders got away," Ray answered.

Nancy squatted on the floor in front of Billy. "Wow. Billy called and said Gunders shot a cop, and they had his place surrounded. What happened?"

Ray got up, walking towards the kitchen. "Don't worry, Nancy, everything is under control. Gunders won't be free long, if he's still alive."

Most of the mysteries were solved. But there still were more surprises awaiting the Summers family.

Chapter 30
You Are One Great Cop

Captain Glade was getting frustrated, looking at Chief Ford's silver badge clock on the wall. The two interrogations up in Charlotte had been going on for over an hour, and he still had no news on either. He walked outside to smoke a cigarette, trying to avoid all the press on the sidewalk.

A reporter stuck a microphone in his face as he walked towards his squad car. "Captain, is it true that you finally got a suspect in Chief Ford's killing?"

Glade pushed the microphone aside, moving past the questioner. "No comment. I've got no comment at this time. I'll let you know when we got something concrete. Right now, I don't have anything to tell you. Sorry."

He walked between and around dozens of news people, finally getting to his car, after saying "no comment" at least ten times. After pulling out of the parking lot, he lit a cigarette, trying to collect his thoughts. *Why hasn't there been any news? How far could Gunders have gone in two hours? Should I just go talk to Mom and the brother myself?* He ran his fingers through his hair, exhaling out his car window, when his phone rang.

"Captain, this is Antrum. Jessica Gunders just confessed to the Georgia liquor store killing. Now, we're trying to get her to open up about George."

Glade pulled into an empty parking lot. "Did you read her her rights?'

"Yes, sir, we did, we got it on tape. She seemed relieved after she confessed. She said she carried all that inside for too long. Then she said she doesn't want an attorney. I know that sounds crazy, but that's what she said."

"Do you got a witness to that, Antrum?"

" All three of us heard it, plus it's on tape."

Glade turned the car back on to get some air conditioning. "What did she say about the liquor store killing?"

"She told us everything. It was a Sunday and she wanted to party so she went to Georgia with Steve Summers. She had the fake ID, so he stayed in the car. She said when she went to pay for two bottles of vodka, the clerk hassled her on her bad ID, threatening to call the cops, so she panicked and hit him, breaking one of the bottles over his head."

Glade nodded. "Yep, that's how they said it went down."

"Sir, who are they?"

"Oh, don't worry about it. What did she have to say about Steve Summers?"

"She said he didn't know what happened until later after they got drunk, and she made him promise not to tell anyone."

"So, what else did you get out of her?"

"Only about her moving to Ohio, and getting married up there, then divorced, and finally getting married to a guy who died in Charlotte. We're still working on her about her sons, and what car George drives. I told her George killed a cop today. She cried for quite a while, but she still won't say anything about either one of them."

Glade lit another cigarette, throwing the spent match on the cruiser floor. "Just keep working on her. As long as she doesn't want an attorney, we can keep her there all night.

She's got to know more than she said. Call me if you get anything new."

The captain called Akers, hoping he had some news about the brother Tommy. "Akers, what's up with the brother?"

"Captain, here's where we're at with this guy. He says George borrowed his truck a lot, but Tommy didn't know what he used it for. I told him about the murders, but he keeps saying to talk to George. He said he has no idea why there's dents on the front of his truck. He's sweating like crazy…I know he's lying. Now, he's screaming for an attorney."

"Akers, go ahead and push him to get an attorney. Tell him his mother just confessed to the 1951 killing, and George is looking at a life sentence for Walter's death. Make him think he needs an attorney because he's looking at a charge of accessory to murder of a policeman, and that carries thirty years minimum. Play the good cop more. Talk him into helping us so we can try to get him a break with his sentence, got it?"

"Yes sir, I'll call you back as soon as he cracks."

Glade drove back to the station, making his way through the press, and finally plopping on the big chair behind the chief's old desk.

Almost instantly, Skiles walked into the office, closing the door. "Captain, we just got word of a white male gunshot victim up at a hospital north of Charlotte. The guy fits Gunders's description. They said he drove up to the emergency entrance with his car running, then he passed out. He's in surgery now, and they expect he'll be there for an hour or so. He didn't have an ID, but it sounds like he could be our guy. Thoms is heading up there with two troopers."

"Great job, Skiles; now call the hospital and see if that guy's blood type matches Gunders's."

Ten minutes later, a smiling Skiles leaned into the captain's office, telling him the guy at the hospital and Gunders's blood types were both A negative.

"Okay, Skiles, let's take a chance. I think we got him and I want to talk to that son of a bitch. Call and get some troopers to guard his room." He picked up his briefcase and hat, heading towards Skiles in the doorway. "Why don't we just head on up there and see what's going on? Now, when we leave, act cool. I don't want the press to know anything."

"Aye, aye, sir," Skiles answered as they went out the front door.

"What hospital are we going to?" Glade asked Skiles as they slowly drove their squad car around some television people.

"Let me see." Skiles pulled a paper out of his shirt pocket. "It's the Lady of Peace Methodist Hospital in a little suburb of Charlotte called Nannan Hills."

Glade wrote in his little notebook. "How long will it take to get there?"

"Oh, I'd say about forty minutes, more or less."

"Good, that will give me time to make some phone calls, but don't worry about your speed. Flip on those lights; I'm anxious to show that bastard my pretty face."

Glade pulled his phone off his belt, calling Carl Williams. "Carl, this Glade. I told you I'd keep you informed on what was happening. Well, to start with, we're heading up to a hospital north of Charlotte to check on a gunshot victim we think is Gunders. One other thing, old lady Gunders admitted to the Georgia killing, and she said Steve Summers wasn't involved, except for waiting for her in the car. He didn't even know what she did until later that night. Pass that on to the Summers; that should make them feel better."

"Thanks, Captain, that's great news. I'm at their house now, I'll tell them. Thanks again."

Glade and Skiles were almost half way to Charlotte when Glade's cell phone rang.

"Captain, this is Akers. I've got some good news. I followed your advice and told Tommy Gunders he really needed an attorney…even offered to call one for him. I convinced him he was fixing to be charged with being an accessory to multiple murders. That's all it took…he's singing like a canary. He even offered to testify against his brother. He wants a deal. I told him that we might be able to help him, but first he's got to tell us everything."

Glade raised his fist in the air. "Great job, Akers; what's he telling you?"

"He knows all about Steve Summers's killing, and the attempt to kill his grandson. Then he told me all about Chief Ford's murder, even telling us where to find the gas can he used. Oh, and get this, Captain…George told him ahead of time what he was going to do."

"And he thinks we'll help him with the DA? Sure. He knew about everything before it went down, and he wants us to help him? He's no better than his brother, that son of a bitch. Don't promise him anything. Charge him with lying to a police officer first, and get him down to Rymont. We need to throw the book at him later. Great job. Is there anything on the car?"

"Oh yeah, you got something to write on?"

"Give me a second." Glade got his notepad out, pulling the pen off the top. "I'm ready, Akers, what do you got?"

"George drives a blue 1999 Chevy Nova, with plate number 5649SHE. Captain, I called the hospital…that's the car up there. We've got him."

"Way to go, Akers. Now we're going to have some fun."

Glade filled Skiles in on everything, then called Thoms. "How close are you to the hospital? Good. Now listen, when you get there, make sure you have someone guarding his room, and be sure he's secured to his bed. The minute he wakes up, read him his rights. The car matches, it's him. Charge him with killing a cop for now. We should get there in about fifteen minutes, pending my sorry ass driver." He punched Skiles in the shoulder. "I've got a few things I want to say to Mr. George Gunders, so you make sure he's ready for me when I get there. See you soon, Deputy Thoms."

Twenty minutes later, Glade and Skiles found the hospital. There was a cop at the front door, who told them that Gunders was on the third floor. When the elevator door opened on the third floor, they found two troopers sitting on chairs on each side of the elevator. Without saying a word to either trooper, Glade was told Gunders was in room 344, a room guarded by two more cops standing outside the door.

Glade and Skiles walked in, seeing Gunders sleeping, with his right arm heavily bandaged and handcuffed to the shiny brass rail that ran along his bed. He had a clear oxygen tube stuck under his nose.

Glade moved up next to the bed, shaking Gunders's right shoulder. He grimaced as he woke up.

"Oh, did I hurt your shoulder? I'm so sorry," the captain said.

Gunders turned his head away from Glade, staring at the wall on his left side. The captain shook his shoulder again, and Gunders screamed in pain.

Glade turned, looking at Skiles. "Damn it, I keep forgetting he's got a bad shoulder."

Glade turned his attention back to Gunders. "Well, what do we have here? Why, it's Deputy Gunders. You've been a busy little deputy, haven't you? I bet you can't guess what we found out today. To begin with, your mother confessed to a murder from way back in 1951. And to top that, we even got a confession from your little brother Tommy. He seems to know all about your little accidents knocking people off the road, and even pouring gas over their cars. Isn't he a great brother?"

Captain Glade nodded. "I just wanted to come by and personally give you all the good news, you son of a bitch. You've already been charged with shooting a cop. That carries a thirty-year sentence, minimum. Now, guess what? We're going to charge you with first degree murder, too. Let's see," he started counting on his fingers. "Chief Ford, that's one count of murder. Oh, there's Trooper Walters…you know, the trooper you killed behind your house…that makes two. Wait a second, we can't forget Steve Summers; I guess that makes three.

"Let's see, I'm forgetting someone. Sure, you will be charged with attempted murder on the Summers boy, too. Yes sir, I'd say you are an amazing shithead. All this to protect your mama because of what she did fifty years ago. And now, you won't see her again. You see, it looks like both of you are going to die in jail. Guess it wasn't worth it, huh?"

Gunders didn't say a word, he just glared at the wall.

Glade grabbed Skiles arm. "Wow, isn't this great? In a few minutes, Skiles here…he's my deputy, as you know. Anyway, he'll be reading you your rights and charging you with three counts of first degree murder and one count of attempted murder; and guess what? I bet the DA will charge you with a few other things, like leaving the scene of an accident, or obstructing justice, and who knows what else? So, what do you think about that, Gunders? Doesn't that sound like fun, you asshole?"

The captain reached over to the rolling tray next to Gunders, pouring himself a glass of water from a light green plastic pitcher. "Man, that was good water. Georgy, just think, you're going to meet a lot of neat guys in prison. Hell, one of them may end up being your boyfriend. And just think of all the wonderful men who will just love you for being an ex-cop."

Glade poured another glass of water in his white Styrofoam cup. "God, my job can be fun sometimes. Oh, Mr.

Skiles, why don't you do me the honor of reading Mr. Gunders here his rights? As they used to say on TV, 'Book em Danno.' I'll be waiting for you outside. I can't take any more of this scumbag."

Skiles did as he was told, then met Glade in the hall. "Captain, didn't you want to try to get a statement from him? Maybe we could have gotten a confession."

"We can do that later," Glade answered, popping a piece of gum into his mouth. "I kind of liked doing it that way, Skiles. We're going to hang him no matter what. What a shithead. I just want him to remember our little talk the rest of his life. Besides, I've been wanting to do that to an asshole like him for years."

Skiles stopped walking, turning to his boss. "Captain, I just want you to know I thought that was cool."

"So did I," Glade responded. "So did I."

When they got into the squad car, Glade called Carl Williams again. "Carl, I thought you'd want to know we just charged Gunders with three counts of murder, as well as attempted murder of Billy, and he'll have other charges filed against him later by the DA. His mother and brother are both going to prison for a long time, too, as more evidence comes out, just like what happened in the case study you copied for me. Anyway, it's officially over; we've got all the bad guys in jail. Now, do me a favor and pass all of that along to all of the Summers."

"Will do, sir."

"One more thing, Deputy Williams; I need you to thank everyone who met me at that school. I thought they were all crazy, and man, was I wrong. That's a great bunch of guys, and because of them, we'll put that asshole in prison for the rest of his life. Thanks Carl, and like I said, thank all of the other guys for me, will you?"

"And thank you, Captain Glade. You are one great cop."

Chapter 31
That's Grandma's Bench

Carl called all the Summers, along with Nancy, back into the living room. They all looked at him as he sat next to Billy on the sofa. "I just got a call from Captain Glade. They've got George Gunders in custody, and they've charged him with three murders and the attempted murder of Billy, along with some other charges. Glade said it's an airtight case, so let me be the first to tell you all it's over."

Nancy started crying and Billy put an arm around her shoulder. "Are you okay, baby?" he asked.

"Yeah, I'm okay...I'm happy. I'm happy for all of us, but mostly I'm happy for Grandma." She turned, wiping her tears from her cheeks with her arms, looking at Grandma. "It's over, Grandma, it's over."

Granny stretched her arms out. "Come here, Nancy."

Nancy walked over and gave her a hug, and they both cried. Grandma looked over Nancy's shoulder at Billy. "You better not lose this one, you hear? She's awful special. She's like a daughter to me. Don't let this one get away, son."

"You can count on it, Grandma, she's mine forever; or should I say she's ours forever?"

"Billy, how about doing me a favor?" Grandma asked. "Get Frank Fatha over here, will you? I want him here. He's part of the family now, too."

Billy called his coach, filling him in on everything, then asked him to come over. Fatha was there in fifteen minutes.

Grandma stood up, looking at Billy and Gary. "Billy, I know you're anxious to get back to school, with all the classes you missed, but do you think you and Gary can take me over to see Steve tomorrow? That would mean a lot to me."

"Of course we can; right, Gary?" Billy answered, looking at Gary.

"Hey, you don't have to ask me twice about skipping school," Gary answered with a big smile.

The Summers, along with their annexed family, spent the rest of the evening talking about Grandpa. They laughed and cried, remembering all the things Steve had done over the years. It was like everyone had a story that touched everyone else. Granny nodded dozens of times as the stories filled the living room of that old house.

"I hope Grandpa is listening to all this. I hope he's proud of us," Billy said as he looked at his grandmother smiling.

Grandma twisted her little head, raised her shoulders and looked around the room at her family. "I'm sure Steve is up there, laughing with us. I can hear him now. He's saying, 'At least I did one thing right; look at that great family.' Yeah, I'd say he's proud of us tonight."

***

After Billy woke up the next morning, he grabbed his bath robe, picked up his crutches, and hobbled by Gary's room, seeing his brother sleeping. When he glanced into Grandma's room, he noticed her bed was already made, and there was no sign of her anywhere. The mystery was solved when he smelled bread baking. She was making their big Saturday buffet breakfast two days late.

As he walked into the kitchen, she was stirring something on the stove. She turned around with a dripping spoon in her hand when she heard Billy.

"Well, look who's up. Good morning, Billy; how'd you sleep?"

"Wow, what a night, Grandma. I guess those pills really worked. I don't remember ever sleeping better, even before this damn cast. Maybe all that stuff that happened yesterday kind of knocked me out. Did you sleep good, too?"

"I sure did. It felt like Steve was with me last night. I could feel his arms around me all night. Do you know he cuddled me every night of our marriage? And I loved it. For the first time in what, three weeks, it felt like he was with me. I miss him so much." She dropped her spoon, crying.

Billy skipped over to her, keeping her from falling, then hugged her for over a minute. When he sat back down at the table, he was amazed at the spread she put out for the boys. There were fried eggs, pancakes, biscuits and gravy, along with sausages and bacon. She even made his favorite...homemade cinnamon rolls loaded with little pecan pieces on the top.

"Go ahead and dive in," Grandma said, squeezing a small plate of toast onto an open spot on the table. "Now, don't wait for your brother...you just get going before everything gets cold."

"What do you mean, 'don't wait for your brother'?" Gary asked, rounding the corner. "Holy shit, Grandma, look at all this food. There's enough here for the whole football team. You are really something."

"It just made me feel good to cook for you boys this morning. You just go ahead and eat up. It's just a regular football season Saturday breakfast, except it's on a Monday."

Billy picked up a cinnamon roll and poured a glass of milk. "So, Grandma, what time do you want to go the cemetery?"

"Oh, about noon would be fine, Billy."

"Only thing is we'll probably still be eating then, Grandma, with all this food," Gary said with a chuckle, as he grabbed two pancakes with his fork.

At twelve thirty, Gary helped Grandma and Billy get into her car. She insisted on driving. When they pulled through the gates of the Rymont Cemetery, they weren't talking, just thinking about Grandpa. Grandma knew exactly where to go, turning left on the second alleyway. It was easy to spot Grandpa's grave even from a distance, because Ray had bought a white cement bench to put in front of his brother's headstone, so Grandma could sit and talk to him.

A white limousine was parked next to Grandpa's grave, with a well-dressed black man leaning on the long, fancy car. As they got closer, they could see an older lady sitting on Grandma's bench. They parked behind the limo.

Gary got Billy's crutches, helping his brother stand up. The three of them walked over to the bench, studying the visitor. She looked up at them, wiping her eyes, then put her pink lacey handkerchief into the purse. She looked like she was about seventy, with kindness in her soft but wrinkled face.

"Oh, excuse me," the lady said, as she looked up at the Summers. "I'm just saying goodbye to an old, dear friend. Are you here to see Steve, too?"

"Yes, I'm Steve's wife Mary. These are our grandsons, Billy and Gary," Grandma answered as she sat next to the lady on that special bench, almost like she was reclaiming her territory.

The stranger wiped the tip of her nose with the black glove on her left hand. "I am so sorry for your loss. You have my sympathy." She looked down at Billy's cast. "Young man, you need to sit down. I've got to go, anyway." She stood up as Billy sat on the edge of the bench.

"That's all right," Billy said. "I've got enough room. There's plenty of space for all of us."

"How did you know Steve?" Grandma asked, watching their new friend sit back down.

"Steve and I went to school together. He was one of my best friends. My name is Suzy Thompson," she answered, shaking the hands of the three Summers. "In high school, my name was Suzy Blakely. I got into some trouble the year we graduated, and Steve was the only one who tried to help me. I never forgot that...I mean, he didn't have to do anything for me. We dated a few times, but he was more like a big brother to me. Do you know he was the only one from Rymont who showed up at my trial?"

She stared at his headstone. "It was the lowest point in my life, and I really needed a friend, just one friend. He stood up for me when no one else would, not even my parents." Her voice trailed off as tears rolled out of her baby blue eyes.

Grandma looked at Suzy. "I heard about you. Steve wanted to be sure you had a friend at your trial. He talked about you a lot."

Suzy blew her nose with the pink hanky. "I just found out Saturday that he had passed away. It broke my heart. That's why I'm here...I had to come by and see him one last time, he was so special. There I was, a nineteen-year-old kid, thinking my life was over. I didn't have a single soul who even acted like they cared, except Steve. I will never, ever forget him." Her tears were rolling down her face uncontrollably. "I'm sorry, please forgive me." She stood up, walking towards her expensive carriage, then turned back towards Grandma. "I've got to go now. God bless all of you."

They could tell she was sobbing as the limo pulled away. Her shoulders were shaking as she looked back at them over the half-open tinted window. The three Summers sat on the bench without making a sound, just watching the limo leave, until Grandma spoke up.

"Isn't it something? I mean, how some things turn out. Who would've thought I'd meet that woman, especially after how much I hated her when she was on trial? Now I realize how silly it was and how nice she is. I feel bad now for how much hell I gave your grandfather over the whole thing. All he ever wanted to do was to help a friend."

Billy looked at the headstone. "Man, Grandpa was something." He put his arm around his grandmother, feeling Gary's arm on her, too. The three of them sat there for a few minutes, holding on to each other. Billy looked over at his brother, seeing giant tears bouncing down his freckled face.

"Maybe it will all come out now," Billy whispered to Grandma.

She just nodded.

No one heard the car come up behind Grandma's car until it was almost there. Billy looked over, not believing what he saw. He looked at Grandpa's grave, then back at the car. It was the black Cadillac that had been chasing him for so long.

An old man got out of the car, wearing a red and black English-looking cap from the sixties or seventies. He slowly walked towards the bench.

Billy shielded his eyes with a hand, trying to see who was heading towards them. He grabbed a crutch, standing up. He recognized the old guy, and his mouth flew open in shock. "Oh my God, Grandma, look. Look, it's Bob Atlas."

Grandma and Gary turned their gaze towards their old friend, trying to understand what was going on.

Atlas wiped his forehead with his hand. "Ray told me I could find you all here. Man, it's hot, even for September. Hey, can you spare me a little space on that there bench? My legs are killing me."

Gary stood up, opening some space on the bench as Grandma and Billy slid over, giving Atlas the edge of the marble seat.

"Mr. Atlas, it's you. You're the guy who's been tailing me, and I bet you're the fourth Promiser, aren't you?" Billy asked.

Bob caught his breath, then exhaled slowly. "Yes, Billy, you're right on both counts."

"Wow, I never would have guessed it was you," Billy said, shaking his head. "You weren't even in Grandpa's group in high school, were you?"

"No, not really. Your grandfather and I were just friends in school, but not real close friends. That's why I was so surprised that right after our graduation he asked me to join the group. I didn't think it meant all that much, but it was kind of neat, because everyone thought Steve was so cool. I think he wanted me to be a Promiser because he figured I was more stable than Tim or Brad."

"So, Mr. Atlas, why did you follow me all the time?" Billy asked.

"That was the Promise; to be there to protect each other and our families. I was just watching out for you, Billy, the best I could." Atlas caught his breath. "I knew all about Gunders and I figured you were in danger, so I did what I could to protect you."

"So, you knew about the drowning and the killing in Georgia?" Grandma asked.

Atlas wiped his forehead with his shirt sleeve. "Yes, I knew all that. Steve did, too. But you've got to understand, we couldn't tell anyone. Gunders made it clear, in his little hints, that if we said anything, our families could be harmed, and he was a cop. That scared both Steve and me. So that's why I sent you those notes, because I was afraid for my kids and grandkids. I knew you'd eventually figure out what they meant and get that SOB."

Billy turned, looking at Atlas. "So, why didn't you tell me all about everything when I came to the bank to see you?"

"I wanted to, but I figured you didn't have any hard evidence. You had to discover it...you know, without me, because of Gunders's threats."

"If you all were so concerned about Gunders, why did Grandpa call Chief Ford the day before he died?" Grandma asked.

Atlas took off his cap, running his fingers through his few remaining hairs. "Steve told me he could trust Ford, and after he found out he had cancer, he decided to take a chance and clear his conscience. That's when he called the chief's office. That one phone call probably got him killed."

It was quiet for a few seconds until Grandma spoke up. "Bob, is that why you followed Billy, to be sure he wouldn't get hurt?"

Bob nodded. "After Billy came to see me, I knew he was looking at the wrong murder. He was more interested in the drowning, and at that time he had no idea about the killing of that liquor clerk. I figured the more Billy kept asking questions about what happened in 1951, the more nervous Gunders would get. That's why I tried to follow him, and despite that Gunders almost killed him anyway. I guess I'm not such a good James Bond, huh?"

Billy laughed, looking at Bob. "Oh, you weren't so bad. I mean, we never did get your tag number."

Granny leaned over, touching shoulders with Atlas. "Bob, if you were going to send clues to Ray, why didn't you just write him a letter and tell him everything?"

"I had to be careful...that's why I made sure there were no fingerprints on anything. I was so afraid of Gunders, the last thing I wanted was him knowing I was involved in anything. After Steve was killed, I was the last one who knew anything about his mother murdering that kid in Georgia. No, I had to be careful, especially for my family. I hope you all understand."

Granny looked at her grandsons. "Of course we understand, don't we, boys?" They nodded.

She grabbed Atlas's hand, squeezing it hard. "Why did you do all this for us, Bob?"

"Listen, I made a Promise, a Promise to a saint of a man. He turned out to be my best friend. I honestly believe he would have given his life for me, and me for him. Everything I did was for Steve, and the Promise."

They all sat there for a few minutes, just looking at the grave, interrupting each other's thoughts with sniffles and sighs. It had turned into a love party for Steve Summers. There was a peaceful feeling being shared by the four of them that Monday afternoon in the Rymont Cemetery. They'd learned so much about Grandpa, and so much more about themselves.

Billy stood up, reaching for his crutches. Gary and Atlas helped Granny get to her feet, and they all headed back to their cars.

Someone's cell phone rang. Billy struggled to get the ringing phone out of his pocket, seeing that Nurse Clark was calling him. He didn't answer it.

He looked back at his best friend's grave. "Grandpa, I miss you so much. Thanks for being a super father. I love you."

The End

ACKNOWLEDGEMENTS

The little lady that stood by me for so many years helping me with everything, from friendship to editing all my books, is in heaven now. I miss her every second and can never repay Nancy for all she did for me. What an angel.

Special thanks to my beautiful daughter, who was proofing and reading my works even on her death bed. She undoubtedly is with her mother watching over me and my grandbabies.

To my wonderful neighbors who have supported me so long with this story: Bob and Natalie, Frank and Norma, Kevin and Kim, even Valerie. Thanks for being my sounding board in so many ways.

To Bob Atlas, who taught me how to listen, how to care, and how to be totally honest and always be sure to "walk in everyone else's shoes".

To my son Chris, who gave me a nice contrast to his sister. They showed me a mixture of life spices that were wonderful to experience.

To Jim Huntington, who continually challenged my thinking, always striving to make me want be the best.

To Vickie. What a sister. She has been there every day for a lifetime. She helps me with everything I need. She has supported all my endeavors completely and it's a joy to even know her. She is amazing.

To Linda and Beckie, who at times were wonderful for my family.

And finally to my new set of kids, my grandkids. Yes indeed, they are the sails on my life raft. Helping Connor and Kaylee grow up with an appreciation of life, an appreciation of God, and an appreciation of the family makes every day mean a lot for me. I'd hate to think where my mind would be without them.

About the Author

E.G. Lander was born in a tiny spec of a town in northern Minnesota called Deer River. He grew up on a fishing resort his parents owned, telling guests, almost as soon as he could talk, about his family of eight, the woods, the local Chippewa Indians, the lakes and the native game. It was there that he realized he would one day be a storyteller, a writer of what he knew and learned as a youngster. He postponed much of that to raise his own family, and build a career to launch him back into writing. He worked his way through college by writing papers for other students, then graduated with a BA in pre-law and political science. From there he joined the U.S. Marine Corps, becoming a teacher and a facilitator of MCI (the Marine Corps Institute). He got married and became a leader for a national retailer, honing his communication and writing skills with speeches and motivational leadership. But he was always dreaming of writing, especially telling stories about families and their ups and downs.

E.G. retired early to start that second career- the storytelling one. In the last four years, he has completed four manuscripts, (3 fictional and 1 non-fictional) and he's working on a fifth one and getting ideas on #6. His first work was What's in the Rear View Mirror? an 80,000 word saga about a family in South Carolina caught up in murders from 50 years ago that haunt them today, creating even more murders. It's being published now, as is a 117,000 word story called Damn It, Wake Me Up, the drama of an American family that can't endure the husband who gambles and cheats on his wife and eventually tries to kill her. However, she doesn't die from the "perfect murder plan" he and his mistress devise. She ends up in a coma where she can hear and think. She learns their plan and wakes up and finds such sweet revenge. The 3rd fictional work is entitled The Incredible Bucky Berrot, a fantasy about a family of birds in Australia and how Bucky changes the way all the birds in Bayberry Hills think about their laws and their enemies, as well as the possibility of God (why can't a bird believe in God?). This colorful family and community fable was co-authored with E.G.'s grandson (10 year old Connor) to give a slant of assorted creatures probably not seen anywhere (60,000 words).

E.G.'s most recent work is called An Email From God. It's the accounting of how he struggled to face his wife's death and what God did to not only curb his suffering but to give him hope for the future. It is only 20,000 words but tells a remarkable story of love and miracles.

That's his program: one manuscript/18 months. He is ahead of schedule.

34335422R00176

Made in the USA
Lexington, KY
01 August 2014